Anasa Maat

A Little Bit of Honey

THE QUEST FOR A SOUL MATE

A ROMANTIC NOVEL

Maat

"A Little Bit Of Honey"
© Copyright 2005 Anasa Maat
ISBN 0-9754719-0-2

Second Printing: April, 2005

Book layout Design & Printing:
Cypruss Communication, Iselin, NJ

Nutany Publishing Company
Newark, New Jersey 07102
Tel. 973.242.1229

Printed in Canada

Acknowledgments

Writing this book has been a revelation for me in so many ways. Like so many things that we put a lot of effort into and manage to complete, we owe thanks to those who helped make it possible. I am first thankful to the Creator, owner of the heavens and then to others who are dear to me and who helped me along the way.

I thank my family: my mother, Lula Echols, for always being there for me; my children Danielle and Eric Screven, who have given me little concern, enabling me the freedom from worry that one needs to be their most creative. Shonté, thanks for your helpful suggestion. Paris and Hasjonn Simmons, thanks for linking me up with a copy-editor and helping to coordinate the services. I thank my grandchildren (Tamara, Ebony, Tayari, Little Hasjonn, Nuru, Jordan, and Faraji) for bringing such joy into my life and giving me a respite from work.

I thank my friends for their time and support, especially Virginia Moore for taking the time to read the first draft, Mildred Booker, thanks for taking the time to read for me. Your critique was very helpful. Joe Evans thanks for providing me with information on the schools in Richmond Virginia. Tunde Dada, thanks for helping me with the Yoruba names. Shaka Taylor, thanks for helping me learn more about the religion of Ifa. I thank Diane Raintree, a wonderful editor, who put me on the right track, Claudine Perry, for doing a great job as copy editor, and okerry@.net for your 100 words free, your suggestions were right on target.

Last but not least I thank my husband, Hadren W. Simmons, who meticulously read each of the drafts, and whose support, critiques, suggestions, time, and love made it possible for me to reach deep down into my soul and pull out the words that comprise this book. I love you Hadren; you are my soul mate.

Introduction

Spinster and old maid are terms those of us born before 1950 are familiar with. They were terms used to refer to unmarried women over the age of twenty-five in the decades before the nineteen seventies. Today, thank God, we have come to better appreciate women who have chosen to remain unmarried in order to pursue careers, or those who just may never had met their soul mate. One of the things I wanted to show, through this work is that women, over twenty five and unmarried, are in a better position to find their soul mate now that stigmas such as old maid and spinster have become obsolete. Women are under less pressure to get married before they turn twenty-five just for the sake of having a husband.

Modern women that choose to marry and raise a family while building careers at the same time have my greatest respect. I know how difficult it can be. Yet, while it is a challenge that millions of women take on it is also a challenge that many women won't even try. Some women who accept that challenge ask themselves "Did I make the right choice?" What married woman working and raising children hasn't wondered if she could have been more successful in her chosen field if only she had not taken on the responsibilities of a family? How many of us wonder if we could have been another Oprah or maybe another Condoleezza Rice if we had remained single as they did?

On the other hand, single women who make the choice not to sacrifice career for family must wonder if they have made the right choice, too. Like the character Teyinniwa in the story, "A Little Bit of Honey," how many of them reach fifty and wonder if they would have been happier to have a husband and grandchildren to comfort them in their old age.

I must give credit to those women who manage to reach the pinnacle of success in their chosen field, and at the same time raise well adjusted children and hold families together. These are your superwomen. When I think of women like this Hillary Clinton, who may just become the first female president of the United States, and my own personal hero, Ida B. Wells, come to mind, though I know there are many more. Ida B. Wells, in her struggle to stop the lynching of her people through writing and public speaking, managed to make a name for herself that eventually was included in history books while holding a family together. One of my favorite stories tells of her travels across the country on a train with a nursing baby stopping along the way to speak out about the atrocities of lynching Black men in the south during the first decades of the twentieth century.

In order to achieve this level of career success and relationship success a woman has to have a very special man. Few men are comfortable when their wives pursue interests that take her away from him, or that supersede his own level of importance. So many marriages fail because one spouse is not willing to compete for attention with a career. Women are generally the ones to make the sacrifice allowing a man to have both career and family. To make this work in the reverse, a woman needs more than just a man; she needs a soul mate.

The heroine in "A Little Bit of Honey" wants marriage and career. Not stigmatized by the now obsolete "old maid" term ascribed to women of her mother's generation, Aliyah Neal does not settle for just a relationship, she wants more and holds out until she finds it. In the meantime she uses her time well to pursue career goals, develop meaningful friendships, travel, and explore unconventional means of getting what she wants out of life. "A Little Bit of Honey" will introduce many readers to Ifa, an ancient African religion, for the very first time. Perhaps they, like Aliyah Neal, will determine that sometimes going out of your own experiences can help you fulfill your destiny, and might just pay off in the long run.

Chapter 1

Loneliness

"Your thong must be too tight," he whispered under his breath, but loud enough for her to hear it.

She looked up in shock, and then glanced over her shoulder to see if maybe he could be talking to someone other than her. No. Just the two of them were on the elevator. She quickly caught the door before it closed, stared at the handsome stranger in disbelief, and then stepped out of the elevator onto the seventeenth floor.

"Pervert," she said disgustedly, then gave him a dirty look as the door closed and the elevator continued to ascend.

An hour later she found herself looking into his handsome face again when she entered the conference room on the eighteenth floor, where her boss, Joe Simmons, editor-in-chief of *Enigma Magazine*, had summoned her.

"Aliyah Neal, say hello to Mark Griffin," Joe said. "Mark's a freelance photojournalist, one of the best. We're going to be using some of his work in future issues of *Enigma*. Mark, Aliyah is one of our top editors. She'll be editing some of your work."

The look of surprise and embarrassment on Mark's face was almost enough to make her feel sorry for him. She ignored his extended hand though. "I'm sure working with you will be a challenge, Mr. Griffin," she said, hoping her icy stare added to his discomfort.

Exiting Joe's office, Mark opened the door for her. "I'm so sorry about this morning in the elevator, Miss Neal," he said with a look of genuine sorrow. "It's just that you came across so stuck up when you first entered the elevator. I was only trying to be friendly when I said good morning to you, and you wouldn't even speak."

"You should quit while you're ahead." She hastened her pace to the elevator.

"Please let me make it up to you. How about having lunch with me?" He moved aside, allowing her to step into the elevator first.

"You've got to be joking. Lunch is out of the question. I'll have my secretary call you when I've had a chance to review your work." She got out of the elevator on the seventeenth floor again.

"Please don't hold what I said against me. I didn't mean to offend you," she heard him say, just as the elevator door closed.

Flowers arrived the next day with a little note from him begging her forgiveness. He sent her cute little "I'm sorry" cards at least twice a week, and made up all kinds of excuses to stop by her office to discuss his work, always asking for a chance to make up for his initial crudeness.

"Are you going to hold that remark against me forever?" he asked on one of his visits to her office.

"I told you that I've forgiven you for that."

"Then what's the problem? Why won't you go out with me, Aliyah?"

Why won't I go out with him? she asked herself. Aliyah hadn't had a serious love interest in months, and she wanted a man in her life. Two of her best friends were happily married. She wanted the same thing they had. But she was tired of dating men who later turned out to be creeps.

Finally, after three months of being fiercely pursued by Mark, she gave in to his charm, despite his reputation for being a player. She was lonely, not to mention horny.

Mark wore his hair in locks. Aliyah, proud of her African heritage, had been wearing long box braids for the past ten years and felt that Mark demonstrated pride in his African heritage, too, by wearing his hair in a long, natural style. Since her first visit to Africa ten years ago, as a student representative to the International Conference of Women in Nairobi, Kenya, she had become attracted to African-American men who were conscious of their history.

8

Mark had recently relocated to New York from Los Angeles. He was an excellent photographer. His accompanying stories, appearing in leading newsmagazines around the world, were always interesting, and he appeared to be genuine. Aliyah was impressed when he told her that he had tickets for them to see Bring in Da Noise, Bring in Da Funk, the popular Broadway musical highlighting the history of tap dance.

For this first date, Mark drove through the Holland Tunnel from his apartment on the Lower East Side into downtown Newark, New Jersey. Checking himself out in his rearview mirror, he wondered if he would be spending the night with Aliyah in Newark. He certainly hoped so. He arrived at her eighth floor apartment, in a well-maintained building, at two-thirty on a Saturday afternoon. He was dressed casually in beige khakis, an open collared white shirt, and a black sports jacket. He felt confident of his well-groomed appearance.

"My, but you're punctual," Aliyah said when she opened the door, not quite ready yet.

Flashing an innocent boyish grin, and not waiting for an invitation, Mark walked past her and into the sunny, spacious, attractively furnished apartment.

"The performance doesn't start until four. We have a little time to get better acquainted." He plopped himself down on her plush green sofa.

"Make yourself at home," she said, noting that Mark had done that already. "I need a few minutes to put on the finishing touches."

"You look great, but then you always do, Aliyah."

"Thanks, you look pretty good yourself." She checked Mark out. His body was lean and taut, his smile charming.

"I hope we make it in time for curtain call," he said, watching Aliyah sashay into the bathroom.

"Fix yourself a drink. I'll be out in a few."

Twenty minutes later Aliyah was ready to go.

"I didn't know it would take you so long to get ready," Mark said, when they were leaving Aliyah's apartment.

"Don't worry, we have plenty of time." She walked around to the passenger side of the car and let herself in.

His five-year-old black Volkswagen Jetta sped them through the Lincoln Tunnel and up Broadway. They parked the car in a garage near the theater district then walked the short distance to the theater, arriving twenty minutes prior to curtain time. They were seated fifteen minutes before the show was to start. The fourth row center, orchestra seats provided an excellent view of the stage.

"I told you there was nothing to worry about," Aliyah said, once they were seated.

Mark ignored her comment. "I think you will enjoy this show, particularly since Savion Glover is starring in it. He's from Newark, too, you know. He must be in his mid to late twenties by now, close to your age, Aliyah. Did your paths ever cross in Newark?"

"No, I was born in Newark but I didn't grow up there. My family moved to South Orange, New Jersey, when I was a little girl."

"I'll bet you were a beautiful little girl, too," he said, just as the curtain opened. The sound of clicks and taps on floorboards drew Aliyah's attention to the stage where a spotlight was focused on a dark mass, huddled on the floor of a slave ship. A hush fell over the audience as they anxiously waited to see what would happen.

"What did you think of the performance?" Mark asked, as they left the theater.

"The choreography was wonderful. So were the drummers. The narration of the story was especially moving," Aliyah said.

"Tap dancing was a wonderful way of telling this story," he said, taking her arm as they stepped off the curb to cross the street. "I'm glad you enjoyed it."

Mark impressed Aliyah by taking her to a trendy midtown restaurant, which nightly featured entertainment in the Motown style of the 1960s and 1970s.

"I've been reading some of the stories you've written for *Enigma*," he said once they were seated. "I must say I am very impressed with your writing. I've been waiting patiently to get to know the woman behind the words though. Tell me about yourself, Aliyah. How did you get interested in writing?"

"I've always loved to read. I was very young when I decided to become a writer. Even though my father tried to discourage me, I never gave up my dream of becoming a writer. Now I dream of becoming editor-in-chief for a popular magazine one day, maybe even *Enigma.*"

"You strike me as a woman who gets what she wants out of life, Aliyah. I am confident that you will be all that you want to be. I have a feeling that you and I are right for each other."

"Why do you feel that?" Aliyah took a sip of her water.

"I'm a go-getter, just like you, Aliyah. I have dreams and I don't let people or things discourage me from getting what I want out of life. My dream is to become an internationally renowned journalist, reporting on world affairs. I can feel your energy. I can tell that you'll inspire me and vice versa."

"You think that maybe I can be your muse." Aliyah laughed softly.

"Yes, something like that." Mark flashed his boyish smile again.

After they left the restaurant, he drove Aliyah back to her apartment. It was only nine-thirty when they arrived at her front door, and he waited patiently for an invitation to come in this time. Aliyah hesitated before she turned to him and said, "I had a wonderful time, Mark. I hope you won't mind if I don't invite you in. I am really tired; it's been a long day."

"I'm not going to lie and say that I don't mind, Aliyah. I respect your decision not to invite me in, as long as you won't let me leave without telling me when we can see each other again."

"I would love to go out with you again, Mark. When did you have in mind?"

He looked relieved. "How about next weekend?"

"That's fine. Call me during the week to confirm. Okay?"

Just as she was turning to enter the apartment, Mark reached out and turned her to face him. He planted a gentle kiss on her lips.

11

For their second date, Mark came by her mid-town office on a Friday evening and they took the subway to a downtown comedy club. The club was small, but cozy. The lights were dim and candles flickered on the tables. A small platform with a single stool on it was used as a stage.

One comedian after another, six in total, entertained them for almost three hours. One of the six comedians, a young Jewish woman, joked about single life after thirty and living alone in the city. Aliyah never laughed so hard, prompting Mark to ask, "So you really relate to this single life in the city thing, Aliyah?"

"Oh yes! Especially the part about how men think that women are all desperate to get married and willing to go to any lengths to hook them. She's right; the only hooks most of these men want to know about are the hooks that unfasten a woman's bra. And the only hooks a lot of single women are interested in are those that will pull her up the ladder of success."

"Does that mean that you're not desperate to get married?"

"No, I am not desperate to get married, Mark, although I want to get married some day when I meet the right man."

"Who knows, maybe you already have." He smiled at her.

During the intermission, Aliyah excused herself to go to the powder room. She smiled to herself thinking that a relationship with Mark could possibly work. That thought left her mind quickly as she spotted Mark flirting with the waitress as she made her way back to their table.

"I ordered you another martini," he said, as she took her seat.

"Another?" Aliyah said, thinking that she was already feeling a little giddy from the first one.

"Yes, there's a two-drink minimum at this club. Don't worry you're in good hands."

After leaving the comedy club, they headed for a local outdoor café to grab a quick bite to eat. The night air felt good. Shimmering stars lit the sky, and the moon appeared to be smiling at them as they walked holding hands, recalling some of the jokes they had just heard. At the café, Mark ordered a burger and fries. Aliyah ordered a Caesar salad with grilled chicken.

"Are you always such a sensible eater?" Mark took a big bite of his burger.

"I try to be. I stay away from red meat and try to eat a lot of raw fruits and

nodding his head, waiting for her to admit it.

Aliyah thought back to the incident. *Maybe I did act a little snobbish when I entered the elevator that morning. I could have acknowledged his pleasant "good morning" instead of ignoring him and focusing my attention on the floor indicator. But I had a lot on my mind that morning.* She dismissed any blame on her part.

"It took me months to get a date with you," Mark reminded her.

"I was being cautious. I like to know a little about the men I go out with before the first date."

"What did you find out about me?" Mark rested his arm on the back of the sofa, behind Aliyah.

"Well, you do have a reputation as a flirt with the women in the office."

"Rumors, rumors," he laughed. "Do I look like a player? They're just jealous because they know I only have eyes for you." He gave Aliyah his most charming smile and a look of pure innocence. Then he took her into his arms and kissed her passionately on the lips. Aliyah returned the kiss with even greater passion.

Encouraged, Mark kissed Aliyah softly on her face and throat before exploring her mouth with his tongue. With expert fingers he unzipped her dress, slipping it over her shoulders, and then unhooked her bra. His kisses continued on her breasts, her nipples, her stomach, and finally to her most sensitive parts. Mark lifted her from the sofa and carried her to the bedroom where he finished undressing her and then himself. On his king-size bed, he continued to explore her body with his tongue, his hands, and finally his manhood, making her toes curl in sheer pleasure.

Following a night of incredible sex Aliyah awoke to the smell of freshly brewing coffee and hot cinnamon buns coming from Mark's kitchen. She grabbed one of his T-shirts and headed for the kitchen.

"Back into bed," a naked Mark playfully ordered as he put the finishing touches on the tray that he was preparing to bring into the bedroom. "I'm not finished with you yet."

Aliyah dutifully obliged and returned to the bedroom with Mark at her heels.

"Breakfast in bed? What a treat." She picked up her coffee cup and took a sip.

"Breakfast is not the only treat you're going to get in bed this morning," he said.

Two sips into her coffee and one bite of the cinnamon bun were all that he allowed her before his lips covered hers and his adept fingers removed the T-shirt. This time Aliyah became the aggressor. She straddled Mark's body and covered it with warm kisses. He moaned, caressing her buttocks and rocking her until they were of the same rhythm. Between squeals of passion and moans of delight, they rocked and rocked until finally their fingers entwined, squeezing out the last bit of pleasure.

"I hope I didn't wear you out," she said.

"Are you kidding? I love it when a woman enjoys fucking as much as I do."

They fell into a pattern of dating every weekend and even during the week sometimes. As they got better acquainted, Aliyah discovered they had a lot in common. They both loved basketball. At a Madison Square Garden championship game, they both cheered their team on. Only Mark cheered for the Lakers and Aliyah cheered for the Knicks.

"You're living in New York City now, Mark. You can't be a Lakers fan anymore."

"Why not? I have invested too much time and energy loving the Lakers to switch now."

After the game, they stopped for ice cream. "They make my favorite butter pecan ice cream here." Mark led her into an ice cream parlor near the Garden.

"Butter pecan is my favorite, too."

"Ah! A woman with a discriminating palate, I love that."

As the weeks turned into months, Aliyah kept in mind something that her grandmother used to say to her while she was growing up. "Before you get married, keep both eyes open, after you are married, close one." She wanted to be sure that she kept her eyes wide open before she considered making a commitment to any man. The longer they dated, the more she became aware of the things she and Mark did not have in common.

One evening, while they were driving from Manhattan to her apartment, Aliyah was telling Mark about an article she was writing for the next issue of *Enigma*.

"Obesity is a very serious problem among black women. Did you know that black women are the most obese group in America?" She did not wait for him to respond. "Diet is a primary cause. Black women use too much fat in their cooking. We have got to learn to use healthy alternatives." She looked at Mark and waited for a reaction.

"The only people that will be interested in reading your article will be black women, Aliyah. Don't you want to target a bigger audience? Why not focus on obesity in general or obesity among women?"

"What's wrong with targeting black female readers?"

"Nothing, if you want to limit yourself and your writing prospects. Is that what you want to do Aliyah?"

"What I'm trying to do is to provide African-American women with information that addresses their unique problems and will help them to better understand themselves and improve their lives. Don't you feel the same need to reach our people through your work, Mark? Why does your work focus mainly on white people and their culture?"

"There is more of a demand for the photographs and stories I do about white people. There are many magazines that can use my photographs of white people, but the only demand I get for photos of blacks is from *Enigma*, *Essence*, *Ebony*, or *Jet*. When it comes to making money I am not prejudiced about where it comes from." He turned up the volume on the radio to listen to his favorite hip-hop station.

Aliyah thought about what Mark had said and decided that blacks, regardless of the money involved, should use some discretion about the jobs they took, and it did not necessarily have to mean that they were prejudiced. She had problems with white models being used to advertise makeup and hair care products in *Enigma*. If manufacturers wanted to sell their products to black women, then why wouldn't they use black models to advertise their products in black magazines?

A few weeks later on a Saturday morning, following a Friday night party they had attended at a downtown club, Aliyah was taking a shower at Mark's apartment.

"You haven't forgotten that my friend Charles is getting married next week have you, Aliyah?" Mark's voice came through the shower curtain.

"I haven't forgotten. I have to decide which dress I want to wear and make an appointment to have my hair done the Friday before the wedding so that my braids will be fresh."

"I thought you might want to wear your hair different for the wedding, maybe even straighten it," Mark said, catching Aliyah completely off guard.

"Straighten my hair, Mark? You've got to be kidding."

"Braids are alright sometimes, but why can't you change up sometimes, just for special occasions?" Mark continued to shave, looking in the bathroom mirror.

"I don't ask you to stop wearing your locks for some occasions do I?" Aliyah snapped, stepping out of the shower onto a faded yellow bath mat, and drying herself off with a worn blue bath towel.

"No, you don't. But that's different." Mark furrowed his brow, and gave her a look that showed his patience was wearing thin. "I'm a man, and men are not expected to change their hairstyles for the occasion. My dreads are a permanent part of who I am."

"That's another thing that bothers me about you. No matter how many times I tell you that the word to use for your choice of hairstyle is locks, not dreads, you continue to use the European name that derived from Europeans feeling that locks like yours were dreadful. Why do you insist on calling your locks dreads?"

"Because I wear my hair like this to be different, not to try to make some Afro-centric bullshit statement, Aliyah," Mark raised his voice. "I try not to antagonize people, and you don't care about that. As long as you can keep your job at *Enigma*, that's all you want. You would never be able to work for a white magazine with your attitude or your fashion statements," he shouted at her.

Aliyah ignored his comment, not wanting to get into an argument with him. She dressed hurriedly, thinking that what white people thought overly consumed Mark. She was suspicious of black men who wanted their women to look like white women. She felt that what they really wanted was a white woman, but were willing to settle for a black woman if she changed her look to conform to white standards.

Sometime later, Mark told her that he had to go out of town for a few days to work on an assignment for a newsmagazine. He told Aliyah that he would call her when he returned. Three days after Mark should have left town, Aliyah happened to be driving by his apartment building and saw lights on in his apartment.

Thinking that Mark might have forgotten to turn the lights off, and knowing how frugal he was about wasting electricity, Aliyah thought that she would use the key he kept hidden in a secret place and turn the lights off. When she entered the apartment, she could see telltale signs of a recently eaten meal for two. Dirty dishes were soaking in the kitchen sink. The stove was still warm from the oven. She could smell perfume in the bedroom, Opium, she was almost positive. A Louis Vittone suitcase lay open on the chair in the bedroom. She could see it was filled with women's clothing. She quickly exited the apartment, making sure to leave the lights on.

Aliyah sat outside Mark's apartment building for over two hours before she finally saw him enter the building with a short, blonde, white woman. She was holding his arm and they were laughing. Aliyah felt hurt and betrayed. She cried as she drove through the Holland Tunnel. *How could he?* She asked herself. *Does he think I am a fool? Why did I trust him? Why did Mark have to turn out to be such a jerk?*

Four days later Mark called her office to say that he was home. He volunteered to take the train to her apartment that evening, after she got settled in from work.

"Oh no! Why don't I just go by your place after work and wait for you to get in." She fidgeted with her desk calendar, trying to keep her composure.

"Are you sure? I thought I could spend the night at your place and get a ride back to the city with you in the morning."

That was another thing about Mark that bugged her. He always referred to New York as "the city" as though it were the only city in the world. Newark was a city, too, and she was proud to live there. Knowing that she would not be spending another night with Mark, she was anxious to get the confrontation over with. She knew she would be driving back to Newark alone.

"I prefer to meet at your place if you don't mind. I'll just let myself in and wait for you, okay?" Aliyah put the desk calendar down, more composed now.

"Okay," he agreed.

She left work early that evening, wondering how she should approach Mark. Should she be waiting with her coat on ready for a speedy exit, or should she behave as though nothing was wrong and let him hang himself? When she arrived at the apartment, all was in order. The place was scrubbed clean of all evidence of recent company. She looked in the bedroom; the Louis Vittone was gone. The usual smell of Mark's favorite burnt incense lingered. Aliyah turned on the stereo inserting a Toni Braxton CD. She hung her coat in the hall closet, and then went to the bar and fixed a pitcher of martinis, made just the way Mark loved them with a little more gin and less extra-dry vermouth.

She was sitting at the bar sipping one when she heard Mark's key in the lock. She was shoeless; her beige silk blouse was opened at the collar. She wore matching slacks and a gold leather belt to match her gold jewelry. She quickly caught a glimpse of herself in the mirror behind the bar. She looked calm, relaxed, and sexy. Her feet, with recently polished toenails, were resting on the second bar stool. Toni Braxton was singing in her sultry voice, "Seven whole days, and not a word from you."

Mark sauntered into the room with a huge grin on his face. He grabbed her in his arms and planted a wet kiss on her lips.

"Baby, I missed you," he said, releasing her from his grip. "Did you miss me?" he asked pouring a martini for himself.

Ignoring that Aliyah hadn't answered his question, he sauntered over to the couch, drink in hand, talking about his photo sessions and how much work he had accomplished in the last few days. Before she realized what she was saying, Aliyah blurted out, "Were you lonely without me, Mark?"

"Of course," he replied, his eyes beckoning her to the sofa.

"Were you with any other woman this week, Mark?"

"Of course not. Why would you ask such a question, Aliyah?" His eyes probed her face for an explanation.

The rest poured out of Aliyah as though a dam had broken. Through her tears, she told him how she had come to the apartment, left, waited, and saw him with the other woman. Mark was flabbergasted, however, he regained his composure quickly. He jumped to his feet from the sofa and tried to explain that an old girlfriend from California came out to visit him for a week, and he just could not tell Aliyah about it.

"I knew you couldn't handle it, Aliyah," he yelled as she grabbed her coat, put on her shoes, and fled from the apartment in tears for the second time in less than a week.

"Aliyah, we are not engaged, we never talked about commitment," was the last thing she heard as the elevator door shut.

That was the last time Aliyah was ever at Mark's apartment. She made up her mind that, until Mr. Right came along, she would learn to deal with loneliness the best way that she could. Perhaps she could find a project to throw herself into for a while. Maybe even look for a new place to live. She had been thinking of investing in something of her own. Her family, friends, and work would have to be enough to sustain her until she found a husband. It was better to be alone and lonely than to be in a relationship that was not based on trust.

Eighteen months after the breakup with Mark, Aliyah was a new homeowner. While getting over Mark and readjusting to being alone, she had plunged into finding a place of her own to buy. She had looked at condominiums in Manhattan, which were way above her financial means. She also had looked at brownstones in Brooklyn and Harlem, only to determine they required too much work. Finally, at the suggestion of her father, she had looked at some of the restored brownstones in the city of her birth, Newark.

Aliyah was shocked that the suggestion to buy in Newark had come from her father. Six years earlier, when she first had decided to move all of her stuff out of her parent's large home and into her first real apartment following her college days, her dad had balked because the apartment was in Newark. "You won't be safe living in Newark," he had exclaimed. How ironic; Newark was the one place that her parents were anxious to get out of following the riots of the 1960s, and here she was returning to her roots.

The three-story brownstone Aliyah purchased was in a developing neighborhood, which only five years earlier had been a dilapidated section of the city, but that didn't matter to her. There were definite signs that it was now returning to the status that it had enjoyed before whites had abandoned the city and fled to the suburbs. "White Flight" had enabled her to get the house at a great price. The brownstone, along with her three-year-old midnight blue Mercedes Benz sports car, was her pride and joy.

The four-bedroom home was fully restored, but there were a few things Aliyah wanted to change. It had great potential, but most important it was only a twenty-minute commute by train to her office in Manhattan. It was within walking distance to the New Jersey Transit Trains or the Path Trains.

Once she settled into the brownstone, Aliyah plunged into landscaping and decorating her new home. Gardening was a hobby she took up after purchasing the brownstone. It was a hobby that her mother, who lived in a large English Tudor with a spacious yard in the nearby suburb of South Orange, had hoped her daughter would enjoy as much as she did.

Standing at her bedroom window one morning in late April, and looking down at her garden Aliyah thought, *city courtyards can be just as attractive as the most spacious, meticulously manicured suburban lawns*. The courtyard below her window was bricked in with borders of neatly trimmed ivy. Clay pots that held last year's impatiens, petunias, begonia, and other brightly colored annuals were strategically placed about the courtyard to receive the most sun and to capture instantly the observer's gaze. The forsythia in the corner against the six-foot stockade fence looked like a sunburst, with bits of its glory settling on each branch. It was obvious that the gardener had chosen to let the bush grow to any form it desired rather than shape it with hedge trimmers. Deep purple crocus and shoots of coming tulips completed this day of spring, newly arrived, following a long, hard winter.

The courtyard below her bedroom window was proof of her gardening skills. Last summer her yard had blossomed into a showcase of beautiful flowers, and she looked forward to inviting her family and friends to backyard barbecues to hear their praises of her handiwork. The only drawback to these anticipated gatherings was that the conversation would without a doubt turn to, "Aren't you lonely living in this big house all by yourself?"

Decorating and gardening had taken up so much of her time that she barely thought of her loneliness. Not until the brownstone was almost completely finished did Aliyah begin to focus again on her desire to have a husband. Spring was her favorite season of the year. The last two springs had started the same way. Lonely! She had spent many a cold night sitting in front of her fireplace staring into the fire, wishing she had a warm body to snuggle up next to, and dreaming about the warm days ahead. Now, with the cold season behind her, she looked forward to walks in nearby Branch Brook Park where the cherry blossoms equaled those in the nation's capital. She longed for someone to walk with, someone whose hand she could hold.

No matter how hard she tried to fool her family and friends, she knew they weren't fooled one bit. They knew she was lonely, and they wanted her to find the man with whom she could share her life. She was grateful that they did not pressure her about getting married. They rarely questioned her when she showed up at family functions and social gatherings alone. They took it for granted that one day she would fall in love, get married, and live happily ever after. Until then Aliyah knew she would have to depend on them to help fill in the gaps of the lonely days ahead.

Chapter 2

Kʌɴṃi

"Aliyah, my love, how can I help you today?" Kanmi Olajide, owner and manager of the only fully African department store in the state, greeted Aliyah as she came through the revolving doors of his store. Kanmi and Aliyah were the same age, although he looked older because of his prematurely receding hairline. Their friendship went back to her freshman year at Rutgers University.

"I'm looking for some pieces that will help accent my living room." Aliyah greeted him with a warm embrace.

"I just got in a new shipment from South Africa yesterday. Let me show you." He took her arm and led her to the escalator that took them to the second floor.

His imported inventory consisted of original African artwork and included sculptures, prints, pottery, handcrafted gifts, African-designed clothing, and a huge selection of books by people of African descent throughout the diaspora. Kanmi had been instrumental in helping Aliyah select tasteful items for her new home.

"How's life treating my favorite customer?" he asked, as they browsed about the second floor.

"Things could be better. I'm getting bored now that the house is almost finished." She looked at some throw pillows made of genuine mud cloth that he showed her.

"There is too much to do in the world for anyone to get bored. You need to get out of the house more, Aliyah. Why don't you plan a trip? It will help to relieve your boredom."

"I don't want to go on a trip alone, Kanmi. I'm alone enough already. All I do is work and decorate the house."

"Sometimes just a change of scenery is enough to chase away the blues. Besides you meet some of the most interesting people when you travel, at least I do. Who knows you may even meet the man of your dreams."

"I'm not interested in a long-distance relationship. I hope the man of my dreams lives locally. Enough about me, tell me what's going on in your life?"

"I have been shopping in Southern Africa for merchandise for the store. You know my customers, like you, want a wide range of merchandise to select from. Because you African Americans don't know where you came from in Africa, you don't identify with any one African country. You want merchandise from all over the continent. You are born internationalists," he said, and laughed.

"Most African Americans know that our ancestors were captured in West Africa, and then forced into slavery in the Americas. They are not totally ignorant of their history." Aliyah looked at some Kente cloth napkins.

"Perhaps, but the point I am trying to make, though, is that African Americans tend to view all of Africa as their motherland. They embrace the whole continent. Not that there is anything wrong with this. I wish Africans living on the continent felt the same way. If they did perhaps there would be less conflict and more unity."

When she finished shopping, they had selected pillows and throws made with fabrics imported from all over the African continent. Kanmi's input was helping to give her house a wonderful look and feel of African authenticity.

Kanmi had been living in the United States for seventeen years. He had come from Nigeria as a foreign exchange student his senior year in high school. He stayed after his graduation to study economics at Rutgers, the

State University of New Jersey. His parents were wealthy Nigerians who encouraged him to remain in the United States after he graduated from college because of the instability in his homeland. Kanmi had taken their advice and accepted their money to start his own business. On an earlier occasion when Aliyah had visited the store, Kanmi had told her just how well his business was doing.

"My business has been a huge success," he had said with a look of pride on his face. "My parents are impressed that I can come home whenever I want to. I've even managed to bring a couple of my 'homeboys' to America to work in the store." He had beamed proudly. "They are as grateful to me as I am to you. I will never forget how you befriended me when I first came to America, Aliyah."

Aliyah thought about her first meeting with Kanmi when they were both freshmen. She was living in the dormitory on campus, and he was living with a host family in Somerset, NJ. They were in the same World Cultures class. Aliyah remembered Kanmi's telling the class about his host family.

"They really don't understand me or my culture, and they are not receptive to learning anything about it." He had looked for sympathy from the class.

Out of her curiosity about the motherland, Aliyah reached out to him after class. "It must be hard for you to be so far away from your family and the culture you know so well," she had said while they walked together up College Avenue to the student center.

"It would be easier if Americans were not so fearful of those that are different than them. There is so much that we can learn from each other." They had become fast friends and remained friends ever since.

Shortly after he graduated from Rutgers, Kanmi married a beautiful Nigerian woman, Oya. They purchased a large Victorian home in Plainfield, NJ. Aliyah was a frequent guest in the Olajide home and godmother to their oldest son, five-year-old Mwangi. On one occasion, when Aliyah was visiting them Kanmi tried to persuade her to extend him an invitation to visit her new home.

"When am I going to get to see our masterpiece," he had said, referring to his part in helping to decorate the brownstone.

"Soon, soon," Aliyah had said. She wanted everything to be perfect before she invited guests to her new home.

"You African-Americans are so much like us, yet you are so different. In Africa, there is no such thing as waiting until everything is ready before you invite your friends over. Friends come over right away to help you make everything right. You need your friends to come over to bless the new home. I prefer the African way to the American way."

"Well, it's not like that in America. Here it is all about show. I want to show off my new home. I want it to be just right before I invite my friends over. I want compliments." Aliyah had put off inviting him.

At the Olajide home, Aliyah often got the opportunity to meet other Nigerians. Before she met Mark, she had dated a couple of the Nigerian men she had met through Kanmi. The last date had turned out to be a real disaster. It tested her friendship with Kanmi. She would never forget what Kanmi had said to her when she told him that she did not want to date any more Nigerian men.

"Are you saying that you do not respect my culture, Aliyah?" His face had told her that he was hurt and angry.

"I didn't say that Kanmi. What I said was that I prefer dating African-American men because we share the same culture. African-American men for the most part do not treat their women as though they own them. I didn't like it when your friend, Okolo, behaved as though he owned me."

Oya, always calm and poised, had come to the rescue. "Not all African men behave like that, Aliyah. You don't see Kanmi behaving as though he owns me do you? This particular behavior has its roots in tradition. But it is a changing tradition, Aliyah. African men for the most part, like a lot of other men, feel superior to women. But it doesn't mean that we have to accept this behavior. We get to choose the men that we want to spend time with. When enough African men are rejected because of this behavior, they will learn that the behavior is unacceptable, and they will change."

It was during a visit with Kanmi and his family that Aliyah learned about

Nigerian culture and the religion of Ifa. Shortly after her visit to the store, Aliyah was a dinner guest at the Olajide home. Oya suggested that Aliyah begin to make offerings to her guardian *orisa* to help in her pursuit of a soul mate.

"The *orisa* are like the Christian angels or saints," she explained. "Only followers of Ifa have a guardian *orisa* that looks out for them and helps them in all endeavors." Oya offered her an appetizer from a tray that she sat down on the coffee table.

"How do I find out who my guardian *orisa* is?" Aliyah asked curiously.

"To be really sure you would have to consult a Yoruba priest, a *babalawo*. He will be able to help you determine your true guardian *orisa*. From my observation of you and from what you have told me, I would guess that you are a child of Osun, Aliyah. Osun is the goddess of the rivers and lakes. She is responsible for providing humans with pleasure, happiness, and procreation. The gift of love comes from Osun. Children of Osun are very aware of how they look, and they cannot tolerate boredom. They like the finer things of life. You are a lot like that, wouldn't you agree, Aliyah?" Oya asked, sitting down beside Aliyah on the sofa.

"I suppose that description fits me somewhat." Aliyah reflected.

"Osun can help you acquire what you desire in life. She is a very sensuous goddess. She loves offerings of honey. Perhaps if you poured a little bit of honey into the river occasionally, as an offering, while asking Osun to find a soul mate for you, she would oblige. It could not hurt you to try," Oya persuaded her.

"Maybe I will, Oya. Especially if I get desperate enough," she added as Kanmi reentered the room.

"What are you two yakking about?" He smiled, pleased to see that his wife and his friend were getting along so well.

"Oya was telling me about the *orisa* and how they can help me find a husband." Aliyah laughed.

"Don't laugh Aliyah, the *orisa* will not help you if you don't take them seriously." Kanmi replaced Oya on the couch, who left the room to check on her dinner and look in on the baby.

"You know, the way of Ifa is a very ancient African religion, and it has been helping people of African descent for centuries. It is well known in the Americas too, having come here by way of the middle passage. In Brazil, believers of the *orisa* call their religion Candomblé. In Cuba and Puerto Rico, the religion is Santería. It is called Shango in Trinidad and Tobago; and in Haiti and the southern part of the United States, it is called Vodun or Voodoo. There are millions of *orisa* followers in the world, Aliyah. The African Diaspora is very large and wherever you find a sizable group, you will find believers of Ifa." Kanmi studied her face for a reaction.

Curious to know if Kanmi attributed his own success and wealth to his belief in the *orisa*, Aliyah was about to ask him how the *orisa* had helped him and his family.

"You know only of my life here in the United States, Aliyah." Kanmi appeared to have read her thoughts. "My family comes from a long line of Ifa believers. After the colonization of Nigeria by the British, my ancestors remained Ifa believers while many Nigerians were converting to Christianity. It was much easier for the Christians in Nigeria."

"How so?" Aliyah asked, reaching for one of the appetizers.

"Well, for one thing, their children could attend missionary schools, and they received other benefits that the missionaries provided. You had to abandon your own culture in order to attend a missionary school, though. You were expected to adopt Christianity, even change your name to a Christian one. My family would not abandon the way of their ancestors."

"And this helped you?" she asked, as she munched on what tasted like shrimp.

"Yes, their steadfast belief enabled them to ward off illness, death, and hardship. My father is a very wealthy Nigerian businessman. He is important in Nigerian politics and holds an elected position. My father works hard at bringing about positive change in Nigeria. He believes that, in order for the people of Nigeria to come together for the good of the country, they must return to the way of our ancestors. They must again call on the *orisa* for protection and good fortune for future generations of Nigerians." Kanmi paused to allow Aliyah to question him.

"I always thought that you were a Christian, Kanmi. Isn't what you are saying a contradiction?"

"Not at all. Nigeria is now comprised of mostly Christians and Muslims. Many Nigerians continue to practice the religion of their ancestors; however, they do so in secret. Many believe, as the Europeans taught them, that their ancestral religion is a pagan one, outmoded and obsolete. Many do not practice any religion openly. They have abandoned their traditional belief system and now believe only in power and money. I have been one of the many who has hidden my true belief system in order to advance my education. In order to come to the United States as an exchange student, I pretended to be a Christian."

"That must have been very difficult for you." Aliyah gave Kanmi a sympathetic look.

"Even after I came to America, it was difficult to practice Ifa," he said, sadly. "I remember when I was an exchange student living with my host family how difficult it was to construct an altar in my room to my guardian *orisa*. My hosts could not understand why I had the altar in my room. They certainly could not understand my need to make monthly offerings to my ancestors. They were afraid that I was working some kind of black magic on them. They were uncomfortable with me living in their home and practicing my own culture. I was glad when I got a room on campus, but even then I had to hide my true belief system. Pretending to be a Christian in America has opened doors for me that would ordinarily have been closed."

"So what you are saying is that you lied to get ahead in America, right?" Aliyah asked. "Does Ifa condone lying?"

"Not at all." Kanmi looked at her in amusement. "What I did to get ahead was to use trickery. It was harmless to all involved, yet it got me what I wanted. Trickery is the gift of the *orisa*, Eshu. He is the father of wit and intelligence. Aliyah, you have a lot to learn about the religion of your ancestors. You have never indicated to me that you wanted to learn. Do you think that maybe you would like to learn now?"

"I don't know yet, Kanmi," Aliyah hesitated. "If it means giving up my Christian principles, then I don't think so." She hoped she didn't offend him.

"Believing in the *orisa* does not mean that you cannot believe in the teachings of Jesus Christ. Followers of Ifa believe in one God only, same

31

as Christians. Olodumare is the name that we use for God. We accept that God has many names. We sometimes refer to God as Eleda, the creator; or Olurun, owner of the heavens; or Oluwa, owner of man. The *orisa* are God's helpers. You have to go through them to get to God, just as Christians go through Jesus to reach God. People, the world over, believe that Jesus existed; many believe that he was sent here to save the Jews. Jesus himself says this in the book of Mark and the book of Matthew. Ifa followers believe that the *orisa* are a medium to reach God. People of all races have converted to Christianity; some willingly, some forced. They believe in the teachings of Jesus, which are no different than the teachings of Ifa." He poured himself a glass of water from the pitcher on the coffee table. "Ifa teaches us to use love, friendliness, and goodness among other things in our dealings with people." He stopped and took a sip of the water. "You see Aliyah, you do not have to abandon Christian principles to believe in Ifa."

"Are you trying to convert me, Kanmi?" Aliyah was a little uncomfortable.

"No. I just wanted to give you information about my beliefs, in order to broaden your knowledge and help you to understand my culture. You are a very intelligent woman, Aliyah. You will have no difficulty deciding what is right for you, but to make an intelligent decision you should have as much information as possible." Kanmi finished his sentence just as Oya returned, carrying their youngest son, Yori.

Yori was only eighteen months old, and he was the most adorable child. He had Kanmi's strong jaw and his mother's large oval eyes. He was just beginning to say isolated words in his parent's native tongue. Aliyah reached out to take the baby from Oya, but he tightened his arms around his mother's neck. He looked at Aliyah and said what sounded like "Nuge." Kanmi and Oya laughed.

"What did he say?" Aliyah asked, laughing with them.

"Oya is reading to him from a Nigerian book of folk stories, and he thought you were one of the characters in the book because of your braids."

Kanmi continued to chuckle.

"What a precocious baby to make an association like that at such an early age." Aliyah made a playful gesture toward the baby. "Tell me, where is my Mwangi?" she inquired after her godson and Kanmi's oldest son, a six-year old.

Mwangi reminded Aliyah of herself at that age. From the time she was a little girl, she had been determined. She set her sights high and always got what she wanted. Mwangi was just like that, determined and assertive. He warmed Aliyah's heart.

"Mwangi is spending the night with some friends," Oya said. "They are having a naming ceremony tomorrow for their seven-day-old baby, and they wanted Mwangi to be company for the older child while they make preparations."

"Has the baby been unnamed until now?" Aliyah asked.

Oya explained that in their culture a child was not given a name until the eighth day following his birth. "The first seven days are a period of innocence and all babies are swathed in a protective shield where evil cannot touch them. On the eighth day they enter into the world of mortals. At the naming ceremony, the child will be blessed by the *orisa*, and armed with the tools he will need to be successful in fulfilling his destiny here on earth."

How beautiful, Aliyah thought. There was so much that she admired about Oya and Kanmi's culture. She seemed to recall being at the naming ceremony for Mwangi, however, she had not fully understood what was happening at that time, and it had never been explained to her as Oya just did. Perhaps she hadn't been ready to understand it before now.

"What name will they give the child?" Aliyah looked at Kanmi.

"He is the first-born son. Therefore, he too will be a Mwangi," Kanmi, said proudly. "Mwangi means son of. My first-born son is Mwangi Kanmi Olajide, which means son of Kanmi Olajide.

"Are you a Mwangi, too, Kanmi?"

"No, I am the third son of my father. I was born at the time my father was meeting with great financial success. My full name is Olasunkanmi, which means "My turn to be rich."

"What about the baby's name?" Aliyah was fascinated.

"Yori is a derivative of Ifayori, which translates Ifa outshines them all," Oya said. "My name is Oyafunmi, which translates blessing from Oya." She had a look of pride on her face. "My parents had been childless for the first eight years of their marriage. I was not conceived until my mother sought the help of a *babalawo* who told her to make offerings to her guardian *orisa*, Oya. My mother is now an Ifa priestess."

"Let us go into the dining room to feast," Kanmi said, as though he were starving.

During her periods of absence from the room, Oya had prepared a delicious meal of yam balls, Aliyah's favorite African dish, used to dunk in specially prepared soups. There was rice with a marvelous peanut sauce, and grilled fish that looked and smelled heavenly. Over dinner, Kanmi wanted to hear more about Aliyah and what she was doing to fill up her time. Aliyah told them about the happenings at her job, where she was now a senior editor.

"I am working on an article entitled 'Women-- Red, Yellow, Black, and White: Why Can't We Be Sister Friends?' I feel that there are many reasons that women of all races are not closer, but I believe that the bottom line is that white women are unwilling to accept women of other races as their equal. This is especially prevalent in the work force, where white women feel that they have to be in charge. They have a difficult time taking orders from women of color."

"I think that is true of white people in general." Oya said, feeding the baby some soup. "It is a big problem the world over. Unless something is done about it, the world is destined for destruction."

"Perhaps the upcoming conference on race relations sponsored by the United Nations will have a significant impact," Kanmi said, and poured Aliyah a glass of palm wine. "What about your personal life, Aliyah, are you happy?"

"Happiness is relative, Kanmi." Aliyah stopped eating and put her fork down. "I am happier owning my own home than I was renting an apartment. I am happier being an editor than I was being just a feature writer. And I am happy to have good friends like you and Oya in my life. I could be happier if I had a relationship with someone, like what you and Oya have. I would love to have a man to share my life with, but I am not going to settle for just anyone just to say that I have a man."

"You know, Aliyah, having a man in your life does not always bring you happiness. It's having a soul mate that brings you real happiness," Oya said, smiling with a twinkle in her eye.

"How do you define soul mate, Oya?" Aliyah smiled back at her.

"A soul mate is someone who can read you without your telling them what you are feeling, someone who empathizes with you, who wants for you what you want for yourself." She glanced at her husband for him to agree.

"More important is to have a joining of the physical and the spiritual selves," Kanmi said. "Each individual, in order to be complete, must balance their physical selves with their spiritual selves. In order to have a successful marriage, both partners must be spiritually as well as physically compatible. Oya and I are fortunate that the *orisa* have blessed us with such a relationship." He made eye contact with his wife.

"I don't know many people that have relationships like yours," admitted Aliyah. "My own parents don't have that. My father expected my mother to assist him in reaching his dream of having his own business, a devoted wife, and successful children. I don't think my mother ever had a dream of her own. I want more in a relationship than what they have. Even today, with both her children all grown up, my mother seems so lost, as though she doesn't fit into the world anymore. I don't want to reach fifty only to discover that my life is finished. I want my life as it is, but I want more, too." Aliyah sipped her palm wine.

"How do you intend to get this 'more' that you want out of life, Aliyah?" Kanmi asked, chuckling. "I know how determined you are, but have you ever considered that this 'more' that you want doesn't exist? You are so picky, Aliyah." He said, referring to Aliyah's rejection of his two Nigerian friends.

"You won't let anyone fix you up with someone nice. I can think of a half dozen men that would love to be in a relationship with you, but you won't give any of them a chance. You want a perfect man, and there is no such thing on earth."

Aliyah thought about what Kanmi said before she responded. "Perfection is not what I am looking for in a man; however, I do feel that there has to be some common ground, like those things that we can and cannot tolerate." She put her fork down again. "I will not tolerate a man that does not respect my feelings or my beliefs, and I will not tolerate a man that cheats on me like Mark did. Besides, I hate blind dates. I think that people who agree to go out on them are desperate. I'm not at that point yet. Besides they can sometimes ruin friendships." She smiled at Kanmi, remembering the time she dated his Nigerian friend.

"I agree with you, Aliyah," Oya said, putting another piece of her delicious grilled fish on Aliyah's plate. "I think what you are saying is that men and women, although different, are equal."

"You are going to find out that a lot of men do not agree with that," Kanmi said. "Particularly non-American men."

"I know that cultural differences in a relationship can be crucial; that is why I prefer dating African-American men." Aliyah hoped she did not offend Kanmi again. "At least I will know that we are speaking the same language, culturally. Anyway, what will be will be. I will just have to keep the faith and wait until the time is right."

"Well, while you are waiting, consider what I said about making an offering of a little honey to Osun," Oya said. "She will help you find a soul mate."

Aliyah left Kanmi and Oya's home intrigued with their culture and their religion. She wanted to learn more about Ifa. She was attracted to the idea of bringing more balance into her life. Her physical and emotional needs were clearly out of sync with her spiritual self. She was at times overwhelmed with her physical needs, but she was determined not to let them get the best of her. She wanted a soul mate more than anything else in her life right now. She was interested in Oya's suggestion to make an offering to a guardian *orisa*; however, she didn't give it any more thought until several weeks later.

Chapter 3

Teyinniwa

Aliyah had barely put the key in her front door when she heard the telephone ringing. She quickly opened the door, put her purse and briefcase on the credenza in the foyer, and grabbed the nearest telephone.

"Well, are you coming over or not?" Teyinniwa's booming voice came through the receiver. "Sis is putting chicken on the grill, and she wants to know if she should put enough on for you. You didn't forget it's the last Friday of the month, did you?"

It had been a hectic day for Aliyah. To top it off, traffic getting to the Holland Tunnel had been bumper to bumper. She had left her office at 6 P.M., and it was now after seven and she was just arriving home. She had completely forgotten her standing last-Friday-of-the-month-date with her good friend Teyinniwa.

"Of course I'm coming over," Aliyah said, trying to sound as though it had always been part of her plan for the evening. "Just give me time to take a quick shower and change into something more comfortable. I'll see you in forty minutes, okay?"

"Good, we'll hold dinner until you get here," Teyinniwa said, before hanging up the phone.

At 8 P.M., Aliyah was ringing the doorbell of the Freeman sisters' home. Teyinniwa and Morgan were older than Aliyah, neither was married, and they lived together in their family home in north Newark. Aliyah had met Teyinniwa on her first trip to Africa. They had both attended The International Conference of Women in Nairobi, Kenya. Aliyah had come to love both sisters; however, it was Teyinniwa to whom she felt she owed her rebirth. Standing on the front porch to the Freeman house, waiting for someone to answer the front door, Aliyah recalled her first meeting with Teyinniwa Freeman.

She was only a sophomore in college. Teyinniwa often reminded Aliyah that she behaved like a sophomore, too, when they first met. According to Teyinniwa, with only one year of college under her belt, Aliyah believed that she knew all there was to know about life.

The Black Student Organization at Rutgers had announced its intention to send a student representative to the conference sponsored by the United Nations. Aliyah had been active in black student affairs since her first week on campus. She worked hard for the organization and was dedicated to moving the organization forward.

She had hoped she would be the chosen representative, although she tried not to show how much she wanted it. She even tried to help another candidate who was vying for the opportunity, telling the membership why she believed the other candidate was worthy of being chosen, even though deep in her heart she desperately wanted to be the one to go. She even tried to persuade her father to finance the trip in case she wasn't the chosen one.

Bill Neal had reminded his daughter that it was costing him plenty already to pay her tuition and living expenses at Rutgers. He told her that she would have to find another way to finance her trip to the motherland. Aliyah did not argue with him because she understood his position. She felt fortunate to have a father who could foot all of her college bills. Aliyah knew so many students who were struggling financially to stay in school despite financial aid from various sources. She felt privileged knowing that her family could afford to pay her way and that she would not be in debt when her education was complete.

She was wonderfully surprised when the Black Student Organization finally announced that she was the one who had been selected to represent the organization in Kenya. She attributed this good fortune to her faith in God, and all the time she had spent on her knees praying for this opportunity. It would be the highlight of her life. She was only nineteen years old, and she was going to travel all the way to Kenya without her parents or any other supervision. She would be completely on her own, or so she had thought.

Much to her dismay, even before she boarded the plane at JFK Airport in New York City, Aliyah had been unofficially assigned a chaperone. Shortly after she and her parents had arrived at the airport, a very attractive woman, dressed in beautiful African attire and with long locks of premature gray hair, greeted her dad with a warm smile and caring embrace. Her father had introduced Teyinniwa to his wife and daughter as one of his latest Mercedes owners. Teyinniwa in turn had introduced the Neal family to her equally attractive sister, Morgan, who had accompanied her to the airport.

Teyinniwa had recently purchased her dream car from Bill Neal, and she was extremely grateful for the deal he had given her. Mr. Neal had made little of the transaction, stating that it was the least he could do for such a refined and beautiful sister. Teyinniwa had told them that she was attending the conference in Nairobi, Kenya, to present a position paper, "African-American Women in the 21st Century," on behalf of a woman's organization to which she belonged, The Daughters of Africa. She had been happy to oblige Mr. Neal when he had asked her to look out for his little girl who was traveling alone, halfway around the world. Aliyah had felt disheartened, thinking that this older woman, who was at least thirty-five years old, was going to be giving her dad a full report of her activities in Kenya. She had decided then that she would do all she could to distance herself from Teyinniwa while in Africa.

"Come here and give me a big hug, girl," the tall, buxom Teyinniwa said, opening the front door and jolting Aliyah out of her thoughts.

"Me, too," Morgan, the smaller of the two sisters with a much softer voice said, coming in from the kitchen. "Where have you been, girl? It seems like ages since I last saw you."

"I've been busy working on the house, you know, and my job has been keeping me pretty busy. And last month, you two were in Zimbabwe."

"Let's eat now before my dinner gets ruined." Morgan led them into the large formal dining room.

"I love this house," Aliyah said, sitting down at the beautifully set table. The Freeman home was a huge English Tudor in the Forrest Hill section of Newark. Teyinniwa and Morgan had been raised in the home and had inherited it from their mother when she died. The house had been in the family for over seventy years.

"This house holds a lot of memories for us," Teyinniwa said. "Everything you see is a family heirloom. Practically all of the furniture belonged to our grandparents."

"Some of the stuff we collected from our travels, you know," Morgan reminded her sister.

The Freeman sisters were world travelers. Between them they had visited all of the continents and over fifty cities worldwide. "Was your trip to Zimbabwe as exciting as the time we had in Nairobi?" Aliyah asked Teyinniwa.

"Every trip I take to the motherland is exciting," Teyinniwa said. "The trip to Kenya was special though, mostly because I met you there and we have remained friends all of these years. Do you remember how you tried to avoid me in the beginning of that trip?" She laughed a hearty laugh.

Aliyah remembered that, after she had boarded the jumbo jet that would take them to Kenya, she did not see Teyinniwa throughout the flight. One of her seatmates was a student representative from Spelman College in Atlanta, and they became fast friends. Aliyah had speculated that Teyinniwa was probably sitting in first class with other dignitaries going to the conference, including Coretta Scott King and Dorothy Height. She and Maxine, the student from Spelman, made plans to be roommates while in Kenya and to stick together. Aliyah gave no further thought to Teyinniwa until she and Maxine, exhausted from the long flight and the mass confusion they met at the airport, finished dragging their huge duffel bags up four flights of stairs to their dormitory room at the University of Nairobi. Once they were at the top of the stairs, Aliyah remembered hearing a familiar voice screaming, "Who the hell do they think they are? I don't care if she is the president's daughter. She is no better than I am." The loud voice was coming from the room directly across from hers. When she looked in the open door, she saw that the booming voice belonged to none other than Teyinniwa.

"What are you doing here?" Aliyah remembered asking Teyinniwa through the open door.

Grinning from ear to ear, Teyinniwa had embraced Aliyah and explained that the women from her group had been kicked out of their first-rate hotel accommodations to make room for visiting dignitaries. It appeared that the Kenyan Bureau of Tourism had not realized that they were entirely overbooked for the conference. More than ten thousand women from all over the world had descended on Nairobi in the past two days. Accommodations were not that plentiful, and the Kenyan government had taken temporary control of hotel assignments.

"Dignitaries like the daughter of the president of the United States of America, can you imagine," Teyinniwa had exclaimed.

"She's about as dignified as a sardine. Well, anyway, here we are college students again. By the way, don't forget that 8:3o tomorrow morning I will be making a most stimulating presentation at the University Center, room 3oo. I know that you will be there," she had said.

"I remember the pained look on your face when I invited you to attend the lecture I was giving the next morning." Teyinniwa brought Aliyah back to the present.

"And a most stimulating lecture it was," Aliyah said. "I remember you spoke of the plight of the African-American woman."

"Yes. I remember saying that black women were more prevalent and more successful on college campuses and in corporate America than black men were. Many of the relationship problems between black men and black women are directly related to African-American women having more opportunity to succeed. You, for example, are too successful for most black men, Aliyah."

"Tell me about it." Aliyah nodded her head in agreement. "I remember how impressed I was with your presentation." She also remembered how even more impressed she became with the older woman during the rest of the trip.

"I hope the situation has improved since you made that speech fifteen years ago," Morgan said. "Surely there are more successful and eligible black men around now. Have you met any interesting men lately, Aliyah?"

"Not really. Like I said earlier, I've been pretty busy with the house and work. There haven't been many opportunities to meet any men."

"You must come in contact with some cute guys at work, don't you?" Morgan asked.

"I make it a rule not to get involved with the men at work. Besides, there are few eligible men working for the magazine."

"I don't understand why no one has grabbed you up by now," Teyinniwa said. "I remember in Africa the men wouldn't leave you alone. Do you remember the safari that you and that other little girl accompanied me and the Daughters of Africa on?"

"That little girl's name was Maxine and she was a college sophomore at the time just like me," Aliyah reminded Teyinniwa. "Of course, I remember the safari trip. It was the most exciting thing I had ever done in my life. The Daughters of Africa were the most interesting women I had ever met. They were all seasoned travelers, educated, with advanced degrees, and well read. I was so impressed with them."

"Well, I remember the safari guide we had. He fell in love with you at first sight. Do you remember that?" Teyinniwa gave Aliyah a look that said how could you forget.

"Oh yes," Aliyah said. "He was from the Massai tribe. He drove us through Massai country in his safari van and insisted that I sit up front with him. He told me all about the culture of the Massai people along the way. I'll never forget the sight of grazing zebras along the way. They were as common as grazing cows along the countryside in America."

"I remember when we stopped to buy some soft drinks and snacks from the only convenience store in the vicinity," Teyinniwa said. "An Asian-Indian owned it. I asked our guide why the Kenyan people still appeared to be economically controlled by non-Africans. He never did answer me. All he wanted to talk about was you. Is she married? Does she have a boyfriend?"

"I remember asking him a similar question when we stopped for lunch at that beautiful lodge with the picturesque setting," Aliyah said. "The food was delicious, and although African men, Massai to be exact, served the meal, the owner was of European descent. I asked our guide why African men didn't appear to own any of the businesses in their own country."

"What did he say?" Morgan asked.

"He appeared embarrassed by the question," Aliyah said. "He just looked at me and said that 'Wherever there is money to be made, you will find them.' I remember how abruptly he changed the subject and looked right into my eyes and asked me to marry him." Aliyah laughed from the memory. "If I had known then that his would be the only marriage proposal I would ever get, I might have accepted it."

"Don't worry Aliyah," Morgan said. "You're young; you'll get your chance at marriage. So tell me about the safari guide."

"He was a wonderful guide." Aliyah looked at Teyinniwa for confirmation. "He could locate whatever animal we wanted to see. We chased a family of giraffes and came within a few feet of a lion's den where a male and female lion growled at us, apparently disturbed about being aroused from their afternoon nap. We climbed on top of the safari van to shoot pictures. It was so exciting. When we got back to Nairobi, he asked me out on a date for the next day, but I declined. He was too intense for me."

"What I remember is the long drive back to the city of Nairobi," Teyinniwa said. "We were covered with dust and we couldn't wait to use the community shower at the dormitory and jump into those lumpy cots." She laughed.

"Did you meet any other cute guys in Nairobi?" Morgan asked Aliyah.

"What about that guy you dated who owned the gift shop in downtown Nairobi?" Teyinniwa reminded her.

"You must be talking about Muiru," Aliyah said. "He didn't own a gift shop downtown. All but one of the up-scale shops downtown were owned and operated by Asian-Indians. Muiru had a booth at the Gikoma marketplace. Maxine and I did most of our shopping there and we loved it. African men, mostly of the Gikuyu tribe, owned all of the booths there. They were delightful. I loved the way they called out to us: 'My long lost African-American sister, come here and look at my stuff.' We had so much fun with them."

"Wasn't Jomo Kenyatta a Gikuyu?" Morgan asked.

"Yes he was," Aliyah said. "They are so much like African-American men, sexy, and exciting. What impressed me the most was their command of languages, not only English and their own Swahili, but European and Asian languages as well. Muiru asked me out on a date and I accepted."

"Where did he take you?" Morgan asked.

"He and his cousin, John, took Maxine and me out dancing. He was so cute." Aliyah let her thoughts drift to the night she spent dancing with Muiru under the moonlit African sky in Nairobi. She remembered how hard his body had felt through her thin summer dress. His erection, which bulged noticeably under his loose-fitting trousers, wouldn't stop throbbing.

"John doesn't sound like an African name." Morgan brought Aliyah back to the conversation.

"That was his Christian name," Aliyah said. "He told me that in order to attend any of the free schools in Nairobi, which were run by missionaries, he had to be baptized and take on a Christian name. We learned so much about their culture. They were impressed that I appeared to know quite a bit already about the Gikuyu culture. I told them that before coming to Kenya I had read Jomo Kenyatta's book, *Facing Mt. Kenya*."

"Remember our last night in Kenya?" Teyinniwa asked. "You and Maxine came along with me and some of the Daughters of Africa on an overnight trip to Mombasa, on the Indian Ocean?"

"How could I forget that?" Aliyah finished the remainder of her dinner.

"Don't tell me you met another man in Mombasa?" Morgan started to clear the dishes from the table.

"Oh yes, she did," Teyinniwa said, getting up to help her sister. "What I remember about Mombasa is the bus ride from Nairobi. It was long, hot, and bumpy. The roads were so bad that my seat came loose after the driver hit a big bump in the road, and I had to ride the rest of the journey in a prone position."

"I remember we encountered a little difficulty getting accommodations,"

Aliyah recalled. "It appeared that the best hotels were reserved for European travelers."

"Let me tell this part, Aliyah," Teyinniwa said, sitting back down at the table. "This African hotel clerk at The Diani Sea Lodge, a resort right on the beach, refused to register us, so I told him to go get 'Bwana.' " She laughed at herself for using the word 'Bwana', that she had remembered from the old Tarzan movies. "Well, only after I gave the owner a piece of my mind, in the style that only an African-American woman, who was hot, tired, and angry could deliver, were we allowed to register."

"The hotel owner was a European man of German descent," Aliyah said. "After detecting the southern accent of one of the Daughters of Africa, he warmed up to us. He mentioned that he had lived in Texas for a short time, and that he did not want any trouble. He told us that the hotel personnel were unaccustomed to registering African-American visitors. This was only the second group of African-Americans to attempt to register at the hotel since they had opened five years ago. We later learned that the Massai and Gikuyu people living in the area were not allowed in the hotel at all."

"The accommodations were wonderful though," Teyinniwa said, carrying some more dishes into the kitchen. "Despite the looks and stares of the other European guests, we had a delightful time. The Indian Ocean was so beautiful, and so were the beaches. Beautiful white sand and plenty of lovely shells, including a few cowry shells. You know they were once so valuable they were used as currency?" Her voice carried from the kitchen.

"We met some cute Massai warriors on the beach selling beautiful handcrafted jewelry, a few masks, and some spears." Aliyah spoke loud enough for Morgan, who was loading the dishwasher, to hear. "One of them was wearing Western attire. He lived in a beautiful waterfront home near the beach. He invited us to his home to meet his family."

"They were not accustomed to meeting African-American women visiting in their community," Teyinniwa said. "They fell in love with us. Their English was impeccable. They wanted to know all about life in America and we wanted to know all about life in Mombassa."

"I remember that night, after dinner, we listened to the poolside entertainment provided by the hotel," Aliyah said, smiling from the memory.

"Lucy, a singer from South Africa, was the main attraction," Teyinniwa said. "She'd been living in exile in Kenya for the past five years. She talked to us after the show, and I remember feeling so bad for her. She longed to go back to a free South Africa. She told us how much she missed her family. She loved talking to us," Teyinniwa said, getting misty-eyed just thinking about it.

"Teyinniwa was wonderful," Aliyah said to Morgan, who had come back into the dining room. "She encouraged Lucy to 'keep the faith.' I remember you said that your faith was inherited." She looked at Teyinniwa, who was trying to remember. "Remember you told her that your chosen name, Teyinniwa, meant faith for a brighter future, and that that was what we all have to hang on to. You also told her that your ancestors were slaves in America, and that your great grandfather passed this strong faith on to his descendants by taking the surname Free-man when slavery was finally abolished. You also told her how he refused to pass his slavemaster's name down to his descendants. You were wonderful with her, Teyinniwa. I was so proud of you." Aliyah got a little misty-eyed too.

"I'm surprised that you remember so much," Teyinniwa said. "I have always been interested in South Africa. I remember promising Lucy that South Africa would be free in the next five years, and that she would be able to return home. I told her that freedom was imminent, despite the fact that many white people in that country were in denial. I told Lucy that the daughter of the president of the United States had walked out of a workshop at the conference the previous day because she refused to engage in a discussion about apartheid. The president's daughter had stated that 'apartheid was not an issue to be addressed at the conference, as it was not a problem concerning women directly.' How wrong she was," Teyinniwa said.

"I remember your telling Lucy that you knew apartheid was on its last legs because the other women, representing the majority of countries around the world, did not agree with the president's daughter," Aliyah said. "How right you were."

"Well, that trip to Mombasa turned out to be very exciting," Teyinniwa said.

"So was the overnight train ride back to Nairobi," Aliyah added.

"That's right," Teyinniwa remembered. "That's where you met that other cutie."

"Uh huh," Aliyah said smiling.

"I recall a very attractive young man who introduced himself to us at the train station while we waited to purchase tickets to take us back to Nairobi," Teyinniwa said. "He was tall, dark, and handsome, right, Aliyah?"

"Very handsome. He was wearing a three-piece suit and carrying an attaché case. He asked if he could have the pleasure of our company at dinner," Aliyah remembered, and smiled.

"All of us? We asked him in unison." Teyinniwa laughed.

"His name was Cam," Aliyah said. "He wanted all of us to join him in the dining car for dinner. He was so cute. Beautiful smile with pearly white teeth. He wrote me a few times after I returned to the States."

"I remember he was really impressed with you, Aliyah," Teyinniwa said. "I think he said his father worked for the railroad, and that he received free passes for his passage and dinner. He was a manager for one of the large hotels in Nairobi."

"Why are you still smiling, Aliyah," Morgan asked. "Did anything happen with the two of you?"

"Not really." Aliyah was still smiling.

"All I know is that the rest of us left him and Aliyah alone in the dining car to retire to our respective compartments," Teyinniwa said. "I didn't see Aliyah again until we got off the train in Nairobi."

"Cam invited me to visit with him for a while in his compartment," Aliyah said. "We talked until the wee hours of the morning and I must have fallen asleep. I remember waking up at 5 A.M. after hearing him whisper in my ear, 'Look out the window, there is a surprise for you.' When I looked out the window I was in awe. For the next two hours Cam and I watched the wildlife in Kenya take flight, hunting for their breakfast. We saw giraffes and elephants, zebras, gazelles, and even hippos as the train sped on a snakelike path toward Nairobi. Kenya was such a wonderful adventure." Aliyah sighed, still in awe fifteen years later.

"Do you still hear from Cam?" Teyinniwa asked.

"No. We kept in touch for a little while. But Kenya is on the other side of the world. He's probably married with five or six kids by now."

"Or maybe five or six wives," Morgan said.

"Have you always enjoyed traveling?" Aliyah asked the Freeman sisters as they led the way into their parlor for an after-dinner brandy.

Teyinniwa told Aliyah that she had taken her first trip abroad when she was only eleven years old. She had competed in an international debating team runoff in London. She attended Branch Brook Elementary School in the city, and was a member of the youngest debating team in the school system. Her school and her family were so proud of her that everyone helped to raise the money for the trip. Her team came in third, but it was still such an honor.

"After that I was bitten by the travel bug." Teyinniwa laughed.

"She passed it on to me," Morgan admitted.

Aliyah had spent many a Friday night sipping brandy in the large Freeman parlor over the last fifteen years. She learned that the sisters had always lived in the home their grandparents had purchased in the 1930s. At one time, the whole Freeman family, consisting of Teyinniwa and Morgan, their parents, their uncle and his wife, three of his children, and of course their grandparents, lived in the six-bedroom home. Sitting in their spacious parlor they reminisced about their lives.

"Now, of course, there are just the two of us left," Morgan said, sadly. "Everyone else has either died or gone to live somewhere else."

"Oh, but we had some wonderful times in this old house." Teyinniwa attempted to cheer her sister up. "If these walls could talk, they could tell some stories."

Shortly after her first visit, Aliyah remembered asking the sisters; "Will you continue to live here if either of you get married?"

"Who knows," Morgan had responded. "Perhaps that is why neither of us has taken the plunge, yet. We are too damned comfortable living here".

"Speak for yourself," Teyinniwa had said loudly. "If I meet Mr. Right, I am out of here, leaving you all by your lonesome."

"Who else do you think can put up with you, besides me?" Morgan had laughed.

Now that both of the sisters were over fifty, talk of marriage had ceased, and relationships with men were only spoken of in the past tense.

"We have both had our share of men," Teyinniwa was now saying. "We've both moved out on occasion to spend time trying to build a relationship with a man. But, we both have always come back to what we have here. We have always been able to come and go as we please, whenever we please, for as long as we please, with no consequences. Neither of us has had to answer to another person since our parents died thirty years ago. They left us this house, their life savings, and our independence." She sipped her brandy.

"And we have made the most of it." Morgan poured herself another brandy. "I don't know about you, but I only have a few regrets."

"Now, when I look back on my life, I do wonder if my choices should have been different," Teyinniwa said. "Would I have been happier being a wife and raising children to keep me company in my old age?"

"You've got me to keep you company in your old age." Morgan looked at her sister, and laughed.

"You may still get married one day," Aliyah said. "You are never too old, you know."

"It will never happen," Teyinniwa said. "We don't date anymore."

"But you are only fifty, you still have time." Aliyah was optimistic.

"Only fifty? Thank you, sweetheart." Teyinniwa smiled at Aliyah. "But I am looking fifty-five right in the eye. Besides there hasn't been a serious candidate for a husband in over fifteen years."

"What happened to him?" Aliyah asked.

"Oh honey, at the time I just wasn't ready to make a commitment," Teyinniwa said. "I was just beginning to realize my dream. I was one of the founders of The Daughters of Africa, you know. It had always been a dream of mine to found an organization that would help black women and children get out of life what they deserve. I couldn't be all that he wanted me to be as a wife and follow my dream at the same time," she sighed. "We had a wonderful relationship that lasted eight years, but he wanted more, and I wasn't willing to make the sacrifice. Listen to me, honey, if the right man comes along and wants a commitment, think carefully before you make a decision that could send him away. You may not get another chance. The right man comes along only once in a lifetime, maybe twice if you are lucky."

"I appear to be having trouble recognizing Mr. Right." Aliyah looked forlorn.

"Oh, you will know him when you meet him," Morgan chimed in. "There will never be a time when you won't want to be with him, and there will be little about him that you will want to change." She laughed to lighten the mood.

"Have you let a Mr. Right slip by, too, Morgan?" Aliyah asked innocently.

"Is the sky blue?" The sisters said together, and then laughed.

"I'm sorry that I didn't have someone experienced to talk to when I was a young woman," Morgan said. "I made so many mistakes when I was younger that I now regret. I try not to focus on them because it does no good. What's done is done." She shrugged her shoulders.

"We all make mistakes when we are young," Teyinniwa said. "But young love rarely works out anyway."

"Sometimes it does," Morgan said. "I have noticed in some cultures young love is encouraged and nurtured. I have witnessed a Jewish colleague of mine nurture a relationship between her daughter and a young man whom the family considered a good catch. When her daughter was fifteen, she started dating a seventeen-year-old genius. He had been accepted into Harvard University to study biochemistry. Instead of discouraging the relationship because the girl was so young, her mother nurtured it because she knew the potential of the young man."

"What does a fifteen-year old know about love?" Aliyah asked. "It sounds as though the mother was just seeing dollar signs. Infatuation at such an early age just leads to sex."

"The mother told me that she cautioned the young woman about the dangers of unwanted pregnancy and encouraged dialogue about sex in order to help her avoid pregnancy when they would become sexually active, something she believed to be unavoidable." Morgan became defensive. "The couple didn't get married until they both finished college, and now they have a wonderful life together." Her mood changed and she looked sad.

"Fifteen is too young to know what you are doing," Aliyah said. "I remember when I was fifteen. It's a good thing that I didn't end up with any of the choices in boys I made then. Ugh!"

"I regret that my parents did not have the foresight to do the same thing for me," Morgan said, as though she didn't hear Aliyah. "My first love was a young man that had great potential, but I was only sixteen and my parents felt I was too young to be in love. They discouraged the relationship and caused us to break up. This young man went on to become a very prominent lawyer. He married someone else, and appears to be content now. However, I have always regretted that I didn't hold onto him while I had him. I've been looking for someone like him ever since." She had a faraway look in her eyes.

"Our grandparents on both sides got married at early ages and the marriages lasted until they died," Teyinniwa said. "I know that times have changed, but we have to look at the circumstances of each relationship before we make a determination about whether it will last or not. Sometimes you can fall in love at an early age and it can work. We cannot make blanket statements about love, because each situation has its own uniqueness. Morgan and that young man were so much in love at the time. It probably would have been better for her if our parents had nurtured the relationship and helped them along. I often think that the reason she has never married is because she never got over her one true love." Teyinniwa looked at her sister sympathetically.

"I've got to get out of here," Aliyah said, getting up from the comfort of the chair. "I have a lot to do tomorrow."

At the front door, Teyinniwa told Aliyah her how much the once-a-month girl talks meant to her and Morgan. "We really look forward to your visits." She gave her a hug.

"We never got a chance to talk about your trip to Zimbabwe." Aliyah suddenly remembered.

"That's okay, we can save that for next month." Morgan reached out for her hug.

Aliyah had always been one to learn from other people's mistakes.

She was glad that she had met the sisters while she was so young. She remembered thinking that perhaps they could help her to get all out of life that they had gotten and more, too. She had decided after her first visit to the Freeman home that she would take them up on their offer to visit them once a month. It never occurred to Aliyah, then, that fifteen years later she would be in the same position that Teyinniwa was in when they first met, accomplished in her field, well traveled, unmarried, and childless.

Chapter 4

"You want to grab some sandwiches and eat lunch in the park?" Claudia said into the telephone, while Aliyah continued to edit the story she was preparing to submit to her editor-in-chief.

With Claudia on speakerphone, Aliyah continued to write feverishly. "I don't think so," she said. "This story is still not quite right, and today is the deadline for submission. I need to stay right here and work on it a little more. Maybe I'll order something from the deli and eat lunch at my desk. I want to get it perfect before I turn it in this afternoon."

"Then why don't you come by after work?" Claudia asked. "Ebony would love to see you, and so would Kwame. It's been ages since you spent the night with us. I'll leave work a little early and make something special for dinner, okay?"

"That sounds like a plan. I'll see you later on then." Aliyah turned the phone off.

Spending the night with Claudia and her family was always an enjoyable experience. Claudia's marriage was one of the happiest Aliyah had ever known. The joy she felt, as a guest in her home, was the closest feeling she had to being married herself. Claudia was like a sister to Aliyah. They had shared everything as children growing up together in South Orange, New Jersey.

Claudia had been Aliyah's best friend since sixth grade. Her parents had separated when she was eleven; her father was an abusive alcoholic. Claudia and her two younger siblings had fled with their mother from Brooklyn to live in Claudia's maternal grandparent's home in South Orange, New Jersey. The house, an old colonial, in Aliyah's neighborhood had been in their family for years. Despite obvious financial difficulties, it was apparent that the family was warm and loving. Aliyah remembered how happy she had been when Claudia was put into her class. She remembered thinking, *Now I won't be the only black in the class.*

It was almost seven when Aliyah finally left the office. She'd accomplished a lot by working through her lunch hour. The traffic going up to Harlem was only moderately heavy. When she turned left off Malcolm X Boulevard onto 145th Street, she saw Kwame, Claudia's husband, walking toward Convent Avenue. Kwame, only five feet eight inches tall, about the same height as Aliyah, was walking at a fast pace. It was evident from his athletic build that he worked out regularly. Aliyah eased the car towards the curb, rolled down her window and called out to him.

"Hey, mister, you need a ride?"

"Are you trying to pick me up lady?" Kwame teased, recognizing the voice before he saw the car.

"I guess you're surprised to see me today." Aliyah reached over and unlocked the car door for him.

"No," Kwame said. "I knew you were coming for dinner. Claudia is making something special for you, and she sent me out to get fresh garlic and French bread. You're in for a treat."

"Knowing Claudia, that doesn't surprise me. She's the only woman I know that can put in a full work day and prepare a gourmet dinner for guests, all before 8 P.M.," Aliyah said, remembering how much Claudia had accomplished before they even graduated from high school.

As one of the top secretarial students in their graduating class at South Orange, Maplewood High School, Claudia had landed a summer job with NBC just before entering her senior year. She fell in love with the corporate world, and did not mind the forty-five- minute bus commute into Manhattan everyday. She loved having her own money to spend, and spend it she did, becoming the best-dressed girl in the senior class. Claudia continued to work part-time for NBC all through her senior year. She became a member of the work-study program which enabled her to get an early release from school each day in order to commute to New York.

Aliyah barely saw Claudia in school that last year, but they continued to spend weekends together. They often ventured into Manhattan to shop or eat lunch, and occasionally to go to one of the hottest discos for a night of fun, meeting attractive guys. Claudia quickly learned her way around the Manhattan circuit, and Aliyah loved tagging along for the ride.

"My wife is one amazing woman," Kwame said as Aliyah parked the car in front of their house. "I worry about her taking on so much, though." He waited for Aliyah to turn off the engine. "Did you know that she is taking classes at City College three nights a week?"

"No. She never mentioned it to me."

"Then don't say anything to her about it," Kwame said. "Wait until she's ready to tell you." He jumped out of the car and came around to Aliyah's side to open the door for her.

Aliyah wondered why Claudia had not told her that she was going to college. She recalled that Claudia had opted not to continue her education after completing high school, stating that she had had enough of school for a while. She remembered Claudia saying that she wanted to work and make some money in order to buy some of things that Aliyah took for granted because they came so easy to her. By the time Aliyah was a junior at Rutgers, Claudia was making her way up the corporate ladder as an administrative assistant for NBC.

"Something smells wonderful," Aliyah said as soon as she entered the house.

"Dinner is almost ready," Claudia, petite and pretty, announced from the kitchen. She came into the foyer and gave Aliyah a hug. "Where's the bread,

Kwame?" she asked her husband. "I want to make some garlic toast before we sit down to eat."

"What are we having?" Aliyah gave Kwame her jacket to hang up.

"I made vegetable lasagna and some broccoli rabe. Aliyah, come and sit in the kitchen with me while I make the garlic bread."

"Where's Ebony?" Kwame asked.

"She's up in her room. Check on her for me will you? I'll call you when dinner is ready."

Leaving the room, Kwame made eye contact with Aliyah. He put two fingers up to his lips to remind her not to mention that she knew Claudia was going to college. Aliyah gave him a wink, implying that the secret was safe with her.

Like Claudia, Kwame was a native New Yorker. They were both from Brooklyn, but unlike Claudia, he came from a middle-class family. He was the only child of professional parents. His father was the pastor of a Baptist church in Brooklyn with a large congregation. His mother was a social worker. Kwame grew up in the church. He was a member of the choir and reportedly had a beautiful voice. He loved music both secular and non-secular. He once thought he wanted to be a preacher like his father, however, after doing some missionary work in Africa with his mother, he decided to become a teacher. He taught history at Washington Irvine High School in Manhattan, but his dream was to teach in Ghana.

"Is Kwame still investigating teaching positions in Ghana?" Aliyah asked Claudia while she set the kitchen table.

"He's more serious about it than ever girl. He's made up his mind that he is going to do this one way or another," Claudia said, putting the garlic bread in the oven.

"How do you feel about it?" Aliyah arranged the napkins and silverware on the table.

"Whatever makes him happy," Claudia said. "I would love to see Africa myself. I remember your first trip there when you were in college. I never knew a person could change so much," she recalled. "Your whole attitude changed. Remember how you condemned materialism as a white man's value. Telling me materialism and capitalism is what led to the white man's

56

destruction of the African civilization."

"I remember," Aliyah said, recalling how Claudia had erupted one day while she was visiting Aliyah in her dorm room in New Brunswick. "You really gave me a piece of your mind and helped me put things back into perspective," she said, remembering Claudia's anger.

"Whoa!" She had shouted at Aliyah. "I don't want to hear that crap, especially from you. You're the one who grew up demanding that daddy buy her all the latest designer clothes, all the latest compact discs and stereo equipment. You're the one who was very disappointed when daddy presented you with a brand new Mazda as a high school graduation gift, because you had been praying for a Mercedes. How dare you, Aliyah! Now that I am finally in a position to get a small portion for myself of what has been handed to you on a silver platter all of your life, how dare you have the nerve to tell me that I should abandon my attitude of materialism because of some bullshit you've been reading and listening to. Are you willing to give up hoping that daddy will buy you that Mercedes for a college graduation gift? Will you refuse it if he does?" Claudia had asked angrily.

After some thought, Aliyah had to admit that material things had a place in each of their lives. She had said to Claudia, "I don't believe in putting materialism above love for people." Somewhere she had remembered reading that "You are supposed to use things and love people, and not the other way around." To love things and use people was a sin as far as she was concerned. She and Claudia had vowed then that they would never cherish diamonds the way that some women did, and they would not accept a diamond as an engagement present from their future fiancés. It was the love of diamonds that led to Africa's destruction.

"You were right, Claudia. I did go a little overboard when I got back from Africa. But you have to admit I was right about a lot of stuff. Especially about attending the African history lecture series up in Harlem. We learned a lot from Dr. Ben and Dr. Clark. And as I recall, you met Kwame in the class that I insisted we take with Amos Wilson. Those classes were a wonderful means of meeting good-looking brothers with a little something under their caps. Too bad it didn't work out for me," Aliyah said, recalling how many guys she had met and dated during that time. "Six months after we started attending the lectures, you met Kwame and three years later you were married. I don't know why, but I just never met the right guy." Aliyah thought of Claudia and Kwame's happiness.

"You're right," Claudia said. "If it hadn't been for you, I never would have met Kwame, and we wouldn't have Ebony or this house. The day we married, the day Ebony was born, and the day we moved into this brownstone were the happiest three days of my life."

"The experience you got working on this brownstone sure helped me when I bought my own brownstone in Newark, even though I didn't have anywhere near the work you had when you moved in here," Aliyah said gratefully. "Things have really worked out wonderfully for you, Claudia. When will my time come?"

"Things are going well for you in other ways, Aliyah. Look how well you are doing at *Enigma*. I was so happy when you got a job in Manhattan. All I could think about was that I would be able to have lunch with you at least once or twice a week. Now you're a senior editor. You're making a lot of money. Driving a Mercedes Benz. And how many single women do you know who purchase their own home at your age?"

"Claudia, you always know what to say to make me feel better," Aliyah said.

Kwame's den was the favorite room in the house for entertainment or intellectual discussion. The room was very comfortable, with a soft leather sofa and a large screen television. In the winter, Kwame would make a fire in the fireplace while the women cleaned up the kitchen. Ebony always begged to stay up late on the nights that Aunt Aliyah spent the night. No one argued with her, knowing that she would fall fast asleep within the hour. Sure enough, ten minutes into the American Music Awards, Ebony was fast asleep.

"Why African Americans even participate in these charades is beyond my understanding," Kwame said after his favorite recording artist lost an award to a white artist who was obviously less talented, in his opinion.

"How else can they get the recognition that they deserve?" Claudia asked.

"Do you think they get the recognition they deserve on The American Music Awards?" Kwame almost shouted, mindful of the sleeping Ebony on the sofa. "Whenever African Americans are in competition with people of European descent they almost always lose if the decision has to be made exclusively by European Americans. They cannot be fair; it is always race first."

"How else can African Americans get the recognition they deserve?" Aliyah asked, reiterating Claudia's question. "Do you think that it would be any different if African Americans were the dominant race, would they show fairness?"

"African Americans have a history of being fair, Aliyah," Kwame answered her. "We are the quintessential model for treating others as you want them to treat you, don't you know that? We treat others better than we treat each other a lot of the time; for fear that someone will think that we are not being fair. As far as what else they can do to get recognition, they should concentrate on recognizing their own. What would be wrong with an African-American Music Awards Show?" Kwame looked from Claudia to Aliyah for support.

"It would be racist and un-American," Claudia said. "Furthermore it will be considered less valuable than the American Music Award."

"Less valuable to whom?" Kwame asked.

"Less valuable and less accepted in the overall music industry," Aliyah interjected. "African Americans want to make just as much money for their creativity as their European American counterparts, and if their contributions are to be considered less valuable, they will not be able to demand as much money for their work."

"Do you honestly think they get as much now? Do you really think that African-American entertainers get contracts that are equal to those that European Americans get? If you think that, you are very naïve, Aliyah," Kwame said, laughing so loud that he woke the sleeping Ebony, who looked at her daddy and started laughing with him, causing everyone in the room to laugh.

"On that note, I think we should all retire for the night," Claudia said. "We have to get up early in the morning," she reminded them.

"I want Aunt Aliyah to put me to bed," Ebony said.

Once Aliyah and Ebony climbed the stairs to the bedrooms, Ebony insisted on sleeping in the guestroom with Aliyah. She snuggled her little body into the cavity Aliyah provided for her by curling into the fetal position. Then Ebony in her sweet innocent little way told Aliyah, "This is how mommy and daddy always sleep. I want to sleep with my husband just like this one day, don't you aunt Aliyah?"

Aliyah sighed.

In the morning, Claudia fixed them a large breakfast. Aliyah watched Claudia as she bustled around her large, well-equipped kitchen while listening to Kwame and Ebony discussing an important issue over breakfast. "What should I do if Warren tries to kiss me on the cheek again, Daddy?" she asked.

"You have to tell people not to touch you when you do not want to be touched, Ebony," Kwame said. "You can let this boy know that you mean business without offending him."

It was times like this when Aliyah would yearn for a family of her own. She was filled with the desire to be a wife and mother. After breakfast, they all headed off in different directions to their respective jobs downtown, Kwame dropping Ebony off first at the neighborhood day care center.

As much as Aliyah loved sharing Claudia's family on occasion, she enjoyed the time she had with Claudia more. Claudia knew her better than anyone else in the world except her mother. There was nothing that she could not discuss with Claudia. Since she was eleven years old Claudia knew all of her secrets, loves, desires, and aspirations. It was Claudia who comforted her when a romance went sour and Claudia who encouraged her when she went after a promotion on the job. Claudia was one of her biggest supporters.

Driving to her downtown office, Aliyah thought about Claudia's friendship and just what a good friend she had been. *Claudia was always there for me when I needed her*, Aliyah remembered.

When Aliyah thought she was pregnant in her junior year at Rutgers, it was Claudia who told her what to do. Claudia took a day off from work and drove down to New Brunswick to Aliyah's apartment near Rutgers, bringing with her a kit to determine if she were pregnant. "If you are, Aliyah, please consider having an abortion. You have worked too hard to get this far only to throw it all away on a jerk like Melvin. Why did you go out with him in the first place?" Claudia had asked her.

Why did she go out with Melvin in the first place? Aliyah thought, trying to remember as she maneuvered the car through midtown morning traffic. It had been shortly after she returned from the Conference in Kenya that she had begun to wear her hair in a short natural style. Her love life had dropped off considerably following that. Some of the brothers at school just told her straight out that they didn't like women with short nappy hair. *Tough*, she thought, *who needs them*. If she had to be something that she wasn't, then it wasn't worth it. *Besides if they think of my hair in a negative way, what must they think of their own hair?*

Surprisingly though, her new look got a different response from the white guys on campus. She had first noticed this when she fell off her bicycle while riding on campus and had to be taken to the infirmary. An attractive young white doctor had examined her. Although it was her ankle that was beginning to swell, and her wrist that was throbbing, she had noticed that the young doctor was massaging her head. When she realized what was happening, she had asked him, "Are you feeling for lumps?"

"No," he had replied. "I just like the way your hair feels."

Taken aback, Aliyah had responded, "If you want to feel it again you will have to get yourself an African-American girlfriend."

"Finding one that wears her hair natural is as rare as finding a pearl in an oyster," he had quipped.

The decision to wear her hair natural was taken by many of her friends to be a statement. After making the statement, Aliyah didn't have to worry about guys coming on to her because they liked her long straight hair, guys that used a European standard of defining beauty in women. The guys that were attracted to her now were guys that liked the statement she was making because they were making the same statement themselves; proud of who I am, the way that I am.

Melvin was one of the guys who liked the statement Aliyah was making. He was a senior history major. History had always been Aliyah's worse subject in school. She could never distinguish between all of those European kings she had to study for her Western Civilization course. The French Revolution was boring to her. When her history professor assigned the topic for the term paper, "Implementations of the Mystique of the French Revolution," she thought he was kidding. She had no idea of what he was talking about. She never would have made it through the course if Melvin had not helped her. She saw his sign on the school bulletin board advertising his services as a history tutor for reasonable fees. She didn't know, at the time, that he was going to become her first real lover.

Melvin was vice president of the Black Student Organization (BSO) on campus, and he had hopes of reviving the Black Power movement of the sixties and seventies. Malcolm X, Huey Newton, and George Jackson were his heroes. Melvin could not understand why he was having so much difficulty waking up the rest of the BSO as to their mission. He had no patience with Aliyah's explanation that people were afraid.

"Look," she had said to him one evening while he walked her to the campus library. "Malcolm, Huey, and George all died violently because of what they believed and what they tried to do. No one wants to take that risk."

"We can make a difference this time," Melvin had insisted, gently taking Aliyah's arm as they ascended the steps to the building. "People were afraid of the Black Panthers because they were intelligent and they looked threatening in their military garb. This time we can use our intelligence to advocate truth. Don't you know that the truth will set us free? We can begin with HIS STORY; it's the biggest lie that was ever told," he had said.

"Shhh, we can't discuss this in the library, Melvin," Aliyah had shushed him, glad that she did not have to respond to his remark. Although he had lowered his voice, he could not be shushed.

"The truth is that black people had a positive and active role in shaping the history of mankind and not the role that whites have historically assigned to them, a history of unproductivity and slavery," Melvin had whispered in her ear while they browsed the book stacks. "Don't you understand that, Aliyah?"

"Yes," she had answered in exasperation.

The only time Melvin stopped speaking truth, as he called it, was when he was making love, and his passion for making love equaled his passion for truth. The small off-campus furnished apartment that Aliyah had been living in since the end of her sophomore year provided the perfect setting for the relationship with Melvin to bud and blossom. The first time Aliyah had made love with Melvin was her first time ever having sex. Oh, she had come close many times, but she had never before allowed penetration. Melvin was different than anyone she had ever been with. He was a master at foreplay. He explored every part of her body with his tongue, even sucking her toes. His sweet kisses aroused her to such erotic frenzy that she found herself guiding him into the private chamber of her body after their third tutoring session.

Later, as Aliyah lay in Melvin's arms he had whispered into her ear, "You were screaming."

"Was that me?" she had asked, hugging him tight to her. Aliyah had wished the relationship would never end.

They became inseparable after their relationship had been consummated, however, something was missing, and Aliyah could not put her finger on what it was. She had listened to all of Melvin's rhetoric, rarely commenting. She had learned to listen without offering any protest. Perhaps that had been the problem. Her silence must have led Melvin to believe that she did not share his passion for "truth."

Once he had said to her, "How can you be so gullible, Aliyah? You believe everything you are told by people who have only wanted to maintain the status quo of keeping people of color at the bottom. In America, our people are discriminated against by the justice system, the education system, in the entertainment field, in the workforce, in just about every aspect of our lives. We fool ourselves into believing that desegregation laws will end discrimination. Believe me, what's to come will be economic segregation. African Americans are being priced out of areas that whites want for themselves, like the best neighborhoods, the best schools, restaurants, etc. To do this they have to control how much money we earn. That means an end to affirmative action. It's coming you know." He had looked at her and had waited for a response.

Aliyah had said nothing. Melvin had just looked at her and sighed.

After his graduation, Melvin had moved to California to enroll in a master's degree program at UCLA. He was looking forward to making a connection with the remaining members of the Black Panther Party. Before he left, though, Melvin had told Aliyah, "Ours was a good fucking relationship, and they're a dime a dozen. What I need in my life is a woman that will support me in my effort to awaken our people, a woman that shares the same vision for our people that I have, a woman that will not settle for less than equality for our people by any means necessary."

It was Claudia who had consoled Aliyah during the difficult time following Melvin's departure. It was Claudia who had taken her to the abortion clinic. It was Claudia who had listened as she vowed never to trust another man. It was Claudia who had held her while she cried, and cried, and cried.

Then it was Claudia who had told her, "Enough is enough, Aliyah. Get over him! It is time to get on with your life. You are only twenty-one years old. You did the right thing. How dare he try to change you! From now on never trust another man that wants to change you. You are a wonderful person just the way you are. You are still growing, Aliyah; things will change in your life when the time is right. Until then just be patient and wait until that time is here. In the meantime, pursue your own dreams."

Aliyah had taken Claudia's advice and had pursued her own dreams. For the most part she was happy with the choices she had made. Ending the relationship with Mark, ten years after the disaster with Melvin, was proof of the strength she had gained. She had learned how to get over a bad relationship and move on to more productive things. Her motto had become "and this too, shall pass." She was conscious of her actions and always cognizant of the advice from her friends and family. Heeding their warnings, Aliyah was sure that she had not met her Mr. Right, and when she did she would do as Polonius had told his son in Shakespeare's Hamlet,

"Grapple him to her soul with hoops of steel."

Chapter 5

family

"Thanks for coming downtown to meet me for dinner tonight," Aliyah said to her mother, while they waited for a table at the Maize Restaurant in downtown Newark. The Maize, located in the newly renovated Robert Treat Hotel, was upscale for Newark. The tables were set with expensive table linen, fine bone china and monogrammed crystal, giving the place a look of real elegance.

"Thank you for inviting me. I can't think of anyone that I would rather be having dinner with, except for your father, maybe. To what do I owe this honor?" Betty Neal asked her daughter.

"Nothing. I just wanted to do something different tonight. I've been dying to see what this place looked like since they remodeled it. I'm glad you were available."

"When have you known me not to be available?"

Still shapely in her late fifties, and very chic, Betty had been a stay at home mom since Aliyah could remember. She was always available for her family.

"Are you alright?" Betty asked, after she and Aliyah were seated at a cozy table in a secluded alcove in the back of the restaurant. She was worried about Aliyah.

"Yes Mother, I just don't like eating dinner alone."

"I know what you mean." She sensed her daughter's loneliness.

"Don't you get used to it after a while?" Aliyah asked.

"I never have. Your dad and I always had dinner together when we first got married. It wasn't until he started his own business that he stopped coming home for dinner. It was okay then because I had you and Jamal, and the two of you kept me pretty busy. But since you and Jamal moved out, I eat dinner alone six nights a week."

"How do you fill in the hours Mom?" Aliyah looked at her mother.

"I watch television, shop, garden, and go to church on Sunday while your father sleeps in, always alone. This has been my life for a long time now."

As Betty gave the waitress her order, Aliyah thought about her parent's marriage. It was true her father rarely ate dinner with the family while she and her younger brother, Jamal, were growing up. Bill Neal had worked twelve hours a day, sometimes more. He was proud that he was able to provide so much for his family. His greatest achievement had been to acquire his own automobile dealership and make a success of it before he was thirty-five. His was the first black-owned Mercedes Benz dealership in the state, and he never lacked time for it. He was passionate about it. It was his favorite topic of conversation and his favorite place to be. His passion, though, did not extend to his children or his wife. Aliyah wanted a man that felt passion for her.

"At least you got married and had Jamal and me," Aliyah said, after giving her order to the waitress. "I'm afraid it's never going to happen for me."

"Oh, it's going to happen for you, honey, just be patient. Don't be afraid Aliyah; remember, the more faith you have the less fear you have. Even if marriage doesn't happen for you, you still have so much to be thankful for. Trust me, being married has its disadvantages. Would you be terribly unhappy if you never got married?"

"It makes me sad to think about living out my life alone. But I don't see a man anywhere on the horizon. I think I have removed myself from the reach of most eligible African-American men. They seem to be intimidated by my success. It's been months since I have met someone that even remotely interests me."

"Where have you been looking, Aliyah?" Betty put her napkin in her lap.

"I haven't really been looking. I thought falling in love would be something that would just happen. Now I'm not so sure. Perhaps I should

68

start looking, but where does one go to look for a husband?"

"How about church?" Betty suggested.

"Oh Mom, you know only women go to church. Think about our church. How many men attend on a regular basis? Those that do, come with their wives."

"Aliyah, there is so much more to life than marriage. You have done so much with your life already. I often wish I had done more with mine before I committed myself to your father. I got married too young. I'm only fifty-eight, and I have been married for almost two-thirds of my life. Aside from raising two wonderful children there is nothing else significant that I have accomplished."

"But, Mom, I'm over thirty years old, and my biological clock is steadily ticking. The longer I wait to get married, the slimmer my chances are of ever getting married."

"It's better to be sure and wait for the right man," Betty said, as she picked at the garden salad that had been placed in front of her. "Honey, you want to marry a man that will make time for you in his life."

"Oh Mom, Dad made time for you." Aliyah defended her father. "What about the trips you and Dad take every year?" she asked, stirring her cream of broccoli soup. "Looking back, I remember the times he took us to Disney World, the Bahamas, and the trip to Egypt."

"Big deal, almost forty years of marriage, and once a year trips for no more than ten days is all I get of him. I appreciate the trips, the luxury car, the big house, and the clothes, believe me I do. But I would trade it all for a small house somewhere where your dad came home for dinner by six, and we could take long walks after dinner, read the paper together, watch television or go to the movies." Betty's eyes became dreamy. "I want to be with him, not home and alone," she said, picking up her fork again and moving the salad greens around on her plate.

While the waitress put the rest of the food on the table, Aliyah wondered if her mother felt useless after the job of raising her family was done. She now recognized loneliness in her mother's eyes. The sparkle was gone and a vacant empty look replaced it. Her children no longer depended on her, and her husband was in love with his own success.

As Aliyah and her mother walked to the parking lot to reclaim their respective cars, Betty wanted to know if Aliyah was coming for Sunday dinner. Sunday dinner was a tradition in the Neal household. After Aliyah graduated from college she had cut down on the weekly visits to her parent's home; but she managed to get there at least once or twice a month.

"Okay Mom. Sunday dinner sounds fine. What time would you like me to come?"

"You know I'll be going to the eleven o'clock service at church. Why don't you come with me? Everyone is always asking me about you; they will be so glad to see you," Betty said with a smile on her face.

"I haven't been to church in a long time, maybe I will go with you." Aliyah said.

"I'll pick you up at 10:30 on Sunday morning." Betty gave Aliyah a kiss on the cheek. "See you then."

On Sunday morning Aliyah was up early as usual. She was enjoying a breakfast of toast and eggs while she read the local paper, The Ledger. A lot was happening in Newark. The waterfront was being developed. The government was putting up a new FBI building about a mile from her house, right on the riverbank. The beautiful new Performing Arts Center was in the same neighborhood. New restaurants and stores were opening to accommodate the art center patrons and all the new workers coming into the city. Newark was again becoming an exciting place to live and work.

When the doorbell rang, Aliyah quickly grabbed her purse and went outside to greet her mother. She was pleasantly surprised when she looked beyond her mother and saw her dad sitting in the passenger seat of her mother's shiny black Mercedes Benz town car. Bill Neal was a handsome man with a full head of hair; the graying hair at his temples gave him a distinguished look.

"I figured if my hot shot editor daughter could get up early to attend Sunday services, so could I," Bill said, seeing the look of surprise on his daughter's face as she entered the back seat of the car.

"Jamal is coming, too," Betty said, grinning from ear to ear. "He and his girlfriend are going to meet us at the church."

Aliyah and her younger brother Jamal had grown up in the church. Although they attended sporadically now, there was a time when they were in church every Sunday. They both sang in the junior choir until they graduated from high school. It was rare for the whole family to be seen in church together now. Betty could sometimes get them together for an Easter Sunday visit, or maybe Christmas or New Year's, but the whole family attending church together on a lovely Sunday afternoon in early spring was extremely rare.

Aliyah felt that all eyes were on the Neal family as the usher led them to the family pew in the front of the church. Metropolis Baptist Church was one of the largest churches in the city. Although only Betty Neal attended services regularly now, the pastor knew that he could count on the whole Neal family for support whenever it was needed. They were all known for their kind deeds, and Bill in particular was known for his generous monetary donations to the church.

Listening to Reverend Doggett's sermon in the beautiful large sanctuary reminded Aliyah of her younger days, when she used to sit with her parents in church, dreaming that one day she would carry on this tradition with a family of her own. That possibility seemed highly unlikely now. Today's sermon focused on loving one's neighbor as Jesus preached in the Gospel.

"We will never come together in unity as a people unless we love each other as we love ourselves," Reverend Doggett was saying to the completely African-American congregation. "We have got to put notions of superiority, based on financial wealth and material gains, out of our systems. We are all God's children; there is no favoritism based on material possessions. Love is the key to enriching our community," he said.

The choir at Metropolis Baptist was one of the best in the city. Many of the church members had joined specifically to be able to sing in the choir. Aliyah remembered when she was a member of the junior choir. It was one of the happiest periods of her life.

"Just a closer walk with thee
Grant it Jesus if you please

71

Daily walking close with thee
Let it be—Dear Lord—let it be"

As the choir sang, Aliyah looked around. People were moved to tears by the words of the hymn. Many were standing and swaying with the music. Arms were raised towards heaven. Babies were soothed by the music. Children looked at the choir in amazement. Men and women hummed along with the choir, faces smiling, feet tapping, and knees jumping to the tune.

Aliyah looked up at the altar. The flower arrangements were beautiful. Gladiolas, roses, mums, zinnia's and other colorful summer flowers provided a warm feeling to the sanctuary. The candles burning on the altar added a glow to the setting. Sitting behind the podium, the pastor, deacon, and assistant pastor smiled and hummed along with the choir. Aliyah was in awe. Nowhere else could she go and get this feeling. Nowhere else could she go and sense everyone feeling the same thing at the same time. The looks on the faces of the congregation could be summed up in one word, LOVE.

As the Neal family walked out of the church together, many people that Aliyah had known all of her life came up to greet them with smiles, hugs, kisses, and kind words. It was such a good feeling to be in the midst of so much love. Aliyah understood why people attended church for Christian fellowship. Your spirits could not help but be lifted after attending a Sunday service at Metropolis Baptist Church.

"I've got to attend church more often," she said to her mother, "I need to feel this more often."

"Why do you think I'm here every Sunday?" Betty smiled at her daughter.

It was three in the afternoon when they arrived at her parent's spacious suburban home. Jamal and Sheniqua had left them after church to attend a matinee at the New Jersey Performing Arts Center. They promised to be back in time for dinner. Once they were in the house, Bill headed for the den to watch his favorite baseball team on television. Aliyah and her mother headed for the kitchen to get Sunday dinner together. Betty told Aliyah that she had prepared most of the food the night before. She had made fresh collard greens, pot roast, roast chicken, candied yams, yellow turnips, and macaroni and cheese.

"I'll make some cornbread while you make a salad," she said to Aliyah.

"Mom don't you think you have enough food already?" Aliyah got the salad bowl out of the cupboard.

"It's better to have too much than not enough." Betty got the milk out of the fridge.

While she and her mother worked together at the center island in the spacious kitchen, Aliyah talked about her responsibilities as an editor. "I'm doing what I have always wanted to do Mom," she said. "Working for *Enigma* is so exciting. As an editor, I get to travel, research, and write. I am so glad that I chose to be a writer."

"I always knew you could be whatever you wanted to be," Betty said. "Even as a child you were determined, setting your sights high but always getting what you wanted. I remember when you decided that you were going to play the part of Harriet Tubman in the school play. You were only six years old, but you made up your mind to get that role by any means necessary," Betty recalled. "You had a lot of confidence then, nothing could shake it."

"Shake what?" Bill asked, coming into the kitchen to find out what was being served for dinner.

"I was just reminding Aliyah about how confident she was as a child," Betty said.

"I remember her telling me that she was going to be a writer despite my concerns about the difficulty she would have breaking into the writing field," Bill said taking a piece of lettuce out of the salad bowl and munching on it.

"Let's get the food on the table, Aliyah," Betty said. "Jamal and Sheniqua should be here any minute and I don't want your father to spoil his appetite before we all sit down to dinner."

"Just told me to mind my own business when it came to making a career choice is what you did," Bill said to Aliyah, ignoring his wife's comment.

"Daddy, I remember telling you that I would find a way to support myself doing what I wanted to do just like you did."

"And she was right," Betty said, picking up a platter of food to take into the dining room. "Our daughter is now firmly established in the publishing business as a writer and an editor and she's only thirty-five."

"Thirty-four. I won't be thirty-five until my next birthday."

"You have to be confident in this society." Bill remained fixated on the subject. "I knew when I was a junior at East Side High School that I was going to go into business for myself. At that early age, I knew that the only way a black man can make it in America is to be his own boss. White people are never going to help us compete with them by giving us a break," he said, just as Jamal and Sheniqua came into the kitchen.

"Is dinner ready yet," Jamal's loud voice interrupted them. "Something smells good and I'm starving," the tall lanky Jamal said.

"Everything's on the dining room table, Betty said. "Let's go and sit down to eat."

Throughout dinner, Aliyah could not help but notice how her brother couldn't keep his eyes off his very attractive girlfriend, Sheniqua. Sheniqua's giggles made Aliyah think that Jamal was squeezing her leg under the table. *My little brother is in love,* Aliyah thought before turning her attention to her father.

"It's nice having you here, Sheniqua," Bill was saying over the sound of his wife's best silver scraping the china plates she always used for Sunday dinner. "Our family has always been a small one you know. Betty's mother and younger brother died in a fire when Aliyah and Jamal were very young. My own mother died when Aliyah was in high school, and I was an only child. For a long time it has been just the four of us having Sunday dinner."

"Thank you Mr. Neal," Sheniqua said, and giggled. "I love your home. I have never lived in a house before. This is so nice."

"Sheniqua grew up in Baxter Terrace Projects," Jamal explained.

"My parents died when I was seven," Sheniqua added. "My aunt raised me. Don't you ever bring your boyfriends home for dinner Aliyah?"

Jamal broke the silence following Sheniqua's remark by changing the subject. "Have sales picked up at the dealership since you hired a new manager, Dad?"

Jamal had been working for his father at the dealership managing the service and parts department since he graduated from technical college. It was at the technical school that he first met Sheniqua, who now worked as a computer analyst for a telecommunication company in Newark. They had been dating only a few months.

"The sales department is doing just fine son. The new manager is working out fine. How's the service department coming along?"

"The service department is doing fine, too," Jamal said, as he and his father retired to the den to watch another game on television, leaving the women to clean up.

"I would love to have a big house like this one day," Sheniqua said to no one in particular. "I hear you have a nice big house, too, Aliyah. Aren't you lonely living there all by yourself?" The sound of the doorbell saved Aliyah from having to answer Sheniqua's question.

"Who could that be?" she asked, looking at her mother.

Betty Neal did not make eye contact with her daughter, but instead walked to answer the front door.

"This is my daughter, Aliyah," Bill said when Aliyah walked into the den where her mother had escorted the newly arrived guest. "You know the rest of my family. Aliyah hasn't been to the dealership in ages. That's why you haven't met her. Honey, come over here and meet Richard Bishop. Rich is my sales manager. He's been with us for about five months now, right, Rich? He came over to watch the game with Jamal and me."

"Hi," Aliyah said, taking the hand that Richard Bishop extended towards her."

"It's so nice to meet you at last," the tall, light-skinned man with the hazel eyes said, holding Aliyah's hand until she pulled it away.

"Excuse me," Aliyah said after exchanging pleasantries, and returned to the kitchen with her mother to join Sheniqua.

"Don't you think he's cute, Aliyah? He's very nice," Sheniqua said. "I see him at the dealership all the time when I go down to visit Jamal. I think he's single, too," she volunteered.

Aliyah looked at her mother and asked, "Mom, was this a setup?"

"Not on my part," Betty said to her daughter in all earnestness.

After all the food was put away, and the dishes neatly stacked in the

75

dishwasher, Sheniqua went to get Jamal.

"We have things to do," she said.

"Yeah," Jamal said, giving his sister a wink and a quick kiss on the cheek as they made a speedy exit.

Aliyah talked to her mother for a while longer before going into the den to inquire of her father if he was ready to drive her home.

As if on cue, Richard Bishop said, "I can take you home. It's on my way."

"Would you mind Rich?" Bill asked, already out of his seat and moving toward the front door. "That would be a big help to me, and I know that I can trust you to get my little girl home safe and sound," he said as Aliyah gathered her belongings.

Once outside, Aliyah felt the need to apologize to Richard for her father's erratic behavior.

"No need to apologize," he said. "Your father is a wonderful man. I owe him a lot. I would do almost anything for him."

Aliyah wondered just how much he would do for her father as they drove to her house in silence. When they arrived at the brownstone, Richard stopped Aliyah as she was about to get out of the car.

"I've heard so much about your brownstone from your dad," he said. "I would love to see the inside."

"I still have some work to do before it's completely finished, but I guess you can come in for a minute," Aliyah said.

Once inside Aliyah asked Richard if he wanted something cold to drink. "Ice tea, water, or a soft drink is what I have."

"A glass of water would be just fine."

"Make yourself at home and feel free to look around." She went into the kitchen to get the water.

Alone in the kitchen, Aliyah wondered if her father were trying to play matchmaker. *He must really be worried about me if he has gone this far,* she thought. Her parents started dating when they were in high school. They got married shortly after her father graduated from Jersey City State College. Neither of her parents knew what it was like to be really alone, without a significant other.

"I see you like to read," Richard said when she returned with the water.

"Yes, what about you?"

"I don't have much time for reading, maybe some trade journals every now and then. I love your place. You're doing a great job decorating. Why the African theme, though?" he asked.

"Why not?" Aliyah responded, wondering, *Does he have to ask?*

"Well, thanks for showing me your place. Maybe I'll see you around sometime."

"Maybe."

"Stop by and say hello the next time you drop by the dealership to see your father," Richard said as Aliyah let him out the door.

"I will," Aliyah said, thinking, *Who knows when that will be?*

As she went upstairs to get ready for bed, the telephone rang. Aliyah knew who it was before she answered it. "Yes, Daddy," she said into the phone.

"I just wanted to make sure that you got in alright."

"Yeah, right!" Aliyah said, sarcastically. "Daddy, please don't start playing matchmaker. I am quite capable of finding my own man."

"Honey, I'm just looking out for you. Richard will be a good catch for any woman. This is a man that's going to be making a lot of money one day. He'll be a good provider for his family."

"I think I provide for myself quite well, Dad, don't you?"

"You know what I mean Aliyah. No one wants to be alone."

"I'm not alone, Daddy. I have my family and my friends. I'll talk to you later," Aliyah said annoyance, coming through in her voice.

"Don't be angry with me, sweetheart. I'm only trying to help."

"Don't try to help me Daddy. This is something I have to do by myself."

"Give Richard some thought, Aliyah. Don't make a hasty decision because you're angry with me."

"There is nothing to decide."

"Did he ask you for a date?"

"No! And please don't encourage him to. Promise me."

"Okay, I won't."

"Good night, Daddy. I'm getting into the shower now."

"Goodnight sweetheart," Bill said as Aliyah was hanging up the telephone.

A LITTLE BIT OF HONEY

Chapter 6

Distractions

Running up University Avenue, Aliyah could hear the eastbound train pulling into the Broad Street Station. By the time she ran up the long flight of stairs to the platform she was almost out of breath. It was not unusual for her to leave the house at 7:15 A.M. to catch the 7:20 train. It put her at Penn Station in Manhattan by 7:35. The walk to her office building on Thirty-Eighth Street was only ten minutes. By 7:46 she was on the elevator pushing the button to take her to the seventeenth floor.

"Hold the elevator," a male voice yelled out just as the door was closing. Aliyah reached out, and pushed the open-door button just in time for the door to reopen. She was surprised to see her boss, Joe Simmons, enter the elevator. He rarely got to his office before nine or ten.

"Good morning, Aliyah," Joe said, in his usual gruff manner, and pushed the button that would take him to the executive suite on the eighteenth floor.

"Good morning Joe," Aliyah said as the elevator door closed and began its upward ascension.

Joseph Simmons was getting on in years. He was at least sixty-nine, but he had energy and creativity that made him invaluable at the magazine. Aliyah admired him, but she believed that he would be productive for only a few more years before his body gave out. She wanted his job, and to prepare herself for consideration when the time came, she stuck by him as though she were glued to him. She wanted to learn all the tricks of the trade, and he was willing to teach her.

"Early morning meeting?" Aliyah asked.

"Yes, I'm meeting with the publishers in a half hour." He gave her a quizzical look.

Joe knew that Aliyah looked up to him, and he was flattered by the admiration of such a young, intelligent and attractive woman as Aliyah. He helped her whenever she came to him, and he sometimes shared trade secrets with her over lunch. He knew that she was vying for his job.

"Have they expressed an opinion about the story I wrote for last month's edition?" she asked, referring to the publishers.

"Not one way or the other. Don't worry, Aliyah, if the publishers were unhappy, I would be the first to know and you would be second," he said, as the elevator door opened on the seventeenth floor.

The publishers were two bright African-American women who had started *Enigma Magazine* ten years ago. They were directly responsible for its success. The circulation had grown to over seven-hundred-thousand subscriptions in the first decade.

"It's just that I haven't received any feedback lately, and I was wondering if they were satisfied with my performance," Aliyah said, holding the elevator door preventing its ascension to the eighteenth floor.

"Don't worry," Joe said again. "You're doing just fine. Why don't you call me later this morning and we'll have coffee and discuss the job you are doing," he said impatiently.

"Okay." Aliyah released the door and walked slowly down the corridor to her office. The quiet told her that she was probably the only one on the floor. When she walked into her office, the digital clock on her desk read 7: 55.

The receptionist and the rest of the staff didn't get in until 8:30 or 9 A.M. Aliyah liked the quiet and peace of the early morning. Getting to work a half-hour before everyone else gave her a chance to organize her day before the telephones started ringing and other interruptions began. For pretty much the same reason, she generally stayed at the office until six when everyone else left at five. By keeping to such a schedule, she missed the rush hour traffic coming into and going out of Manhattan. Besides, putting in ten-hour days at the office helped to distract her from her loneliness. She hoped it would pay off one day in the near future.

At 10 A.M. Aliyah was sitting in Joe Simmons office in the executive suite, sipping a cup of tea and listening while her boss gave her a report of the magazine's progress.

"The publishers are pleased with the work coming out of this department," Joe was saying. "The editorial staff is the best that we have had in the ten years since I have been here. Subscriptions are up, and our circulation has expanded at an astounding pace not only on a national level, but on an international level as well."

"That's wonderful," Aliyah said, grateful for some positive feedback.

"I hope I have alleviated some of your anxiety," said Joe. "Your hard work is not going unnoticed. Keep it up, and it will pay off for you."

Returning to her own office, Aliyah felt reassured that she was on the right track to becoming *Enigma's* next editor-in-chief. Although competition at the magazine was brutal, she knew that she had as good a shot as anyone else. Competition made it difficult to develop any real friendships at the office. She was grateful for the lunches she had with Claudia. They gave her a chance to get away from the office and talk about something other than *Enigma*.

Reaching for the telephone to call Claudia and invite her to lunch, Aliyah decided to check her telephone messages first. She was surprised to find that she had a telephone message from Richard Bishop asking her to call him at the dealership. *How did he get my number?* she wondered. Was her father meddling again? Richard seemed nice enough, but he didn't appear to be her type. What was that crack he made about her choosing an African theme for her house? Maybe he didn't relate to his African ancestry. Why the interest in her then? Besides she wasn't partial to light-skinned men.

Back to Roots, a small health food restaurant on Forty-Eighth Street, made the best falafal sandwiches in the city. Aliyah and Claudia ordered their lunch at the counter, and grabbed the only available table. They had barely sat down when Claudia suggested Aliyah have her first party in her new home. It had been almost two years since Aliyah moved into the brownstone. Although work had become the major distraction from her loneliness, she knew she needed more than just work in her life.

"Maybe I should," Aliyah agreed with Claudia. "Teyinniwa and Morgan are anxious to see what I have done in the house. They haven't been there since I first moved in. Kanmi, too; the last time I saw him he asked me when I was going to invite him over."

"Wonderful!" Claudia said excitedly. "I'll help with the food. I just discovered this recipe for paella that is out of sight."

"I think Memorial Day weekend will be perfect; we'll have an extra day to rest up before heading back to work. What about the guest list Claudia? You know I don't have many friends anymore. I have lost contact with all of our old friends from high school, as well as those people I used to hang out with in college, except for Kanmi. And I don't have any friends at work."

"What about that guy you told me your father introduced you to? Have you had any further contact with him?" Claudia asked, while putting a little hot sauce on her sandwich.

"He called the office and left a message, but I haven't called him back."

"Why not?" She scanned Aliyah's face, looking for a clue.

"I don't know. He doesn't turn me on, besides I don't like the fact that he works for my father. I don't like my father meddling in my love life, which I don't have anyway."

"Then just have a nice little gathering of your closest friends and family. It will be fun." She gave Aliyah a reassuring smile.

Leaving the restaurant, Aliyah felt good. She had a project to keep her busy at home for the next two weeks, another distraction from her loneliness. Besides, she looked forward to entertaining a small gathering of her friends and family. It would give her a chance to show off her garden. Claudia had convinced her to have a barbecue in the backyard rather than a catered affair.

"It will be more intimate," she had insisted. "You know the thrill your Dad gets working the grill. And your mother will feel slighted if you don't give her something to do; cooking is the thing that she does best. Besides I want everybody to try my paella."

On the morning before Aliyah's barbecue she awakened earlier than usual. She wanted to make sure that she had things in order before leaving for work. Not sure what time she would be returning that night, she did not want to wake up the morning of her party to find that she still had a hundred things to do.

She checked the house to make sure that she hadn't forgotten to clean, polish, or sweep something. The house looked good. She had even remembered to put her best towels and her favorite scented candles in the guest bathroom. Aliyah liked to keep a scented candle burning in the bathroom whenever she had company. She didn't want her guests stumbling to find the light switch, and the candlelight gave a nice warm glow to the room.

Aliyah went over the menu to make sure that she had all of the necessary condiments. She checked to see that she had all the tools her Dad would need to barbecue. She looked at the cute barbecue apron and matching hat she had picked up the week before at Macy's. *Dad will love this*, she thought. She planned to stop at her favorite fish market on her lunch hour to pick up fresh salmon steaks. Then she would go to the butcher for fresh ground turkey. She then checked to make sure that she had enough wine and soft drinks for everyone. The fresh cut flowers she had purchased the day before still looked good.

Lastly, Aliyah went into her garden. It was May 27th, and already her roses were in full bloom. The ivy had shiny new green leaves, and the hostra was gleaming. She still had a few late blooming tulips and daffodils. She'd spent last weekend potting impatiens and begonia. The deck furniture was hosed down, and the umbrella was ready to go up. Everything was to her perfection.

On her way back into the house to shower for work, she noticed three large bags of trash piled up near the deck. *What an eyesore*, she thought as she grabbed one of the three bundles to put out at the front curb. Lucky for her it was garbage day. She had forgotten to put the trash out for the last couple of weeks. Still in her bathrobe Aliyah carted the trash through the house and out the front door, one bag at a time. *It would be much easier on me if I could remember to do this every week*, she thought as she was making her last trip.

When she opened the front door for the third time that morning, to her surprise there was someone going through the two bags of trash that she had just put out. Tightening her robe around her, she set the last bag at the curb. When she looked up, the man was staring at her. For a brief moment their eyes met. When he caught her eye he politely said, "Good morning." Quickly, Aliyah lowered her gaze. She wondered if he was looking for food. That was one of the drawbacks to living in a neighborhood that was recently redeveloped. All of the homeless people that were displaced continued to hang around. *He doesn't look homeless*, she thought. Besides he was wearing gloves and expensive tennis shoes that looked new. "Good morning," she said quickly as she hurried back into the house.

At 7:30 Aliyah was on the New Jersey Transit Train headed for her office. She was at her desk by 7:59 answering her first telephone call of the day.

"Daddy, what's up," she said to the sound of her father's voice over the telephone.

"Hi baby," Bill said into the phone. "Are you all set for tomorrow? Your mother thought you could use some help getting your trash out."

Mom never misses a thing, Aliyah thought. "No, Daddy, everything is under control," Aliyah said sweetly to her father.

"Your mother and I will come a little early to help out anyway. Honey would you mind if I brought Richard Bishop to your barbecue tomorrow?" Bill asked his daughter.

"Yes, I would mind, Daddy. I told you before that I don't like it when you play matchmaker."

"I'm trying to do a good deed, Aliyah. The man doesn't know many people, and he wants to make some friends. Is that a crime? He said that you have not even returned his telephone calls."

"How did he get my telephone number in the first place?"

"Didn't you give it to him?"

"No!"

"What difference does it make Aliyah? The man is interested in you."

"I'm sorry Daddy," Aliyah apologized to her father. "But, I would rather you not bring a stranger. Everyone coming will already know each other. We all have things in common. I want this gathering to be special. Besides, I don't want someone there that will want to talk business with you all night. I want your full attention. Some other time, okay?"

"Sure, baby, whatever you say. I'll see you tomorrow then."

"Goodbye, Daddy," Aliyah hung up the telephone with a smile on her face, thinking *he means well.*

"Who is it that can put such a smile on your face so early in the morning?" a familiar voice said from the doorway. When she looked up, Dorothy Caprio was standing in the doorway looking at her. "It must be someone important." Dotty gave her a sly look.

"It was my father," Aliyah said, surprised by the question. Although she got along fairly well with Dotty, they rarely ever stepped over the boundary into their personal lives. With them, it was strictly business.

Dorothy, or Dotty as she preferred to be called, was *Enigma's* other senior editor. Although *Enigma* was a magazine targeted to an African-American woman readership, a few key people on the staff were white. Dotty was one of them. Dotty, an attractive blond, had left a job as a staff writer for a fashion magazine in Canada to become an editor for *Enigma* ten years ago. She, too, was vying for the job of editor-in-chief.

"You must have a good relationship with him," Dotty said.

"I do," Aliyah said and then quickly changed the subject. "What can I do for you Dotty?"

"I need a favor, Aliyah," Dotty blurted out, and walked into the room. "I know that this is short notice, but I have a family emergency, and I have to go out of town for a week or two."

"Oh." Aliyah wondered what favor she needed.

"I won't be able to make the deadline for next month's feature article. Can you do it for me? I'll take your turn the following month if you want me to."

Senior editors alternated writing the editorials or feature articles each month. Aliyah liked this schedule because it gave her a month to do her research before the next article was due. The editor-in-chief wrote an article whenever he wanted. He would bump either one of the senior editors, putting his own article in place of theirs, postponing their work until the next issue in many cases.

Remembering that it was Dotty who suggested that she play up the "equality" angle in her article "Red, Yellow, Black, and White: Why Can't We Be Sister Friends?" Aliyah knew that she owed Dotty a favor. "When is the deadline?" she asked, ignoring Dotty's offer to take her turn for the following month.

"The old man wants it on his desk by the fifteenth of June." Dotty said and sat down in the chair facing Aliyah's desk.

Aliyah didn't like it when Dotty referred to Mr. Simmons as "the old man", she thought it was disrespectful.

"Okay, Dotty, I'll do it," she said. "If you had asked two weeks ago, I wouldn't have had the time, but after this holiday weekend, I'll have plenty of time."

In addition to writing her own articles, Aliyah supervised five staff writers and a junior editor. She had to edit and approve all of the articles they wrote before presenting them for publication.

"Thanks, Aliyah, I knew I could count on you. I owe you." Dotty got up from the chair and started back to her own office.

Aliyah didn't mind the extra work. It would give her something to do after the barbecue. Besides, it would remind Mr. Simmons how well she worked under pressure, and she would not take Dotty up on her offer, but would write her own article for the following month as well.

It was after nine when Aliyah put her key in her front door loaded down with packages. The light on her telephone answering machine was blinking rapidly, indicating that she had a telephone message. Richard Bishop's voice came over the machine when she pushed the button. "Sorry I missed you again, Aliyah. Please call me when you get a chance," he said. *Not tonight,* Aliyah thought. She had had a busy day, but now she looked forward to a hot bath and an early retirement for the evening. She was exhausted. She would get up early in the morning and get things started.

On the morning of her barbecue, Aliyah awakened feeling refreshed although she had dreamed throughout the night. She rarely remembered her dreams, but for some reason she remembered a pair of eyes. The eyes were very expressive, sometimes laughing but also somber. They had followed her everywhere she went in the dream. She shivered at the thought of them and then hurried to start getting ready for her guests.

It was already seven, and she had told everyone to be there by two. She still had to marinate the salmon steaks, wash the chicken for barbecuing, and make up turkey burgers. She also had to prepare a vegetable salad. Her mother was making potato salad and desserts. Teyinniwa had insisted on making a tasty Ghanaian dish, and Claudia was bringing her special paella.

By noon everything was ready. She decided to take a short nap before showering and dressing. She dozed off as soon as her head hit the pillow. Almost immediately she started to dream again. Haunting eyes were following her to the supermarket, to the bank, and peering at her over the counter at the dry cleaner. Everywhere she went, they were there. She woke up to the sound of the doorbell ringing. She glanced at the clock; it was only one o'clock. "Who could that be, an hour early," she said out loud to herself. Running downstairs to get the door, she remembered that her parents were coming early. She opened the door to their smiling faces, arms loaded with delicious smelling desserts.

"Come in and make yourselves useful while I shower and change," Aliyah said, brushing both their cheeks with her lips. She went back upstairs while they made their way into her large kitchen at the back of the house.

By the time Aliyah showered and dressed in faded blue jeans with a red knit top and put on her red moccasins, the doorbell had already rang twice. Her guests were arriving. She came down the stairs to find Teyinniwa and Morgan busy in the kitchen with her mother. After warm greetings, Aliyah asked, "Where's Dad?"

"He's in the yard with Jamal and Sheniqua," Betty said, putting the potato salad in the fridge.

Aliyah went outside to find that her father had already started the grill and was deeply involved in a conversation with her brother about the dealership.

Sheniqua was sitting nearby, looking at the two of them with an amused look on her face. Aliyah greeted her brother and his friend and kissed her father again tying the apron around his waist, and placing the chef's hat on his head.

"You've got to look the part," she said over his protests.

"You look like one of the great chefs of the century," Jamal said, and laughed.

Sheniqua joined in the laughter as her mother, followed by Teyinniwa and Morgan came out to find out what was so funny. The doorbell sounded again, and Aliyah rushed off to answer it. The party had begun.

Aliyah played the part of the perfect hostess, moving among her guests and joining in on the different conversations as everyone delighted in the food and drink. She helped her father and brother at the grill, making sure that the salmon was grilled to perfection. She tried to persuade Sheniqua to try the potato salad, but Sheniqua, who could not have weighed more than one hundred and ten pounds, said that she was watching her weight and did not want to eat anything that was too fattening.

"I'll stick with the vegetable salad. Maybe when I'm over thirty, weight won't matter that much to me either," she said to Aliyah.

"What do you mean by that?" Aliyah asked in a tone that implied her hurt feelings.

"She didn't mean anything negative," Jamal said quickly. "Sheniqua always says what's on her mind, and you are putting on a little weight, sis," he said as if that was a defense.

"Aliyah has always been too thin, the extra weight looks good on her. My mother used to say that 'nobody wants a bone but a dog,'" Bill said, trying to get his son off the hook.

I better leave this conversation alone, Aliyah thought, excusing herself and going over to where her mother and Teyinniwa were sitting at a table and talking about their traveling experiences.

Betty, to a lesser degree than Teyinniwa, was also a seasoned traveler. One of the things Bill did to make up for all the time he spent at his business was to take his family on an extravagant, no expense spared, vacation every year from the time Aliyah was a little girl. Now that the children were grown up, Bill continued to take his wife on a trip every year. The trips with the children had been to Disney World, the Grand Canyon, Yellowstone National Park, and other places of interest that Mr. Neal felt enhanced his children's wealth of knowledge. Now he and his wife went to places that interested them. Last year they visited London and Paris; the year before, they toured Spain.

Teyinniwa was telling Betty Neal about her trip to Southern Africa, shortly after Nelson Mandela was released from prison in 1990. "It was such a wonderful experience," she was saying. "The countryside was the most beautiful I have ever seen. We traveled from Johannesburg to Durban by bus. We went through the Eastern Transvaal making stops at an Ndebele village. Oh! And we stopped to see Blyde River Canyon and what the Africans call 'God's Window.'" It was obvious Teyinniwa was still in awe more than ten years later. "It is the most beautiful view in the world," she said, with a look of sheer delight in her eyes.

"It sounds wonderful," Betty said. "What other countries did you visit in Southern Africa?" She took a sip from the glass of wine Aliyah placed in her hand.

"We also visited Swaziland and Lesotho during that tour," Teyinniwa said. "Morgan and I visited Zimbabwe a couple of months ago. We got to visit Victoria Falls and the Great Zimbabwe Ruins as well as Matopos National Park where we saw bushman caves and some of their original paintings. One of the most magnificent sights I have ever seen was at the top of a mountain where we saw 'Gods View of the World.'"

"It sounds like an unforgettable experience," Betty said in awe.

"Oh, it was. I think what I loved the most was the people of Southern Africa. They are so warm and spiritual in nature. Even the names they gave to God's creations are indicative of their spirituality. Africans used names like 'God's Window' and 'God's view of the World.' When the Europeans came, they changed the names to their liking and to take credit for themselves. They renamed God's creations, and called the Great Falls in Zimbabwe, Victoria Falls, and named Kruegar National Park after Paul Kruegar, as well as giving Cecil Rhodes the credit for 'God's View of the World.'" Teyinniwa sipped her wine.

"I'm going back to Africa one of these days," Aliyah said.

"Another thing that impresses me is the culture." Teyinniwa interrupted. "In what other culture would you find men creating a dance that gives thanks to their women for being good wives and good mothers to their children? We saw men perform this dance in Zimbabwe."

"I would love to visit Africa one day," Betty sighed, still in awe.

"Mom, you were in Africa. Don't you remember when Daddy took the family to Egypt?" Aliyah looked at her mother in disbelief.

"Oh, but no one considers Egypt to be part of Africa, I think they call it the Middle East now," Betty Neal said, looking at her daughter as though she just realized she was there.

"Egypt is in Africa." Teyinniwa corrected Betty. "The greatest civilization in the world culminated in Africa, and we must never forget that, regardless of who says differently."

"Well, I'm going to ask Bill to take me to Africa on our next trip. It is totally unacceptable to visit so many places in the world without spending more time visiting our own motherland," Betty said. "You need a vacation, too, Aliyah." She looked at her daughter. "You work so hard."

"Aliyah is turning into a workaholic," Teyinniwa said. "She needs to get away to one of those resorts where they pamper you for a week or so. Maybe an island in the sun with exotic foods and men that love African-American women," she said smiling in Aliyah's direction.

"It would be nice if Aliyah could meet some nice young man that could appreciate her," Betty said, turning to see Aliyah's reaction.

"I'm out of here," Aliyah said, getting up to go. "I don't like the way this conversation is turning, besides I think I hear Claudia calling me."

She quickly moved towards the bench under an apple tree at the back of the yard where Claudia and Kwame were talking to Kanmi. Kwame was telling Kanmi all about his desire to build a high school in Ghana for children that excelled in math or science and could not afford the high cost of tuition at private schools.

"Why Ghana?" Kanmi asked. "Schools like that are needed all over the African continent, including my home, Nigeria."

Kwame told Kanmi about his experiences as a missionary in Ghana, and how it was always his dream to go back and start a school there. He was preparing to leave by mid August to spend two weeks there with some other teachers to explore the possibility. While the two men talked about Kwame's plans, Aliyah asked Claudia what she planned to do while her husband was in Africa for two weeks.

"I don't know, but I have some vacation time coming up. What about you, Aliyah?" she asked. "Are you going to take a vacation this year? Maybe we can do something together."

"I don't know, Claudia, I'm going to be busy in June and July doing research and writing, but maybe I'll be able to take a break sometime in August. I'll let you know," Aliyah said.

Bill and Jamal joined Kwame and Kanmi and the four men continued talking about Kwame's plan to build a school in Ghana. Aliyah and Claudia drifted over to the deck, where Betty, Teyinniwa, and Sheniqua had joined Oya and Morgan. Oya was holding her baby while Mwangi and Ebony were coloring pictures in the coloring books that Aliyah had purchased to keep them occupied. Morgan was telling the women about a seminar she had attended at City College in New York.

"Marta Vega, the well-known Santería priestess, was one of the panelists," Morgan said. "I was so impressed that Santería priestesses get so much respect."

"Santeria and my religion, Ifa, are related you know," Oya said. "Although the religion started in Nigeria hundreds of years ago, women still have a lesser role there. Only men can become a *babalawo*." She looked disheartened. "*Babalawo's* are priests and often diviners. They can help you fulfill your destiny."

"Well, it's quite different in Santeria," Morgan said. "From what I hear, women are also very important members of the religion. A Santeria priestess can become a diviner and can read a person's *odu* as well as a priest."

"Women are taking on significant roles in many religions," Betty said. "We had a woman pastor speak at our church last week and she was wonderful."

"How did the men respond to her, Mom?" Aliyah asked.

91

"They appeared receptive enough, although I am sure that some objected. Most men are just not ready for women to move into the pulpit." Betty shrugged her shoulders.

"That might be a good topic for my next article," Aliyah said. "I have two weeks to do an article and I haven't even thought about it."

"That doesn't sound like you Aliyah," Claudia said. "You're always on top of things."

"I'm helping a colleague," Aliyah explained. "Women as spiritual leaders, sounds like a winner to me."

"Me, too," Oya agreed.

"I'll toast to that," Teyinniwa said, holding up her wineglass. They all clicked their glasses, as the men joined them to find out what was going on and when they could start eating.

Although it was late May, the weather turned a little chilly after the sun went down. The party moved into the house. Aliyah gave a grand tour to her friends that had not seen the house since she had finished it. Kanmi was pleased with the effect of his decorating suggestions. Teyinniwa admired Aliyah's taste in her selection of colors and the African theme. Claudia pointed out that she was mostly responsible for finishing the wood trim and helping with the other restorations. Betty praised her daughter's gardening skills, but wondered why she had so many garbage cans in the backyard.

"Aliyah you have got to find a better system of recycling your cans and bottles." Bill said to his daughter. "You must have four or five large trashcans filled with cans and bottles in the yard. You can't even lift one of those cans, how are you going to get them out of there?" he asked, shaking his head at her.

"What Aliyah needs is a man to help her with the heavy work around the house," Jamal joined in. "She was never responsible for taking out the garbage or recycling when we both lived at home. I always took care of that," he reminded his parents. "She needs someone to do that for her now. She needs a husband. I would suggest that she find herself one before she gets too fat and unattractive." Jamal joked at his sister's expense.

"I found myself one," Sheniqua said, out of nowhere, grinning from ear to ear. "Jamal asked me to marry him and I said yes."

While everyone gathered around the happy couple offering congratulations, Aliyah felt grateful that the focus was taken away from her man-less state, yet she felt a twinge of jealousy that her little brother was getting married before she was.

It was after 10 P.M. when the last guest left the house. Aliyah looked forward to the next two days of rest before she had to be back at the office. As she walked up the stairs to her bedroom, she recalled her recurring dream with the haunting eyes. *Who do the haunting eyes belong to?* she wondered.

Chapter 7

more distractions

"Yep, there are definitely a couple of extra bulges on my hips and thighs," a naked Aliyah concluded, as she examined herself in the full-length mirror in her bedroom. Always proud of her tall lean body, she became more conscious of her weight following the Memorial Day barbecue. At five feet eight-and-a-half inches tall, she had always carried her weight well. Despite her father's comment that "Nobody but a dog wants a bone," she knew that few men wanted a fat woman either.

Her scale confirmed what she already knew; she was gaining weight. All through high school, she belonged to the track team and ran long distances. There was a time when she even considered running in the New York Marathon. Time never permitted the vigorous training it required though.

Aliyah knew what she had to do if she was going to attract a man. She put on her jogging suit and mapped out a route that would take her along the waterfront. She estimated it to be about five miles round trip. When she left the brownstone, with a small jar of honey in her pocket, it was 5:45 A.M. The streets were empty, and the sky was just beginning to light up. She ran south through Washington Park. Homeless people were still sleeping on the grass. The benches had been removed years earlier to discourage them from sleeping in the park. Now they slept on the hard ground, covering themselves with whatever they could find, including newspaper.

She continued running south, past the new performing arts center, as far as city hall. Then she ran east towards McCarter Highway. Traffic was beginning to pick up, although there were still few pedestrians on the streets. On the way back, Aliyah felt an ache in her leg and decided to walk for a while before resuming her run. She walked along the riverbank, noting the pollution of the water, wondering if it could ever be cleaned up.

Watching the flow of the river, she pulled the jar of honey out of her pocket and slowly poured it into the river. "River goddess, Osun, please accept this offering of honey from me, and please help me to find my soul mate."

Just as she finished, she heard someone walking toward her. She looked up to see a man pushing a supermarket cart filled with something she couldn't make out. She continued to look out over the water. Across the river was East Newark, a city that had broken away from Newark years ago, establishing itself as an independent city. East Newark was comprised of mostly working class European and Asian immigrants. Aliyah resumed her run and, as she passed the figure pushing the cart, she noticed that he was collecting cans and bottles along the riverbank.

"Good morning," he said as she passed.

"Good morning," she said without changing her pace.

The voice sounded familiar. She quickly turned to look at him as he bent over to pick up a bottle. She recognized the tennis shoes and the gloves. It was the same man that she had seen going through her trash right before Memorial Day.

Aliyah got into the routine of waking up early and running before getting ready for work. She wanted to get back into shape. After the initial shock to her system, her legs stopped aching, and she could actually say she felt better after her morning run. She had more energy, and although the haunting eyes continued to follow her in her dreams, she slept better at night. She noticed that her mood, when she arrived at the office, was also better.

During the time Dotty was out of the office Aliyah had completed the article on "Gender Discrimination in Religious Leadership." The new issue had only been in the hands of the readers for a couple of days now, and the story was already creating quite a stir. The publishers loved it and had requested a follow-up to the story. At a meeting in Joe's office Aliyah found out just how well received it was.

"'Gender Discrimination in Religious Leadership,' was a real hit with the readers Aliyah. Tell me, what will you do for a follow-up to the story?" Joe looked at her from the other side of his desk. They were discussing the lineup for the next edition of *Enigma*.

"I'm working on an article titled 'Women in Spiritism.' As a matter of fact, I need approval to visit Brazil for a few days. A Candomblé initiate from Bahia contacted me after the story was released. She has invited me to Bahia to learn more about the Candomblé religion. I'll get a chance to see first hand how Ifa worshippers communicate with the *orisa*," she said, and leaned back in her chair.

"How long will you be gone?" Joe asked, and picked up his desk calendar.

"Three or four days at the most. I hate to leave when Dotty is still out though. I know things will be hectic around here without the two of us." Dotty had been out of the office for almost a month now.

"She called me yesterday to let me know that her father died more than three weeks ago," Joe said.

"Why didn't she say something?" Aliyah asked, sitting up in her chair again, with a look of concern on her face.

Joe said, "You know what a private person she is. She'll be in tomorrow, and you can ask her yourself."

When Aliyah left Joe's office she had received approval to visit Bahia, Brazil, for four days in July. She had a lot of work to do before the submission deadline. She was hoping to get an interview with Marta Moreno Vega, the well-known New York Santería priestess, and at least a telephone interview with Iyanla Vanzant, the very popular Yoruba priestess.

The morning after her conversation with Joe Simmons, Aliyah arrived at the office at 7:40 A.M. She had taken an earlier train. She was making herself a cup of tea in the staff kitchen when she looked up and saw Dotty standing in the doorway.

"So, you finally came back." Aliyah said.

"I'm sure that you heard by now that my father died." Dotty appeared rather nonchalant for someone who had just lost her father.

"Why didn't you tell me before you left?" Aliyah was sympathetic.

"I wasn't in the mood to talk about it," Dotty said. "Besides, my father and I were not that close, so I am not in mourning. I hadn't spoken to him in ten years."

Aliyah could not imagine not speaking to her father for ten years. "Are you all right?" she asked with genuine concern in her voice.

"I will be. I needed to spend some time with my mother, you know, going over the will and other things. She's alone now, and I wanted to help her make the adjustment. Frankly, her life will probably be much better now with him gone. He was very controlling and extremely selfish. The only thing my father ever did for me was to leave me his beach house in the Bahamas. How have things been around here?" Dotty asked, deliberately changing the subject.

"Great," Aliyah said and told Dotty all about the article she wrote in place of hers, the reaction it received, the follow-up article she was doing, and the up-coming trip to Brazil.

"Sounds like you've been a busy girl," Dotty said, sounding a little relieved that she did not have to meet a deadline any time soon, but a little jealous that Aliyah's article was getting so much attention. "I really appreciate your help. By the way, you're going to need a vacation when you finish this project; feel free to use the beach house in the Bahamas whenever you like."

"Do you mean that?" Aliyah smiled. "I have been thinking of taking some vacation time in August."

"Consider it done. Besides I need for you to go away, it will give me some time to catch up with all you've done." Dotty smiled back at her.

Aliyah spent most of the next week in the library. She visited the New York Public Library in midtown, but she found that there was more information available at the Schomberg Library up in Harlem. The Schomberg had a wealth of information and resources related to topics of interest to people of African descent. On the weekend, Aliyah visited the Newark Public Library, which was close to her home. Her eyes and rear end ached from all the time she spent sitting at the computer, but at least her hips were not spreading due to her new exercise regime. She also spent hours on the telephone talking to Oya, whose mother was an Ifa priestess. Oya was providing her with a wealth of information about women in Ifa.

"Remember, Aliyah, only men can become a *babalawo*, but women spiritualists have a significant role in the ceremonies," Oya had said to her during one of their many telephone conversations on the subject. "Two very important *orisa* are female you know, Osun and Yemanya, who is the mother of all the orisa. By the way, have you been making an offering of honey to Osun, the river goddess?"

"Yes," she told Oya. "Ever since I started running along the river bank, I have been making offerings. But so far I have not met my soul mate."

"Be patient and continue to make your offerings," Oya said

.

The day before Aliyah was to leave on her trip to Brazil, she woke up early enough to get in her five-mile run. She didn't know if she would have an opportunity to run the four days she would be in Bahia. She had been running at least four days a week now and she was beginning to notice a change in her body. She was really toning up. Her thighs and hips were noticeably firmer.

After jumping into her warm-up suit and running down the steps, Aliyah remembered to stop in the kitchen and take out a small jar of honey from the cupboard. Running along the riverbank, she headed toward the bridge connecting Newark with Kearny, New Jersey. Once on the bridge, she stopped and unscrewed the lid on the jar of honey, leaned over the railing, and poured the honey into the river. She watched as the current took the honey downstream.

"Osun, I hope you accept this honey as an offering of my devotion to you, and I ask in return that you help me find my soul mate," she said out loud. "I want someone to share my life with. I want a husband." Quickly she looked around to see if anyone was watching her. Satisfied that no one was, she continued her run back towards the brownstone to get ready for work.

It was a beautiful day, warm and bright with sunlight. There wasn't a cloud in the sky. Aliyah decided to drive into Manhattan for a change. Even with the traffic, she was at her desk by eight. By ten o'clock she was busy at her computer doing her research when the telephone rang.

"Well, I finally get to hear your voice again," a male voice came through the receiver.

"How did you get this number?" she asked, recognizing Richard Bishop's voice.

"I just called the *Enigma* operator and asked for you. I hope you don't mind."

"And my telephone number at home?" she asked.

"It's listed in the telephone directory, didn't you know? I gather you received my messages."

"Yes, I did. But I have been quite busy with work."

"Well, you have to stop working to eat sometime. I was wondering if you would have dinner with me. I know we only met that one time, but I would like to get to know you, Aliyah. Your father can vouch for me. How about it?"

"I'm going out of the country on business for a few days, and when I get back I'm planning to go on vacation for a couple of weeks. I don't know when I can go out with you, Richard."

"Can't you squeeze me in for dinner before you go on vacation, Aliyah?" He sounded so sincere she could not say, no.

"Okay," she said. "I'll have dinner with you before I leave for vacation."

"Thanks, Aliyah. I'll make sure you have a good time."

As soon as she hung up the telephone it rang again.

"How about lunch in Central Park today?" Claudia's voice came through the receiver.

"Sounds good to me. Noon all right?"

"Great. I'll meet you on the corner and we can pick up something to eat."

Exactly at noon, Aliyah and Claudia met on the corner facing Central Park. They stopped to pick up falafel sandwiches and mango Mystics to drink, and made their way to their favorite park bench facing the museum. Aliyah told Claudia about her upcoming trip to Brazil, and Claudia told Aliyah about Kwame's plan to visit Ghana.

"I think I can arrange to go on vacation with you in August, Claudia," Aliyah said. "Our vacation can coincide with Kwame's trip. Dotty offered me the use of her beach house in the Bahamas. I think this will work out just fine."

"Wonderful, I'll make arrangements while you're in Brazil," Claudia said excitedly. "We'll fly first class. My mother and grandmother will love having Ebony stay with them for two weeks. We are going for two weeks, right Aliyah? Oh this is going to be so much fun, just like old times. Remember when we were teenagers, and your father invited me to vacation with your family in the Bahamas? We had so much fun, remember, Aliyah?"

"Of course I remember, Claudia, but that was in Freeport. Dotty's beach house is on New Providence Island where the city of Nassau is located. Nassau will be even more fun." She grinned at Claudia.

When Aliyah got back to the office she confirmed the use of the beach house with Dotty, who appeared preoccupied since her return from her father's funeral.

"No problem, Aliyah," she said. "Just remind me before you leave in August to give you the key. I'll give you all the information you need before you go."

Her mood was so depressed that it prompted Aliyah to ask, "Are you all right?"

"I don't know," Dotty said. "I didn't think I would be so affected by his dying. There is so much that I wish I had said. Silence is never the answer. Now, it's too late to do anything or say anything."

"Losing a parent is never easy, regardless of how grown up you are," Aliyah said, trying to be comforting.

"But you don't understand, Aliyah." Dotty's eyes filled with tears. "I have hated him since I was a little girl growing up in Ontario." She tried to fight back the tears. "He always belittled me; he never approved of anything I ever wanted to do."

Dotty got a tissue from her desk and walked over to the window. "He used to punish me into obedience," she said, a little more composed now. "He never showed me any love or gave me any affection," she said, with her back to Aliyah, gazing out the window. "I moved to New York to get away from him. He tried to lure me back with things. He knew that I loved the ocean. That's why he bought the house on the beach in the Bahamas. But to show him that I could not be bought, I never went there. I think that's why he left it to me. He left everything else to my mother, but he is still trying to force me to come to the beach house."

"That's sad," Aliyah said. "Maybe you should see someone professionally to help you deal with this. It's a heavy load, too heavy to handle all by yourself."

"Maybe you're right, Aliyah," Dotty said, returning to her desk. "I can't seem to focus right now. I haven't been able to write a word since I got back."

"Promise me that you will see someone while I'm in Brazil," Aliyah implored of Dotty.

"Yes, ma'am," Dotty said, smiling now.

The flight to Brazil went by quickly. Aliyah tried reading to help pass the time. She had a copy of Toni Morrison's *Paradise* with her. After reading for a couple of hours, she felt herself dozing off. As soon as she fell asleep, the haunting eyes appeared. They were following her to Brazil. She woke up abruptly when the plane hit an air pocket; the book fell from her lap. The gentleman sitting next to her retrieved the book and asked Aliyah if the book was interesting. He said that his wife was a Toni Morrison fan.

"I'm enjoying it so far," she told him.

"Your first trip to Brazil?" he asked.

"Yes. What about you?"

"No. This is my third trip. I'm a sportswriter. This trip I am going to interview Pele, the famous soccer player. Do you know him?"

"I know of him. He was the greatest." Aliyah put her book away.

"He sure was. Will you be staying in Rio?" he asked.

"No, I have a connecting flight to Bahia."

"You'll love Bahia. Make sure you eat at the Castile Restaurant. You'll find it fascinating. It was once a holding fort for slaves, and it has an authentic auctioning block. They do a live performance of the capoeira during dinner."

"What's capoeira?" she asked, curiously.

"It's a form of martial art developed by slaves from Africa. During slavery, fighting among slaves was strictly forbidden and punished severely. Slaves devised the capoeira to look like a dance that they could break into if the master came upon them while they were fighting. In some ways it reminds me of the break dancing from the early 1980's. I think that break dancing and capoeira are related. What do you think?"

"I'll have to wait until I see it," she said, remembering the break dancing of the eighties. Oh, how she had loved it. Talking to him helped the time go by quickly, and before long they had landed in Rio. A short time later, Aliyah was in Bahia.

The Candomblé priestess, María Santos, met Aliyah at the airport. She was a short and rotund mulatto woman with flaming red hair. She drove her to the hotel, which actually was a very quaint old convent that had been converted into a hotel. It sat at the top of a hill in the art district of Bahia.

"Why don't you rest up before dinner," María said in English, with a heavy Portuguese accent. "I have a lot to show you in a short period of time. I'll be back to pick you up at six, okay?"

"That will be fine." Aliyah said and glanced at her watch. It was only two o'clock.

After María left, Aliyah looked around at her surroundings. Her room was very quaint, with hardwood floors, a wrought iron double bed with a rag rug at the foot of it, a small desk and chair, and a chest of drawers. She lay down on the bed to take a nap and dreamed that the haunting eyes had followed her to Brazil. When she awoke it was already five o'clock. *Whose eyes are they?* She wondered as she rushed to get dressed.

María Santos was good to her word and picked Aliyah up promptly at 6 P.M. She drove through the city as though she had lived her entire life there, all the time talking to Aliyah about the Candomblé religion in Brazil.

"Women hold important roles in Candomblé here in Bahia," she said. "In our religion, women diviners are as common as men, not like in Africa or the rest of the Caribbean. Here, women read the *odu* as well as men. They are adept at reading the coconut pieces, kola nuts or the cowry shells. Did you know it was a Nigerian woman, Iya Nasso, who founded the first temple of Candomblé in Salvador, Bahia?" she asked.

"No, I didn't. When was this?"

"Early in the nineteenth century. The temple was called the Engenho Velho."

They toured the city of Bahia with María giving Aliyah the history of Candomblé in Brazil, as she drove. Aliyah listened, with her tiny tape recorder taking down the details for her. She looked out the window at the beautiful city of Bahia. She was fascinated with the highs and lows of the city. There were tall buildings high on the mountain, as well as in the valleys that bustled with activity. It looked like one city built on top of another.

"How does a pedestrian get to the top of the city?" asked Aliyah.

"The elevator."

"An elevator?" Aliyah looked at María in surprise.

"Yes," Maria said. "There is an elevator that takes people up to the top. We can ride it to the upper city later if you wish. Do you have a preference for dinner?"

"A passenger on the plane suggested I eat dinner at the Castile. He said it was once a holding fort for slaves."

"Actually, we just passed that restaurant." María turned the car around and drove in the opposite direction.

The restaurant was interesting, red brick and cement, with thick black doors made of a heavy wood. The auction block was now a stage, but the leg shackles, used during slavery, were still cemented into the floor. The room was windowless, with beautiful chandeliers and sconces providing the only light, and creating a warm glow that was quite romantic. *How ironic*, thought Aliyah. *A place where enslaved Africans met with so much pain, now a place of pleasure for those that can afford to eat here.* The thought gave her chills. María appeared to read her thoughts, and said, "I know the feeling that's why I don't eat here often."

Despite the feelings that they shared, they feasted on scrumptious Brazilian food including *feyoada*, the national dish of Brazil, and *acaraje*. While they dined, beautiful young Brazilian men entertained them with the dance capoeira. Aliyah was fascinated with the gracefulness of the dance.

After dinner, they took the elevator to the higher city. Aliyah could not help but notice the poverty of the people around the elevator. Men and women who appeared homeless lay in the streets near the elevator. Children came up to her begging for money or candy. Each time that Aliyah started to reach for her purse, María admonished her. "Don't encourage them," she implored of Aliyah.

In the upper city, they walked, stopping to check out some of the stores. Jewelry stores were plentiful and beautiful dark women, in gorgeous white lacy dresses with strands of colorful beads smiled at them, inviting them in. Aliyah purchased a small gold ring for Ebony; her birthday was approaching. It was after nine when they returned to the car.

"The Candomblé ceremony itself will take place at 2:30 P.M. tomorrow. It could last several hours," María said when they pulled up in front of the hotel. "I will send a driver for you. Make sure you wear white and red," she added. "We don't want you to look too conspicuous." María laughed.

"What should I expect?" Aliyah asked.

"Each year Candomblé initiates, who claim Shango as their guardian *orisa*, hold a ceremony in his honor. There will be food, music and dancing." María smiled.

"Do the Osun initiates have a ceremony, too?" Aliyah asked as she got out of the car.

"An annual cycle of celebration is held each year for each deity or *orisa*. This will be a most memorable experience for you." María eased the car into the street and drove off.

The next day, her driver arrived promptly at two. He was an older man dressed in a white suit with a red handkerchief in his pocket. He had on a white straw hat with a red band around it. He did not speak English, but he talked to her through the maitre d', saying that they had better hurry if they were going to avoid the traffic. When they arrived at the Candomblé house, Aliyah was astonished to see a huge altar in the middle of the large room. The altar was covered with red satin cloth and decorated with red and white flowers and beads. There were white candles burning at the top. María, dressed in a beautiful white dress with red beads and earrings, came over to greet her.

"You look beautiful," she said to Aliyah, who was wearing a white chiffon skirt and matching off the shoulder blouse with a red-fringed shawl. "Red and white are the colors symbolic of Shango," Maria told Aliyah.

"This is so exciting," said Aliyah, looking around the room.

Bowls of fruit, nuts and other delicacies were placed around the altar in offering to the *orixa*. Men in white pants and shirts were beating drums and people were dancing to the beat. As the ceremony progressed, the drummers and dancers appeared to work themselves to an excited frenzy, pulling others onto the floor to join in the dance. Aliyah found herself drawn to the beat of the drums.

The initiates sang, in the Yoruba tongue, songs that sounded beautiful and alluring. The music was intoxicating. The ambiance was intriguing. Some of the initiates appeared to go into a trance, further exciting the others. María explained to Aliyah that the priests or priestesses that experienced the trance actually became possessed with the spirit of the *orixa*. They would give messages to the other initiates from their guardian *orixa*.

Soon the music lured Aliyah onto the dance floor. The room was stifling. Standing in one spot she swayed hypnotically to the beat with her eyes closed. Her hair and clothing were sticking to her body, moist with perspiration. She sensed the closeness of the other dancers as they danced around her. Suddenly, someone whispered into her ear.

"Osun thanks you for the honey and sends a message," a male voice said. "Soon you will meet the one whose eyes follow you."

Aliyah's eyes popped open, she looked around for the owner of the voice, but she could not discern whom it belonged to. So many people, dancing, singing, and drumming crowded the floor. *How could they know?* she asked herself.

The ceremony lasted several hours as María had predicted. It was after ten when Aliyah's driver returned her to the hotel. María promised to come by the hotel in the early afternoon to take her to lunch before driving her to the airport, where she was booked on a late afternoon flight to Rio de Janeiro where she would spend the night. She was going to use her last day in Brazil to ride the cable car to the top of Sugar Loaf and view the statue of Christ the Redeemer at Corcovado, something she had always wanted to do.

Lunch was at a seaside café. Looking out at the water, Aliyah noticed a small gathering of people at the edge of the sea dressed in brightly colored clothing.

"Those are Iemanja initiates making an offering to her," Maria explained. "Iemanja is the goddess of salt water, she lives in the sea. She is mother of all the orisa. The spelling of some of the words in Candomblé may be a little different, but Iemanja is the same Yemanya of Ifa, or Yemaya of Santería."

The two women walked down to the sea after lunch to witness the group throwing flowers, grapes, and perfume into the sea. One of the women gave Aliyah a few flowers, which she took then threw into the sea. As she watched the waves claim her offering, Aliyah whispered, "Yemanya please accept this offering from me and keep me safe while I travel in Brazil and, please, please, use your influence with your daughter, Osun, and ask her to help me in my search for my soul mate."

The flight from Rio did not arrive at Newark Airport until after 10 P.M. Aliyah took a taxi to the brownstone, arriving at eleven thirty, and went straight to bed. The telephone ringing awakened her. When she looked at the clock it was already 6 A.M.

"Were you still sleeping?" her mother asked before waiting for Aliyah to say hello.

"Yes, but I've got to get up. I didn't mean to sleep so late."

"I thought you would be tired. Your father and I went out to dinner to meet Sheniqua's family last night," Betty informed her daughter. "The aunt who raised her is a lovely woman, but she can't afford to pay for the wedding. Your father and I are going to help the kids pay for the wedding that they want. Sheniqua wants to know if you will be one of her bridesmaids."

"When is the wedding?" Aliyah yawned.

"She wants a Christmas wedding. She wants her attendants to wear red, trimmed with white mink. She's planning to wear a white gown trimmed with white mink. She's hoping for snow. She wants pictures in Branch Brook Park to be taken in the snow."

Aliyah listened half-heartedly, still half awake.

"We didn't get in until after ten," Betty said excitedly. "I wanted to call you, but your father thought I should let you rest and call you this morning," she said, noticing Aliyah's silence. "Are you all right? How was Brazil?"

"Brazil was fine. I'll tell you all about it some other time. Right now I want to get ready for work."

"I thought you would take the day off. You got in so late, and it is Friday. Why not take a long weekend?"

"I can't, Mom. I have too much to do. I probably won't get into the office until after eight as it is. I'll talk to you later."

After hanging up the telephone, Aliyah checked her clock; it was 6:10 A.M. She jumped out of bed and reached for her sweat suit, still hanging behind the bathroom door from the last time she ran. She quickly put it on and headed out the front door. Stopping midway through the door, she came back into the house and went into the kitchen to get a small jar of honey from the cupboard. *I mustn't forget to make an offering to Osun*, she thought.

It was 6:50 when Aliyah came back into the house. While taking a hot shower, she decided to catch the 7:30 New Jersey Transit train into Manhattan. She didn't want to be alone today.

It was eight o'clock and Aliyah was at her desk, going through her mail. A knock at the open door made her look up. Kanmi stood grinning in her doorway.

"What are you doing here so early in the morning?" Aliyah asked Kanmi, laughing and stretching out her arms to get a hug.

"I came over to look at a site for a new store, and I needed the advice of a friend. I was hoping you would be back. Do you have time for a cup of tea?" he asked.

"I'll make the time for you, my friend." Aliyah grabbed her purse and headed towards the elevator with Kanmi. "You are a lifesaver Kanmi. I, too, needed someone to talk to, and lo and behold, here you are."

Seated at a small table at the Roof Top Café, on the fifty-fifth floor of her office building, Aliyah and Kanmi ordered tea and toasted bagels. "What's on your mind?" she asked, in a tone that matched the seriousness of the expression on his face.

Kanmi told her all about his dilemma. It appeared that he had an opportunity to open a new store in lower Manhattan. He wanted another store where he could concentrate just on the handcrafted items that he brought from Africa.

"There is a big market for African handicraft, Aliyah. The Shona sculptures from Zimbabwe are selling like crazy. Wooden sculptures from Kenya are also selling well. So is soapstone from Kenya. These items are hot in Europe, and the interest is growing among African Americans. I know I can make a go of it, but it will take up all of my time and a lot of money to get it up and going. Oya is not too happy about it," he said solemnly.

Oya thought he had enough to handle already and taking on more would be too much. Besides, she thought it would be too risky. She was worried that he was not listening to the signs that the ancestors were giving him through the reading of his *odu*. The ancestors did not look upon greed favorably. Oya was grateful for what God had already blessed them with. She did not feel that this was the right time to invest in a new venture. The ancestors had said as much when Oya cast the coconut for a reading, yet, Kanmi felt that the opportunity was so great that he could not afford to miss it. It could provide financial security for his family for generations to come.

"How can I miss out on such an opportunity, Aliyah?" He folded his hands on the table.

Aliyah did not know what to tell him. She did not want to discourage him from doing something that he really wanted to do, perhaps now was not the right time.

"If Ifa is all that you say it is, then you should know what to do, Kanmi," she said. "You told me that following the Ifa tradition is what saved you and your family from death and hardship in the past. Why would you want to change now? Listen to your heart, and you will make the right decision," she said as she placed her hand over his on the table.

"Do you think I am being greedy, Aliyah?" Kanmi asked.

"What do you think?" Aliyah asked.

"Maybe I am," he said. "I will give it more thought. Anyway, enough said about that. Tell me about your trip now, Aliyah. What did you learn?"

Aliyah told Kanmi all about Bahia. "I even think that I communicated with Osun," she told him. When she finished, Kanmi had a smile and a look of delight on his face.

"It amazes me how the religion of my ancestors has survived in the New World," he said. "Although there are some differences, the religion appears to have remained intact in Brazil and the Caribbean. This New World religion is just as powerful a force in the lives of the initiates in other parts of the world as it is in Nigeria where it originated."

"It must be a very powerful religion," Aliyah said. "From what I have gathered from my research, it is one of the fastest growing religions in the world."

"That's because people are discovering that it works," Kanmi said. "Soon you will find your soul mate and then even you will be convinced."

Back at her desk Aliyah worked fervently to complete her article. She was a third of the way finished when another knock came at the door. Before she could respond, the door opened and Dotty came in.

"Welcome back," she said. "How was Brazil?"

"It was a good trip. I accomplished a lot."

"Well things have been pretty hectic around here," Dotty said, as though she really didn't want to hear about the trip. "The old man was out for the last three days; I think he has been sick. He's back today and he wants a staff meeting right after lunch, so don't be late. Here's a copy of the agenda for today's meeting." She came around to Aliyah's side of the desk to put it in her hands.

"Notice how the old man underlined no exceptions," Dotty said, referring to a part of the memo that said everyone must be in attendance. "He's getting pretty ornery, don't you think?"

Aliyah said nothing, but she automatically became concerned about Joe Simmons. "Is he ill?" she asked herself, barely noticing when Dotty left the room.

Claudia came at noon to have lunch with Aliyah at the same Roof Top Café where Aliyah had had breakfast with Kanmi.

"I made reservations for our trip to the Bahamas," was the first thing she said after they were seated. "We are leaving on the third of August, and we will be returning on the seventeenth. I hope that's all right with you, Aliyah. Kwame is leaving for Ghana on the second of August, so I thought I could drop Ebony off with my mother after I return from taking him to the airport. I'll spend the night with you so that we can leave together from your house." Claudia said, without stopping for a breath. "Did I tell you that we are leaving from Newark Airport? I think that that will be more convenient. Oh, Aliyah, are you as excited about this trip as I am? Two whole weeks of vacation, with no one to take care of but me. I am really looking forward to pampering myself."

"I thought you liked being married," Aliyah said.

"Oh, I do," Claudia said. "I love being alone with the man I love, and with our child, but I also like having some time to myself, away from the wife and mother routine. It's been a long time since I've had some private time. I can't remember the last time I had more than an hour alone."

Strange, thought Aliyah, *I can't remember the last time I was alone with a man I loved for an hour.*

After lunch, Aliyah returned to her office to prepare for the staff meeting. She wanted to make sure that she could answer every question that Joe Simmons might ask of her. Five minutes before the meeting was to start, Aliyah put on the jacket to her suit, and walked down the hall to the conference room. Everyone was in attendance except Dotty and Joe. Joe made it a point of coming to all meetings five minutes late to give the other members of his department some time, but as little as possible, to discuss him before he arrived.

Promptly at five minutes after two, Joe Simmons arrived. He was halfway through the agenda before Dotty arrived. She took the seat next to Aliyah and asked, "How much did I miss?" Aliyah motioned to her that she would fill her in later and focused on what the editor-in-chief was saying. After the meeting, Joe quickly left the room not looking at anyone.

"He doesn't appear well to me at all," Aliyah leaned over and whispered to Dotty. "He looks tired and worn out," she said.

"Maybe he should think about retiring," Dotty whispered back. "What did I miss?" she asked.

"He implied that we are in for some big change and that we had better get ready for it. He also said that he will be doing the lead article for the next issue." Aliyah looked at Dotty who had not written a lead article for the last three issues.

"That lets me off the hook for another month," Dotty said. "What changes do you think he was referring to?"

"Time will tell."

Chapter 8

fun in the Sun

"Come in," Dotty called out in response to Aliyah's knock on her office door, which was always closed. A few days had passed since the department meeting and Aliyah hadn't seen much of her colleague. She was relieved to find Dotty in the office. She wanted to get the key to the beach house.

"Hi," Aliyah said, walking slowly into the office.

Dotty was standing at the window looking out over the city. She appeared preoccupied with her thoughts. She looked at Aliyah and asked, "Do you know how many people there are in New York City?"

"I know there're a lot." Aliyah said, wondering why Dotty was asking such a question.

"Eight million," Dotty said. "Eight million people in this city and not one of them loves me. What am I doing here?"

Aliyah had never seen Dotty look so sad. Not knowing quite how to answer her she said, "It's good to be close to people that love you. I guess that's why I have always stayed close to home."

"I left home because I was feeling unloved there. Now, ten years later I'm far from home and in the same predicament. What can I do for you, Aliyah?" Dotty's voice was tinged with melancholy.

"My vacation starts in a few days, and I would like to get the key to your beach house."

"Oh, yeah!" Dotty said quickly, reaching under her desk for her purse.

"I went down there with my mother the week after the funeral. Everything was in order when I left. Here's the housekeeper's telephone number." She took a piece of paper from her purse and handed it to Aliyah. "You can call her if you have a problem. The house is in the Adelaide Beach section of New Providence Island, which is not too far from Cable Beach. Do you know Cable Beach, Aliyah?"

"Yes. My dad used to take me there when I was a child."

"Well, everything you need should be in the house. My father was very thorough. You'll have to take a taxi from the airport. Here is the key to the house." Dotty handed Aliyah a key ring with two keys on it. "The other key is for the car. You'll need to go to the supermarket right away. My mother and I left the cupboard pretty bare." Dotty smiled as though remembering something funny. "Oh, and don't forget to drive on the left side of the road," she added quickly. "I also wrote down the directions to Cable Beach from Adelaide."

"I hope you know how much I appreciate this." Aliyah quickly scanned the piece of paper Dotty had given her before putting it into her purse. "I feel I really need a vacation. Some fun in the sun is just what the doctor ordered," she joked.

"Well, the Bahamas is just the prescription for what you need. I found the Bahamian people to be very friendly."

"Thanks again, Dotty." Aliyah turned to leave the office.

"I'll try to hold the fort down while you're away, but don't expect too much when you get back. Oh, and have a good time," Dotty said, as Aliyah was walking out the door.

"I have every intention of doing just that," Aliyah said, and smiled. Walking back to her office, Aliyah felt sorry for Dotty; her own problems seemed miniscule compared to hers. Even if she didn't have a man, she had her family and friends that loved her, and they were nearby.

Driving through the Holland Tunnel on her way home Aliyah remembered that it was the last Friday of the month. She decided to stop by Teyinniwa's house. She hadn't seen her good friend since Memorial Day, and she had promised a visit before going on vacation. Happy to find both Teyinniwa and Morgan at home, Aliyah was all smiles as she was led into the kitchen.

"Just in time for supper," Morgan said, as she put the finishing touches on a green salad she was preparing.

"I don't want to intrude. I should have called before coming, but I didn't know I was coming until I was in the car heading back to Newark."

"No problem," Teyinniwa said. "A visit from you is never an intrusion. You are always welcome to share whatever we have. Besides it's the last Friday of the month. We were hoping to see you before you left." She looked up from her task of setting the table, smiled, and then added another setting to the table.

While enjoying a light dinner of broiled salmon, a delicious tossed salad, and a baked sweet potato, Teyinniwa filled Aliyah in on the happenings of the Daughters of Africa.

"We have undertaken a new venture," she said. "We're raising money to open a home for displaced women and their children here in Newark. We hope to provide them with the training and counseling they will need to reestablish themselves in the community."

"Raising the money will be the hard part," Morgan said. "I'm helping them by soliciting funds from various philanthropic organizations as well as government agencies. Hopefully we will have all the necessary funds by the end of the summer, in order to open the house by the beginning of the New Year."

"I love what the Daughters of Africa are doing to help our people," Aliyah said, helping Morgan to clear the table.

"We aren't doing any more than other women's groups have done for their people," Teyinniwa said. "Look at all that Hadassah has done to help the Jewish people. What about you?" she asked Aliyah. "How are you doing? I read your articles in *Enigma*. They were wonderful. I know the magazine must be happy with you. How is your love life, though?"

"I guess you could say it's improving. I have a date for tomorrow night." She followed the sisters as they led the way to the parlor.

"Wonderful! Who is he?" Teyinniwa asked.

"Someone my father introduced me to a couple of months ago." Aliyah was a little embarrassed to admit this.

Teyinniwa sensed Aliyah's embarrassment. She poured some Hennessy into three brandy snifters before making a comment. "Sometimes arranged relationships are the best kind," she said. "Arranged marriages were traditional in Africa you know. The elders seem to know how to pick the perfect mates for their children. Be grateful that your father cares enough to go through the trouble."

"He appears to be a lot like my father." Aliyah said and sipped her brandy, sounding a little disappointed describing Richard Bishop.

"There is nothing wrong with your father," Morgan said. "The man is rolling in money and, from the looks of your mother, he doesn't mind if she spends it."

"There are other things in life that are more important than money to me. I want a soul mate," Aliyah said, using Oya's term.

"As far as I am concerned, men fit into only two categories, those that are good with their pants on and those that are good with their pants off." Morgan said, and laughed. "Men that are good with their pants on are good at making money. They pay creditors on time, do the income taxes, invest money wisely, and all the other things that require them to have their pants on."

"What about those men who are good with their pants off?" Aliyah asked.

"Well, you know what they are good at." Morgan laughed again. "That is usually all that they are good at, too," she added. "They are nothing with their pants on. It's very difficult to find a man that is good with his pants on and with his pants off. I have spent too much time trying to get a man who is good with his pants off to be good with his pants on; it's impossible. Go for the man that is good with his pants on, Aliyah. You'll have better luck teaching him how to be good with his pants off." She gave Aliyah a look that indicated she knew what she was talking about.

"Don't listen to her," Teyinniwa said. "You just wait for the right man, and don't settle for less. In the meantime, enjoy this guy that your dad introduced you to. He may turn out to be a winner. And please enjoy the men in the Bahamas while you are there. When are you leaving?"

"Next week." Aliyah got up from the comfort of the rocking chair she had been sitting in, letting the sisters know that it was time for her to leave. "I'm really looking forward to some real rest and relaxation, not to mention sun and fun. I'll send you a postcard." Aliyah followed as the sisters walked her to the front door.

"Forget about sending me a postcard," Morgan said at the door. "Bring me something back. Postcards from the Bahamas take forever to get here. I love the guava duff that they make in the Bahamas. Bring me some of that back."

"Enjoy your date tomorrow night," Teyinniwa said, giving Aliyah a goodnight kiss on the cheek.

Richard wanted to be prompt for their first date. He left the dealership in plenty of time to arrive at Aliyah's house by 6 P.M. He was wearing gray slacks and a navy blue sports jacket. He thought it best to remove his tie. He had been looking forward to this date for months. Aliyah Neal was just the kind of woman he was looking for. He considered her a good catch. She was ready when he rang her doorbell, and did not invite him in.

"I'm starving," Aliyah said, as they walked to his car parked at the curb. "I'm glad you're so punctual."

"I'm hungry, too," Richard said. "I worked all day and didn't take time for lunch. I usually work until nine on Saturdays, but I left early for this date." He suggested they dine in the Ironbound, a section of the city populated mostly by Portuguese and Brazilians. There were many fine restaurants in the area, making it a big tourist attraction. Most of the restaurants had a reputation for serving food that was tasty, plentiful, and reasonably priced. Richard chose Fornos, a quaint restaurant known for its attractive décor and good food. When the waitress came to take their orders, he ordered paella for two and a bottle of expensive wine to drink with their dinner. He tried to impress Aliyah by ordering in Portuguese.

"I dated a Portuguese girl for a number of years," he said, after the waiter left. "She taught me some Portuguese, as you can see."

"What happened to her?" Aliyah asked.

"Her parents didn't approve of her dating an African American, and she didn't want to disappoint her parents, so we broke up."

"I see." Aliyah looked at him from across the table. *His are not the eyes that are haunting me*, she thought. "So how do you like working for my father?"

"Your father is my role model. I want to be just like him when I grow up."
Richard laughed to show that he was only joking. "You must be very proud of
him." He became serious again.

"Oh, I am. My father has been a wonderful provider for our family."

"I plan to provide for my family in the same fashion that your father
has provided for his family when I get married. My dream is to own an
automobile dealership myself one day."

After dinner, Richard drove out of the city to a neighboring amusement
park. There he made Aliyah laugh as she watched him try to win a stuffed
teddy bear for her by knocking down bottles that appeared to be glued down.
He did manage to win her a stuffed tiger by shooting basketballs.

"I was an all-state basketball player throughout high school," he told her.
"And an all- collegiate player in college."

"Where did you go to school?" asked Aliyah.

"I went to high school in Richmond. It was a predominantly white high
school in one of the better neighborhoods. I was the only black on the team
and the star player," he smiled proudly.

"That must have made you pretty popular in school."

"Oh yes. I have to admit I dated a lot of girls during those four years. And,
since the school was predominantly white, I dated mostly white girls, but I
also dated a few black girls. Color doesn't matter to me," he said.

"So what does matter?" Aliyah was curious.

"So many women are interested in pursuing careers nowadays. I like
women that put their families first. I prefer stay-at-home wives. I want my
wife to excel at cooking, housework, and raising kids." Richard smiled at
Aliyah.

He wants my mother, Aliyah thought to herself. "What if she wants to
work?" She smiled back.

"She won't have time. I want at least four children, two boys and two girls.
She'll have her hands full."

As they walked around the amusement park, Richard told Aliyah that he
came to New Jersey to play basketball for Seton Hall University.

"I lived in the dormitory for the entire four years that I was at Seton Hall.

I was one of the starters on the team the whole time. We had a winning team, and I dreamed of playing professional basketball after graduation. I wanted to play for a northeastern team, and I had a good chance of playing for the Nets. Unfortunately a knee injury snatched that dream away from me during my last year in college."

"That's too bad," Aliyah said sympathetically. "Why did you decide to stay in New Jersey?"

"My parents were pressuring me to stay in school and become a doctor. I had the brain for it and the grades, but I didn't want to spend another six years training to be a doctor. I took a job here as a used car salesman so I could have an income while I was deciding what to do with the rest of my life. Professional basketball was my only dream. I really didn't have a back-up dream. But now I love selling luxury cars."

When they left the amusement park, Richard drove directly to Aliyah's brownstone. After parking the car at the curb, he jumped out of the car to open the car door for her, and then walked her to her front door.

"This has been a very nice evening, Richard," Aliyah extended her hand towards him.

"I hope this is just the beginning of many nice evenings. When can we do this again, Aliyah?" He took her hand and held it.

"I don't know, Richard. I'm leaving next week for the Bahamas. Perhaps we'll talk when I get back."

"I'll call you," he said, releasing her hand and planting a sloppy wet kiss on her forehead.

This wasn't such a bad first date, Aliyah thought as she went into the house.

The next few days appeared to fly by. Aliyah arranged to take the day before she was to leave for the Bahamas off from work. She needed the time to finish packing, and she wanted to get a manicure and a pedicure before leaving. Claudia was coming at seven to spend the night, so Aliyah arose early, as usual, to take her morning run.

As she ran alongside the riverbank, Aliyah noticed that another new building project was going up opposite the Performing Arts Center. She wondered if they were putting condominiums there. She tried to read the sign the contractor had posted as she passed. Not looking where she was going, she stumbled over something or perhaps she just slipped, but all of a sudden, without warning, she felt herself falling. She hit the ground with a thud. "Oh no!" she exclaimed as she lay on the ground. Pain shot up her leg from her ankle as she tried to stand, sending her back to the ground. She cried out in distress.

With her body twisted on the ground, tears in her eyes, Aliyah again attempted to lift herself. The pain was now excruciating. She lowered herself into a sitting position, head between her legs, and waited for the pain to ease.

"Are you all right?" She heard a male voice say to her.

She looked up at him. Their eyes held, and she knew. The mysterious eyes that had been haunting her for months were his eyes. For a moment she felt overcome with weakness. The man was incredibly handsome.

"Let me help you," he said, grabbing her elbows and lifting her to her feet.

It was the same man that she had found going through her trash in the spring. He held her at arms length, allowing her to regain her composure. Avoiding eye contact, she thanked the man and started to limp away. Grabbing his cart filled with empty cans and bottles, the man fell into step with her.

"You shouldn't be walking on that ankle. Why don't you let me give you a lift home?"

Aliyah couldn't help but laugh at the thought of riding in a shopping cart atop a load of empty cans and bottles through the streets of Newark. As if reading her thoughts, he laughed, too, revealing an incredible smile with teeth as straight as a ruler and white as pearls.

"My truck is right over there." He pointed to a somewhat beat-up pickup truck parked at the curb.

"No, thank you," Aliyah said politely and continued limping away.

"Are all the children of Osun as stubborn as you are?" She heard him say from behind her.

Aliyah stopped dead in her tracks. "What did you say?" she demanded, turning to face him.

"I've seen you pouring honey into the river. I assumed you were making an offering to the river goddess, Osun."

"You know the river goddess?" Aliyah was amazed.

"I've read about her and the other *orisa*, too. If you walk all the way home on that ankle you will only damage it more, and you'll probably have to stay off your feet for a week or more," he said authoritatively. "Let me drive you home; you can trust me."

Aliyah thought about what the man said. Her ankle was already beginning to swell. She certainly didn't want to spend her two-week vacation on crutches. "Okay," she said, after thinking the matter over for a few seconds.

Approaching her, the man held out his now ungloved hand. His hand was smooth and brown with clean, neatly trimmed nails. "Jeremiah Jones is my name," he said.

"Aliyah Neal," she said, taking his hand for a brief moment. Together, with Jeremiah pushing the cart and Aliyah holding on and hopping on one foot, they made it to his truck.

Once the cans, bottles, and grocery cart were secured in the trailer of the truck, and Aliyah settled in the cab, Jeremiah jumped into the driver's seat. She could not help but notice how nice the cab of the truck was. It had a nice smell, too. She looked for an air freshener but did not see one. Intrigued with the smell that was emanating from the cab Aliyah asked, "What is that smell?"

"Do you like it?" he asked.

"Yes, I do. It smells so exotic."

"It's Egyptian Musk, my favorite oil to bathe in."

Blushing, Aliyah quickly changed the subject. "Aren't you the same man I saw going through my trash a few months ago?"

On the drive to her house, Jeremiah Jones told Aliyah that he had a recycling contract with the city. He collected cans and bottles in the downtown area, along the riverbank, and in some of the parks. Her street was one of those that he serviced. He had noticed that she never put out cans and bottles for collection, therefore, he was checking to see if she mixed them in with her trash. He apologized for startling her.

"I've been trying to recycle my cans and bottles," she told him. "I started putting them in a large trashcan in my backyard. When I tried to carry it out, though, I discovered it was too heavy. I know it sounds crazy, but I am now on my fifth large trashcan that is filled with empty cans and bottles. I need to find a way to get them out of my yard."

"I think I can help you with your problem." Jeremiah flashed that gorgeous smile of his.

When they reached her house, he jumped out of the truck and offered to carry Aliyah to her door. "No, thanks," she said. "I can manage by myself." Ignoring her, Jeremiah gathered her up in his arms and carried her up the stairs, depositing her at her front door.

"Thanks." Aliyah said, and fumbled for her key. "I can manage from here."

"Put an ice pack on that ankle and stay off your feet for the rest of the day," he ordered. "Tomorrow you will be as good as new."

As he walked back to his truck, he said over his shoulder that he would stop by on Tuesday morning to assess the situation with her cans and bottles. Aliyah watched him drive off before she entered the brownstone. *What a good-looking man he is*, she thought. Then it hit her; "I won't be here next Tuesday," she said aloud.

Bill Neal was at his daughter's house promptly at 5:30 A.M. on Friday morning, August third. The Continental Airlines flight was scheduled to leave Newark Airport at 7:45. He knew from experience that Aliyah and Claudia would have a lot of luggage. They were ready and waiting for him to drive them to the airport when he arrived.

Aliyah's ankle, as Jeremiah had predicted, was as good as new the next morning, although her sandled feet were minus a pedicure. She had followed his instructions, and kept an ice pack on her ankle for most of the night. She had explained to Claudia about the fall she had experienced, but told her nothing about Jeremiah Jones. *We'll have two whole weeks to catch up in the Bahamas,* Aliyah told herself. *If I know Claudia, I won't have a secret left when we return.*

They weren't prepared for the beach house in Adelaide. It was absolutely breathtaking. Less than a hundred feet of beach separated the house from the ocean. The three-bedroom house was impeccably furnished, with a lush tropical look. Every room had an ocean view. Aliyah and Claudia went outside to the carport. The car was covered to protect it from the salt air. When they removed the cover, they squealed at the sight of a beautiful shiny black Jaguar.

They quickly dropped their luggage off in their bedrooms. Aliyah, of course, got the master bedroom. They made a list of what they would need from the supermarket and headed towards town. At the Cable Beach Super Value, Aliyah and Claudia filled their shopping cart with fresh fruits and vegetables, smoked oysters, cheese and crackers, soft drinks, and everything else that they thought would make their vacation enjoyable. They stopped at the duty-free liquor store and picked up several bottles of wine and half a case of Kalik, the national beer of the Bahamas.

Driving along West Bay Street, they marveled at how beautiful the emerald green water looked. They drove east as far as the Paradise Island Bridge where the Atlantis Resort towered magnificently across the water. The castle-like building was painted a deep pink color, making a striking contrast against the powder blue sky and the emerald green water.

"We'll have to visit Paradise Island while we're here," Claudia said. "Ebony is dying to go to Atlantis. She always calls me to come and see their commercials on television. I told her that I would bring her something back from Atlantis."

"Of course," Aliyah said. "I want to check out the casino there."

They bought fresh fish and two very large crawfish to broil for dinner from the fishermen under the bridge. "You are lucky," one of the fishermen told them. "Crawfish season just opened this week, and crawfish are plentiful now."

For the next four days, they stayed close to the beach house at Adelaide. Aliyah continued to get up at sunrise for her early morning run, only now she ran along the beach in her swimsuit. She loved the feel of the moist sand between her toes. She could feel the pull of the sand strengthening her legs. Sometimes she just sat and watched the sunrise, marveling at the wonders of God. She threw large purple grapes into the ocean as an offering to Yemanya. She asked the goddess of the sea to protect her and her friend while they were in the Bahamas. She watched the seagulls dive for fish, and the sand crabs make holes in the sand. Aliyah felt at peace with the world. She wondered if Richard could be her soul mate, and why Jeremiah's eyes had haunted her for so long.

As a teenager, Aliyah had always kept a journal. In it she wrote poetry, essays, and even short stories. For some reason, she had packed the journal for the trip. Listening to the roar of the ocean and the squawking of the gulls, while watching the water gentle rolling towards the beach, she felt a tranquility that she had not experienced in a long time. It inspired her to start writing in her journal again.

Rolling, rolling, rolling
The waves of the ocean
Calling, calling, calling
With its unrelenting motion
Jump in and take a ride
I'll be your guide
We'll go for a visit, just you and me
To the watery, watery home of the goddess of the sea.

On their third day in the Bahamas, Aliyah was still using the time she had to just rest. It was close to noon when Claudia finally arose from her bed. She joined Aliyah on the beach after eating a breakfast of cold cereal.

"How about joining me for a swim?" Aliyah asked.

"Maybe I'll be ready when I get back from my walk. I need to work up my nerve to swim in the ocean. I'm afraid of sharks."

"Don't worry Claudia. Yemanya will protect us from the sharks."

While Aliyah continued to write in her journal and read one of the many books she had brought along, Claudia walked the beach. When she returned an hour or so later she showed Aliyah the treasures she had found.

Seashells, a pretty stone, and an interesting rock were all included in her collection of souvenirs for Ebony.

"Ready to get in the water?" Aliyah asked.

"Let's go," Claudia said bravely.

Both Aliyah and Claudia were good swimmers. Once in the water, they spent hours swimming, snorkeling, and diving for seashells.

Claudia loved to cook. She had learned from her grandmother while her mother was working to support their family. The first few nights that they were at the beach house she prepared scrumptious dinners, which included broiled crawfish, scalloped potatoes, and stuffed peppers. Exhausted from swimming, walking, and running during the day Aliyah and Claudia would relax in the evenings and entertain themselves with video movies that Claudia had brought from home. They watched *Jungle Fever*, *Boyz in the Hood*, *Mississippi Marsala*, and other classic movies that they never got tired of seeing.

On their fifth day in the Bahamas, they decided to venture out. They found a respectable looking nail salon on Cable Beach and went in to get a manicure and a pedicure. They learned from the owner that the hottest nightclub on the island was called the Zoo. "Tourists looking for a good time, good music, and fun always find it at the Zoo," he said. After eating a late lunch of steamed grouper with Bahamian peas and rice at Nesbitts, a local native restaurant, they headed back to the beach house to get ready for a night of fun at the Zoo.

It was after nine when Aliyah and Claudia arrived at the Zoo. From the moment they entered the club, all eyes began to follow them as they were led to their table. Aliyah, tall, bronze and slender with long braids swinging behind her, dressed in a short, sexy black dress, revealing long shapely legs, was gorgeous. Claudia, short and petite dressed in white slacks with a white halter-top showing off the recent tan of her caramel complexion, was stunning. The two of them made quite an appearance. They were the center of attention, and they stayed on the dance floor all night. It was after 3:00 A.M. when the shiny black Jaguar pulled into the carport at the Adelaide beach house.

"I haven't danced that much in ten years," Aliyah said the next morning when she and Claudia met in the kitchen for coffee at noon.

"It was great." Claudia grinned over her coffee cup. "Let's do it again tonight," she said.

"Great! First let's go shopping at the straw market downtown. I want to pick up some souvenirs," Aliyah said.

"We can go to the Cable Beach Hotel later tonight. I heard they have a great band there that plays island music." Claudia said, her eyes getting wider by the second.

"Wonderful," Aliyah said, as they headed out to the beach for a swim.

It was after four when Aliyah and Claudia, thoroughly sunned out for the day, drove the Jaguar downtown for a visit to the world famous Nassau Straw Market. The Straw Market was located between the ocean and East Bay Street. It took up about two city blocks and was packed with vendors selling all types of merchandise.

The mostly female merchants were quite persuasive. "T-shirts, three for ten dollars," they yelled. "Over here, darlings, here, pretty ladies, I have something for you, how about a nice purse or straw bag," they called out, flashing their smiles and trying to coax them to their booths. After two hours of going from booth to booth looking at jewelry, bags of all sorts, T-shirts, caps, beach wear, and an assortment of goods, Aliyah and Claudia decided to grab a bite to eat before heading back to the beach house to prepare for another night on the town.

Unsurprisingly, the two women met with the same reaction they received the night before when they arrived, dressed to kill, at the Cable Beach Hotel in the shiny black Jaguar. They had only been seated a minute or two before the waiter came to take their order for drinks. When he returned with two Bahama Mamas, he told them that the drinks were the courtesy of the gentleman behind them. Aliyah and Claudia turned to thank the gentleman, who took their gesture as an invitation to join them.

"My name is Gabriel," he said, flashing his most charming smile.

"Gabriel, like in angel?" Claudia asked.

"Yes." Gabriel looked directly at Aliyah with this huge grin on his face. "I am your guardian angel, sent here to protect you from all of these men who can't keep their eyes off you."

Gabriel told them that he was the masseur at the hotel. He urged them to pay him a visit in the spa for the treat of their lives. To demonstrate his talent, he grabbed Aliyah's hand and began to gently massage her fingers. It was a heavenly feeling. Aliyah couldn't believe how much his touch aroused her.

"Do her," she said, looking at Claudia.

When Claudia began to feel the same sensation, she quickly snatched her hand back. "I'm a married woman," she said very properly.

Gabriel and Aliyah laughed. Their laughter attracted two of Gabriel's friends who joined them, wanting to get in on the fun and share the company of such lovely ladies. They were welcomed at the table. The five of them talked and laughed well into the night. Finally the women begged to leave. Gabriel invited Aliyah and Claudia to go sailing the next Sunday. Aliyah was happy to accept the invitation. She loved to sail.

Over the next few days, Aliyah and Claudia toured New Providence Island and the Atlantis Resort, spending a little time in the casino. Claudia won one hundred dollars playing black jack and Aliyah lost fifty dollars in the slot machines. They shopped at the mall at Atlantis, ate conch salad at Arawak Cay, and swam at Love Beach, Cable Beach and Cabbage Beach. They ate boiled fish and grits for Sunday breakfast at Mr. T's Restaurant. For dinner, they dined at Johnny Canoes, Señor Frogs, The Poop Deck, The Blue Marlin, or Travelers Rest. They stayed up late every night drinking Kalik and watching movies, but mostly they talked. They reminisced about the past.

"Remember Norman Harris?" Claudia asked, referring to an old beau of Aliyah's.

"How could I forget Norman? He was my first boyfriend. He was a wonderful kisser and he taught me the art of kissing, but he was such a slob."

"I thought he was kind of cute, Aliyah. I was so jealous of your relationship with him. I hated that you got a boyfriend before I did. Besides he took up all of your time."

They talked about the present.

"I'm so blessed to have Kwame," Claudia told Aliyah. "He takes such good care of Ebony and me. I know that he will do anything for me, and I feel the same way about him. Being married to Kwame is like having a best friend and a lover in the same person."

Noticing the forlorn look on her friend's face, Claudia asked, "Is this upsetting you Aliyah?"

The question was so sincere that Aliyah had to laugh. "Yes! I want what you have, a soul mate."

"Don't worry Aliyah, you'll find someone, but don't settle for less than what you deserve, trust me."

"Don't I always?" Aliyah asked, and told Claudia all about her date with Richard.

"Sounds promising," Claudia said.

"We'll see," Aliyah said.

Finally, Aliyah told Claudia about meeting Jeremiah.

"Don't tell me you're going to get involved with a homeless man Aliyah?"

"I don't think that he is homeless Claudia, he has a job and a truck. I think I want to find out more about him. For some reason, which I don't quite understand, I am experiencing a strong attraction for him."

"Just be careful," Claudia warned her. "I don't want anything to happen to you."

"Don't worry, Claudia," Aliyah said. "I'm just tired of picking the wrong guy and dating just for the sake of going out. Since I graduated from college, I am sure that I have gotten serious with at least four or five men, and most of them turned out to be real jerks."

"I think the count is a little higher than that, Aliyah, but who's counting?"

"Well, I've been celibate for the last three years. I feel really clean and virginal now, and I'm not giving it up until I know for sure that he is Mr. Right."

Finally, they talked about their future.

"What do you want to accomplish with the rest of your life, Claudia?" Aliyah asked in all earnestness.

"I want to get a college degree. I've been taking some courses at City College. What about you, Aliyah, what do you want besides a husband?"

"Some day, I want Joe Simmons' job."

"You'll get it. You know what else I want Aliyah? I want us to be friends forever."

"We will be, Claudia. Even when you and Kwame move to Ghana, I will come to visit you, hopefully with my own family."

Early Sunday afternoon, Gabriel came by in his forty-five-foot sailboat, and anchored it almost on the beach in front of the Adelaide beach house. Aliyah and Claudia swam out to where Gabriel had anchored the boat and climbed aboard for a wonderful adventure. They sipped cokes, munched on chips, and allowed Gabriel to take them on a wonderful tour of the island by waterway. An hour later Gabriel turned the boat north, letting it sail smoothly over the waves, and headed out to sea.

"Where are we going?" Aliyah asked.

"I am going to take you to a reef near Rose Island," he said. "It's one of the best places to swim and snorkel."

When they finished snorkeling in the beautiful warm waters of the Bahamas, they explored Rose Island where they followed the sound of drums beating and discovered a private beach party in full swing. Several young Bahamian men and women were laughing, talking, dancing, and eating. Gabriel knew one of the drummers. They were invited to join in the fun, which they did.

There was plenty of steamed crawfish, crab and rice, coleslaw, and conch salad. They drank rum swizzles and "leaded" sky juice, and danced to Junkanoo music until they were exhausted. Gabriel was a perfect gentleman. He delivered the young women right back to where he had picked them up, and made them promise to call him the very next time they were in the Bahamas.

Aliyah and Claudia spent their last day in the Bahamas shopping for last minute gifts. Aliyah remembered to buy Morgan some guava duff at the Swiss Bakery on West Bay Street, near Cable Beach. Claudia found an adorable swimsuit, wrap, and beach bag ensemble for Ebony at the Cable Beach straw market. They ate their last bowl of conch salad at Arawak Cay, where they had become friendly with many of the natives on the island.

Finally, Aliyah purchased a bunch of large purple grapes and a jar of honey at the Cable Beach Super Value to make Yemanya and Osun a final offering before their departure. Driving along Cunningham Lake on JFK drive, Aliyah stopped the car, and she and Claudia walked up to the edge of the lake and slowly poured the honey into the water.

"Osun, please accept this offering as a token of my devotion to you, and please help me in my effort to find my soul mate," Aliyah said.

"Osun, please accept this offering as a token of my admiration for you, and please let the love between Kwame and me last for all of eternity," Claudia said.

When they returned to Adelaide, they went out to the beach where they threw the grapes into the ocean as an offering to Yemanya, thanking her for protecting them from sharks and keeping them safe in the Bahamas.

Chapter 9

Richard Bishop

"Who's that?" Claudia asked referring to the man waving frantically, trying to get their attention as they emerged from the Newark Airport terminal.

"That's Richard Bishop, my father's employee. What's he doing here? Did my father send him to pick us up?"

"I guess he did." Claudia watched as Richard, with a big silly grin on his face, approached them and began to gather up their luggage, taking it to his Mercedes Benz, parked at the curb.

"Where's my Dad?" Aliyah asked, giving Richard a cold stare.

"He had to attend an important meeting, he sent me instead," Richard said, looking rather sheepishly. "I hope you don't mind." He looked at Aliyah with a don't-be-angry expression on his face.

Aliyah said nothing, but she felt the resentment coursing through her body.

Once in the car, Aliyah courteously introduced Richard to Claudia and then quickly went back into her silent mode.

"How was your vacation?" Richard asked, breaking the silence.

Aliyah said nothing.

"It was wonderful," Claudia said, feeling a little uncomfortable with Aliyah's sudden change in attitude.

They were silent for the rest of the trip to South Orange. When they parked in the driveway of Claudia's grandmother's house, Richard was the first to get out of the car. While he carried Claudia's luggage up to the porch, Claudia turned to caution Aliyah.

"Girlfriend, I don't know what's going on, but your attitude is bad."

"How dare my father put me in such a situation. He's gone too far. I resent having this man pushed on me like this."

"He seems nice, and he's not bad looking. Your father means well, give him a chance, Aliyah." Claudia followed Richard to the porch. "I'll talk to you soon," she said, before disappearing into the house.

By the time Richard returned to the car, Aliyah had calmed down a little. When they reached the brownstone, he carried Aliyah's luggage into the house while she checked out the large stack of mail that had accumulated while she was gone. When he finished, she invited him to stay for a while, curious to find out what was going on with him and her father. Were they up to something?

"How did my father happen to get you to pick me up at the airport?" she asked Richard over a relaxing glass of iced chamomile tea.

"I know you must be thinking that it's no coincidence that I keep popping up in your life. But please don't blame your father." Richard apologized to Aliyah. "I have to admit that I have been taking advantage of your father's friendship and using it to try to get to know you better. I hope you're not too upset about it."

"It has been a little strange, Richard. This is so unlike my father."

"I've been smitten with you from the first time I saw your picture on your father's desk. He speaks so highly of you. I just had to meet you for myself. I wanted to find out if you were all that your father boasts you to be."

Aliyah just listened as Richard told her of his motive for persuading her father to let him pick her up at the airport. She wondered if what he was saying was true or if he had an ulterior motive for pursuing her the way that he was.

"My father mentioned that you were new to this area and looking to make new friends. I am sure that you don't have any problems meeting attractive young women, Richard. You're a very charming man."

"Thank you." Richard smiled at her. "We Bishop men are known for our charm. My father and grandfather before me were real ladies men. But once they decided to settle down, they became devoted and faithful husbands. I'm going to be honest with you, Aliyah; I am looking to settle down at this point in my life. From what I gather, you are at that same point."

"What makes you say that?" Aliyah asked, wondering if her father told him that.

"You told me when we went out to dinner that you haven't been dating much, and I know that you are close to my age," he said. "I just assumed that marriage is something you're ready for."

"Maybe. Maybe not. But I will tell you this; I am not about to marry someone just because I may be ready for marriage. I need a lot more than just a man."

"I'm not suggesting anything different. I'm only suggesting that we get to know each other better. Who knows, you may find out that I am just the man you need." He briefly squeezed her hand, and smiled at her.

After listening to Richard apologize at least three more times for surprising her at the airport and beg her forgiveness, Aliyah softened a little.

"I promise you that I will never take advantage of my friendship with your father to see you again. Will you forgive me, Aliyah?" he asked, sincerely.

"Okay, but no more surprises." She made a mental note to have a serious talk with her father to tell him to butt out.

"Scout's honor." Richard gave her the Boy Scout salute.

Aliyah smiled, thinking, *He's okay, I guess.* She was not partial to light-skinned men. She loved her own bronze complexion and tended to be attracted to men of the same complexion or darker. She liked tall men, though, and Richard was well over six feet and muscular. He wore a tiny mustache and a thin goatee. Before he left, they made a date for the following night. He had been invited to a client's backyard swim party in West Orange. He asked Aliyah to accompany him and she agreed.

He arrived promptly at noon to take her to the swim party. He brought her a huge bouquet of mixed flowers that she arranged attractively in a vase while he watched. He was dressed casually with jeans, a T-shirt, and sandals.

Aliyah had on shorts and a tank top. She carried her swim gear in a large beach bag along with her towel.

"How well do you know these people?" Aliyah asked, referring to the hosts.

"Not well at all really. He's been coming to the dealership looking for a deal on one of our more expensive models. He invited me to this swim party, mainly to get me on his turf, so he can persuade me to give him a better price, I think."

"I hope you're not going to talk business all evening, leaving me alone with a bunch of strangers." She eyed him suspiciously.

"Don't worry, I won't do that."

Shortly after they arrived at the party, Aliyah realized that she and Richard were the only African Americans in attendance. The backyard was huge with a fairly large swimming pool. There were about twenty-five or thirty other guests sitting on lounge chairs or at the buffet table that was under a tent. The hostess was friendly and attentive, offering to show Aliyah where she could change. When Aliyah returned from the cabana, Richard had already gotten into the pool. She joined him and they floated together in the water for a while.

"I hope you don't mind that we're the only blacks here," he said.

"No, I've been the only black in many situations. Did you know we would be the only blacks?"

"I thought we might be. But it doesn't bother me. Quite often people don't realize that I'm African American at these gatherings. All of my family has a light complexion, making it difficult for people to tell what race we are."

"Was that by design? I mean all of your family being light skinned."

"You have to know my family history to understand it, Aliyah," Richard said, before swimming to the far edge of the pool.

Aliyah followed. They climbed out of the pool, dried off with their towels, and settled in two lounge chairs on the lawn.

"Tell me about your family," Aliyah said looking at Richard.

"My family is not unique in the south. Being a northerner you may not understand them," he said, hesitating a little.

"I'm listening."

"The Bishops of Richmond, Virginia, can trace their ancestry back to England. They were a well-known aristocratic family whose roots in America extended back to the early 19th century. My father's great, great grandfather started a tobacco plantation that flourished in Richmond until the early part of the twentieth century. My father's great, great grandmother was a slave on that plantation. She bore three children for her master, and her descendants were privileged to share in the master's wealth when freedom came.

"And they have managed to hold onto that wealth all of this time?" Aliyah asked.

"Some of it," Richard said. "The point is they believed that the only way to keep the wealth and privilege they inherited was to follow the rule of marrying lighter. My parents have always been very proud of our near ivory complexion. It is my mother's belief that in due time the stigma of race will be all but forgotten in our family if we continue the practice of marrying lighter."

"Then it's obvious that your family will not approve of me, Richard. So why are you dating me?"

"Oh, they'll approve, Aliyah," he said. "You are a very beautiful and charming woman. Your father is one of the most respected black entrepreneurs in the state. My parents respect ambition, hard work, and one's position in the community. As for the reason that I'm dating you, it's because I like you."

Hmm, she thought. She was just about to ask Richard if he had ever dated anyone as dark as she when the host and hostess approached them. While the host led Richard off in one direction, the hostess escorted Aliyah over to the buffet table to get something to eat.

It was early evening when Richard and Aliyah left the party. They were both tired from all the swimming, but he insisted on coming in for a while. They sat on her backyard deck, which provided them with a clear view of the new moon.

"So, you like selling cars?" she asked, just to make conversation.

"I'm very good at it, Aliyah, and working for your father is wonderful. We work as a team and the two of us practically run the dealership ourselves."

"Along with Jamal, you mean."

"Well, Jamal is really a mechanic. He does well in the service department. I can usually find him under a car with the other grease mon- - - -," he cut himself off before completing the sentence.

"Are you calling my brother a grease monkey?" Aliyah was ready to defend Jamal.

"No. I just meant that he prefers working on the cars rather than selling them. Your father and I handle the front offices. Why do you have so many trash cans?" Richard deliberately changed the subject.

She looked at the large trashcans in the back of the yard and thought about Jeremiah Jones. His eyes had stopped haunting her since their last encounter. Would she see him again? Her life was taking a new turn. She welcomed change, but how could she be sure that the path she was about to take was the one intended for her? She would just have to go with the flow.

"I'm really tired, Richard." Aliyah ignored his question about her trashcans. "Would you mind if we finish this conversation another time? I want to take a bath and get ready for work tomorrow."

"I'm a little tired myself. I'll call you tomorrow." Richard followed as Aliyah led him to the door.

Richard called her the next day, and the following day, and everyday thereafter. He sent her flowers twice a week, a bouquet for the office, and one for her home. They got into a pattern of having dinner together at least three times a week. Sometimes he would meet her in Manhattan and other times Aliyah would insist that they go somewhere locally like Je's Restaurant, The Maize, or Arthur's, all located in downtown Newark. Once they went to the Priory, where they dined in the atrium and stayed for the jazz set.

"I love jazz." Aliyah smiled at Richard, as she tapped her feet to the beat of John Coltrane.

"I prefer classical musical myself. It's the kind of music I grew up listening to." Richard appeared unimpressed.

Once they went to a suburban restaurant where they listened to Brahms and Schubert playing over an intercom while they dined. Richard closed his eyes and seemed to be so much into the music that he blocked everything else out.

"Do you play an instrument?" Aliyah asked to break the silence.

"Shhh," he said and went back to his silent mode.

While they were dining at Je's Restaurant one evening, Kanmi and Oya came in for dinner. Aliyah was delighted. Je's was a real family restaurant, with delicious down home cooking attracting many locals as well as out-of-towners looking for soul food. Aliyah loved dining at places where there was a possibility she would run into someone she knew. She quickly beckoned the waitress to bring them over to the table without asking Richard if he would mind. As the waitress escorted her friends to the table, Richard mumbled, "I thought we would be alone." Aliyah ignored the remark. Smiling and showing her happiness, she introduced Richard to Kanmi and Oya.

"We don't want to disturb your date, Aliyah. The waitress will give us the next available table," Kanmi said, sensing Richard's mood.

"Nonsense," Aliyah said. "You don't mind if they dine with us, do you, Richard?" She barely glanced his way.

Richard nodded his approval, although Aliyah could tell that he was unhappy with the idea.

While they waited for the waitress to come and take their orders, Kanmi told Aliyah that he had decided not to invest in the lower Manhattan project that he had told her about. He decided that he would follow the reading of his *odu*.

"What exactly is an *odu*, Kanmi?" Aliyah asked.

"Every being that descends to earth has a destiny," Kanmi said to both of them. "Not everyone fulfills their destiny during their allotted time on earth though. In order to remain on the right path followers of Ifa generally have a reading of their *odu*. This can be done in several ways. I generally consult a *babalowo* before making any major decisions. My *babalowo* reads my *odu* by casting coconut pieces." Kanmi stopped speaking to allow the waitress to take their orders.

When the waitress left, Kanmi said, "I almost didn't follow my *babalowo*'s advice with the Manhattan project, but thanks to my wife and friends like you, Aliyah, I made the decision to go with what I know. I hope that I made a sound business decision." He looked a little worried.

"He won't be sorry," Oya said. "The readings are never wrong."

Detecting that Richard, who sat quietly throughout the story, was uncomfortable with the intrusion, Kanmi again offered to move to another table.

"Too late," Aliyah said as the waitress appeared carrying a tray loaded with their orders.

"What type of business are you in Richard?" Kanmi asked, shifting the focal point of the conversation.

Throughout dinner Richard talked about the dealership and selling Mercedes Benz cars. "You have not lived until you drive a Mercedes." Richard tried to persuade Kanmi. "You should come by the dealership to see me. I'll work out a deal for you that you will not be able to refuse."

"Maybe I will." Kanmi said to be polite.

Richard insisted on picking up the check for everyone, although Kanmi offered to pay since he felt that he had intruded. Kanmi conceded only on the condition that Aliyah and Richard be guests in his home for dinner in the very near future. Aliyah was happy to accept. She wanted to give her godson the souvenir she had purchased for him in the Bahamas.

The evening ended with a nightcap in Aliyah's living room with just the two of them. While Aliyah poured them both a glass of wine, Richard expressed his feelings to her.

"Aliyah, I don't like it when you take control the way you did tonight. I wanted to be alone with you. There were things that I wanted to talk to you about in private."

"I'm sorry, Richard. What did you want to talk about?"

"Come and sit here next to me." Richard had gotten comfortable and was in a reclined position on the couch.

Aliyah obliged, handing him the wineglass as she sat down next to him. Once she was seated, Richard put his glass on the coffee table and pulled her down, holding her close to him.

"Please, don't," she said pulling away from him.

"That's what I wanted to talk to you about, Aliyah," Richard said, highly irritated. "We have been dating for several weeks now and you will not let me get close to you. What is the problem?"

"Richard, it's been a long time since I've been intimate with anyone," Aliyah admitted, as she moved into her own space. "I've become very accustomed to being alone. Before I get intimate with someone again, I want to be sure that the relationship has potential."

"Trust me, baby, this relationship is going places. It's what I want." Richard began pulling her towards him again.

"Richard, please, don't rush me. I need more time." Aliyah was becoming annoyed herself now.

"Time for what?" he asked in a demanding tone of voice.

"Time to decide if this is what I want." Aliyah stood up.

"Aliyah, when are you going to realize that I am what you need? I'm going to give you all the time you want, but don't keep me waiting too long." Richard stood up and followed Aliyah to the door.

Once they were at the door, he pulled her close to him and gave her a sloppy wet kiss on the lips.

Aliyah pulled away first, thinking, *I'll bet he's good with his pants on, but what about with them off? He certainly needs to be taught how to kiss.*

Aliyah stopped by her father's dealership, a few nights later, after leaving her office. The plan was to pick Richard up in order to have a quick dinner somewhere close by, enabling him to return to work. Richard, like her father, was committed to work. He would meet clients at any hour of the night, at their convenience, if it meant a sale. It was during this stop at the dealership that Aliyah had an opportunity to speak to her father about Richard.

Bill was on the telephone when Aliyah arrived. He waved her to a chair in front of his desk. While her father concluded his telephone conversation, Aliyah looked at the pictures of her mother, brother, and herself that sat on her father's desk. It was an old picture of her, more than ten years old. She could not imagine Richard becoming so enamored with her from that picture. *What is his true interest in me?* Aliyah wondered again.

"Hi, sweetheart," her father greeted her. "I know you must be here to see Richard; you haven't come by to see me in ages. How are you doing? You look wonderful." Bill came around his desk to kiss his daughter.

"I'm fine, Daddy." Aliyah hugged her father.

"Where are you two kids headed?" Bill asked.

"We're just going somewhere nearby to get something to eat. Richard will be coming back soon," Aliyah assured him.

"I'm glad to see that things are working out for the two of you." Bill grinned at his daughter.

"Daddy, I wouldn't say that things are working out as you say." Aliyah could not help but reveal the annoyance she was feeling.

"Is he treating you alright, honey?" her father asked.

"He treats me fine. I just don't want you getting any ideas about us. I don't want you trying to put us together like you've been doing."

"Honey, trust me, I just want you to be happy. Rich was so anxious to meet you. I just thought it would be a good thing."

"Well, Daddy, I am trying to figure out why he was so anxious to meet me."

"What are you implying, Aliyah?" Bill raised his eyebrows, questioningly.

"Don't you think it's a little strange that he pushed so hard to get to meet me? There are probably a dozen or more women that he could easily have. Why me?" she asked.

"Honey, don't sell yourself short, you are a very beautiful and intelligent person. Any man would be proud to claim you as his woman."

"I am also the boss's daughter."

"What are you suggesting Aliyah?"

"It's just that he talks about this dealership as though he owns it. Maybe he expects to one day. Maybe that's why he is paying so much attention to me."

"Richard knows that I am grooming Jamal to take over the business when I retire, which, by the way, is a long way off."

"I know that, Daddy, but I am not so sure that Richard knows that."

"Aliyah, if you find out that's the case, then kick him to the curb. I only know the man's business credentials and his work ethic. I don't know his personality beyond what he has revealed around here. Why don't you bring him to the house for Labor Day, your mother and I are planning to have a little something in the yard. That will give me a chance to find out what his intentions are."

"I don't know about Labor Day, Daddy. Richard has plans to visit his parents in Virginia. He wants me to accompany him. Don't worry, Daddy, I can handle this." Aliyah looked up when she heard a knock at her father's door. Richard was signaling for her to come out.

Once they were in her car, Richard directed her to a trendy French restaurant close to the dealership. European classical music flowed from the speakers. After ordering for both of them in French, a habit that Aliyah was becoming annoyed with, Richard asked her what she and her father were talking about while she waited for him.

"Just stuff." Aliyah made light of his inquiry.

"You are still a daddy's girl," he said and nodded his head.

"My father and I have a close relationship. We talk. If that makes me a daddy's girl, then so be it."

"I guess that's all right for now. Even the scriptures say that it is all right for a woman to cling to her parents until she marries, then she must cling to her husband. Do you agree, Aliyah?" He waited for her to agree with him.

"I'm not in favor of clinging to anyone," Aliyah said. "I like to think that I am my own person. There are some people that I trust, and those are the ones that I confide in. I ask their advice, and sometimes I take it."

"I want a wife that is going to trust me explicitly to make all the major decisions for our family."

"Maybe you will find one," Aliyah said with a hint of sarcasm in her voice.

On another occasion, it was Richard that picked Aliyah up at her office for a late dinner. She directed him to her favorite Szechuan restaurant on First Avenue in upper Manhattan.

"No need to order in Chinese, they speak English here," Aliyah said once they were seated, sarcasm showing in her voice.

"Good, I don't know any Chinese. Does it bother you that I have an interest in languages?" Richard gave her a puzzled look.

"Not really. It's just that I am accustomed to ordering for myself when I dine out, and I've done very well up till now. What other languages have you studied?" Aliyah tried to break the ice.

"I do pretty well with Portuguese, Italian, French, and German. I'm trying to get into Russian now. I love learning about other cultures. I find them fascinating. What about you Aliyah, are you interested in other cultures?"

"I became interested in African culture when I was in college. My interest increased after I traveled to Kenya in my sophomore year. I did some research on African and Caribbean religion for a couple of articles that I wrote for *Enigma.* Have you read them?"

"I don't read women's magazines." Richard fiddled with his chopsticks. "I don't think there is anything I would find interesting in them. I am also not interested in African or Caribbean cultures; they are a bit too primitive for me."

"Aren't you interested in learning something about the culture of your ancestors?" Aliyah waited for the waitress to put the food on the table. The crispy fish she had ordered looked good. She could smell the ginger in the sauce.

"Many of my ancestors, as you may recall, were European," Richard said as soon as the waitress left. "That is the culture that was stressed in our home when I was growing up. I fully intend to carry on this tradition in my own home when I acquire a family of my own. Speaking of home, Aliyah, my parents are looking forward to meeting you at our family gathering on Labor Day. I certainly hope that you can come with me. I would love for you to meet my family."

"I'm anxious to meet them too," Aliyah said, mostly to herself.

When Labor Day arrived Aliyah was very excited. The drive to Richmond would give her an opportunity to spend six consecutive hours with Richard. *This will certainly test my tolerance for him*, she thought.

They decided to take her car for the trip, or rather he decided to take her car. Richard wanted to impress his friends and relatives in Virginia with the fact that his girlfriend drove a sports model "Benz." They were already aware that he had a luxury sedan. Aliyah rarely let anyone else drive her car. It was a gift from her father, and it was one of the few possessions that she cherished. Richard insisted that he be the driver for the trip, as he was familiar with the route, and the car. After all, he sold Mercedes Benz cars for a living.

As soon as they were on the road, he pulled out his stack of compact discs. He intended to control the music throughout the trip. This annoyed Aliyah, but she said nothing. *Keep both eyes open before you marry*, she thought.

"Would you like to hear about the research I'm doing for my next article?" she asked.

"I like to listen to music while I drive; it helps me to relax," Richard said, wondering how his family was going to react to Aliyah. His mother would be concerned about his dating someone so dark. *Well, too bad*, he thought. She would just have to get used to the idea of having dark grandchildren running around. It was certainly his intention to marry Aliyah.

"What are you thinking about," Aliyah asked, hating the silence.

"I want you to learn to appreciate classical music. In order to do that, you have to listen and focus on the instruments."

"I listen to classical music. You know I love classical jazz."

"You know what I mean, Aliyah. Let's just listen to the music," he said, going back into his silent mode.

They listened to Chopin for the next two hours. Aliyah thought she would scream before they reached Richmond. It was not that she didn't like European classical music. As a matter of fact, she enjoyed some of it. Clair de Lune by Claude Debussy was one of her favorite musical pieces. She even liked some of Chopin's music, and most definitely Beethoven's fifth symphony. But that wasn't the point. In her car, she liked to be in control of the music.

When they finally left Maryland, Richard turned off the CD player. He felt, for some reason, that he should instruct her on how to behave in the company of his parents.

"Don't talk about politics or religion with my parents," he warned her. "Your thinking is much too liberal for them. I hope you don't monopolize the conversation with that spiritism stuff you learned in Brazil and, please don't bring up your experiences in Africa. My parents are very conservative. I don't want them to think that I am dating someone who's a radical."

"What should I talk about?" Aliyah gazed out of the window.

"I think you should just listen. My parents are very intelligent and very well rounded. You can learn a lot about our way of life by observing and listening to them."

Aliyah decided that she would do just that.

They arrived in Richmond at approximately noon on Labor Day. Richard began pointing out places of interest to Aliyah almost as soon as they hit the city limits.

"There's my high school." Richard excitedly pointed out the large campus. "I was one of only a few African Americans that attended this high school. Most of the blacks in Richmond attended Central High School, which is really in the ghetto of Richmond. I played basketball against Central High School for four years. They had a winning team, and I wanted to play with them. My parents felt that I would get a better education at Northern so I stayed there. I still received a scholarship to play basketball for Seton Hall. That's why I came to New Jersey, you know," Richard said, glancing at her as he drove. "Seton Hall had a winning team while I played there. Until I hurt my knee, I was headed for the pros, Aliyah. I was really disappointed that my basketball career was interrupted, but I got over it."

Aliyah listened and looked.

"We are entering the black section of town now, Aliyah." Richard continued pointing out places of interest to Aliyah. "This is the Jackson Ward District. I rarely came to this section of town when I lived here, although there are some places of interest here as I recall. This area was once considered the African-American cultural center of the East Coast. There's a black history museum somewhere around here." Richard slowed down the car.

Driving on East Leigh Street Aliyah noticed a landmark denoting facts about a famous African-American businesswoman. "Let's stop," she said to Richard. They read the landmark, which told of Maggie L. Walker, an African American, and the first woman to establish a bank in the history of the United States. She served as the bank's first president. The home she lived in until her death in 1934 had become a national historic site.

"Have you been inside?" Aliyah looked at the well-maintained building.

"No, I haven't." Richard did not appear to be interested.

"Too bad it's closed for the holiday. I would love to visit it one day," she said.

On their way out of the Jackson Ward, Aliyah noticed a statue of Bill "Bojangles" Robinson. "I forgot that he was born in Richmond. Did you know that, Richard?"

"No, I didn't."

When they drove up to the Bishop family home, Aliyah took a good look at the surrounding area. She tried to visualize Richard in this environment as a child growing up. It was a beautiful rural setting, high on a hill, enabling her to look down on the city of Richmond. There were many large oak trees on the property, providing shade and hiding the house from the street and neighboring houses. When they entered the two story brick house, the first thing Aliyah noticed was a huge portrait of what appeared to be an Englishman hanging over the mantle in the large living room. Richard left her standing in the room while he went to find the rest of the family.

During the ten minutes that Richard left Aliyah alone, she looked at the pictures on the mantle. They were old pictures, late nineteenth and early twentieth century. Noticeably absent were people of African descent. Not one of the pictures was of an African American. When Richard returned for her, she asked him about the people in the pictures.

"Those are the Bishop family pictures," he told her. "My paternal ancestors."

Aliyah, though surprised, said nothing. She was there to listen and learn. The rest of the family was in the backyard, where a large tent had been put up to keep the food protected in case of rain. Richard took Aliyah's hand and introduced her to different family members. First his parents, Richard senior and Charlotte Bishop, who were a pleasant looking couple in their mid-to-late fifties, like her own parents. Richard's mother was tall and slim with graying hair. His father was also tall with a receding hairline. Both Mr. and Mrs. Bishop were light in complexion, like Richard, but unmistakably African American.

Richards's sisters also favored their parents in complexion and build. Arlene, the oldest had long straight hair that appeared to be relaxed. She introduced Aliyah to her husband Carlos, a latino. They had two children that looked to be of mixed race. Brenda, the younger sister was married to a white man, who appeared to be Irish, because of his red hair and freckles. Brenda was pregnant with their first child. There were several other relatives in the yard along with some friends. Everyone was light complexioned. Aliyah thought for a second that she was at a Jack-and-Jill reunion. The Bishops were friendly people, and they went out of their way to make Aliyah feel comfortable in their home.

At 5:30 P.M., Richard announced that he and Aliyah had to leave. They had a six-hour drive back to New Jersey that would get them home close to midnight. He had to work the next day, and so did Aliyah. Mrs. Bishop walked with Aliyah into the house. Back in the spacious living room, she told Aliyah about the pictures.

"The distinguished gentleman above the mantle is Richard's great, great, great grandfather, my dear," she said. "Mr. Louis Bishop was a distant relative to William Byrd II, the founder of the city of Richmond. The property that this home is built on was part of an estate that originally included almost two thousand acres of prime real estate."

"That was a lot of property," Aliyah said, not knowing what else to say.

"Oh, Louis Bishop had many Negro slaves that helped him grow tobacco on the plantation. One of the slaves was Amelia, Richard's great, great, great grandmother."

Mrs. Bishop pointed out the pictures of other Bishop ancestors who occupied a place on the mantle in their home. There was Richard's great, great grandfather, Mr. George Bishop. George Bishop, Amelia and Louis' son, grew tobacco on the land he inherited for many years. His son George II was Richard's great grandfather and her husband's grandfather.

"The Bishops made a living growing tobacco here until the early 1900s," Mrs. Bishop said. "Richard's grandfather, Richard Bishop I, willed the remaining land to Richard's father in 1958."

"Do they still grow tobacco here?" Aliyah asked.

"Oh, no, my dear. The tobacco industry had started to decline by then.

The land was sold, or parceled out until it was practically gone. There are only a few acres remaining in the family. My husband and I are hoping that Richard will keep the land in the family when he inherits it after our death."

When Mrs. Bishop finished telling Aliyah the Bishop family history, Aliyah asked her about Amelia Bishop, the wife of Louis Bishop. "What happened to her?"

"Oh, Amelia was never the wife of Louis Bishop; she was just one of his slaves. He never married her. I do, however, have a picture of her and some of her children that was taken while Louis Bishop ran the plantation."

Mrs. Bishop went to a desk in the adjoining room and came back with a photo album. She showed Aliyah a picture of Amelia, a beautiful dark woman of about twenty-five with three small mulatto children hanging onto her apron. The picture was old and faded, but well preserved. Aliyah looked at the other photos in the album; they were also of dark people.

"Who are these people?" Aliyah asked politely.

"Oh, this is Arthur, Amelia's brother. He was not a Bishop as you can see. Here is a picture of Amelia's youngest son by Louis. He married dark and lost contact with the Bishop family after awhile. There are some pictures of his children in this album though." Mrs. Bishop handed the album over to Aliyah.

Aliyah was looking through the album when Richard came in the room with his father and sisters.

"We've got to get on the road, Aliyah." Richard walked over, took the album from her, and gave it back to his mother.

Mr. and Mrs. Bishop both kissed Aliyah on the cheek and told her they were pleased to meet her. Richard's sisters smiled politely and said they hoped to see her again. The ride back to New Jersey was quiet except for the music of Mozart. Aliyah fell asleep.

A LITTLE BIT OF HONEY

Chapter 10

*Change is the one unavoidable, irresistible, ongoing
reality of the universe.*

— Octavia E. Butler

Joe Simmons called a special department meeting the Tuesday after
Labor Day. There had been much speculation going on in the office since
the July meeting when Joe had told the staff to expect some changes. He
had not mentioned one more word about the changes he had implied were
coming, not even at their regularly scheduled August meeting. So Aliyah
was surprised to find one of the publishers at the special meeting, a sure
indication that something important was about to take place.

Enigma's tenth-anniversary issue had created quite a stir among the staff
when it came off the press in mid-August. Although Joe Simmons had given
fair warning about an impending change, Aliyah had not been prepared. She
had been taken totally off guard when she returned to her office, following
her vacation in the Bahamas. She remembered Dotty handing her the
latest issue of the magazine with the feature article that Joe Simmons had
written. Joe had written a chronicle of his own ten-year experience with the
magazine.

"Read this and tell me the old man isn't ready to throw in the towel?"
Dotty had said when she handed Aliyah the article to read.

"Yes, it does sound like he is announcing his retirement to the readers,"
Aliyah remembered saying after she had finished reading the article. "I
remember him warning us that things were going to change at the magazine,
but I wasn't expecting this. Has he said something to you, Dotty?" she had

asked her colleague.

"Not a word," Dotty had said. "But he doesn't confide in me. Maybe he was waiting for you to come back," she had said. But Joe had never mentioned a word.

He started the special meeting by addressing the speculation that had been going on since his article first appeared in the magazine.

"I know some of you are wondering if this means that I am ready to be put out to pasture." He smiled and waved the magazine towards them. "Well, the answer is no, I am not ready for that." Joe was emphatic. "But I am ready for some changes in my life. Changes that will provide me with an opportunity to spend more time with my family and pursue other interests that I have had to put on hold for many years." Aliyah couldn't help but notice the whimsical look on Joe's face when he said that.

"My wife has always wanted to take a cruise around the world," he said smiling. "I promised her that we would do that before we depart this world. In order to keep that promise to her, I've got to make a decision now. Time does not wait for anyone, as we all know. My decision is to retire by the end of this year, and to get on with the rest of my life." Joe hesitated for a few minutes and waited for everyone to recover from his surprise announcement.

Aliyah looked at him, and thought, *He looks tired.*

"The next few months will be a definite transition period for all of us," said Joe, as he looked at his staff. "To enable me to make this transition as easy as possible for you, we at *Enigma* have decided to create a new position." He now looked at the publisher to indicate that it was not entirely his decision. "The new position will be that of assistant editor."

Aliyah sensed the quiet that fell over the room at that point. People were shifting in their seats. Dotty looked at Aliyah for some hint that Aliyah knew what was coming next. When Aliyah shrugged her shoulders, indicating that she had no idea of what Joe was talking about, they both looked up at Joe again, waiting for him to continue.

"The assistant editor will take over many of my responsibilities and assume others that will prepare her for the job of becoming the next editor-in-chief of *Enigma Magazine*. The publishers and I agree that the best person for that job is one of our own." He paused for a few seconds and then said, "Aliyah Neal. Aliyah has made a tremendous contribution to *Enigma* since she joined the staff eight years ago." Joe looked directly at Aliyah. "She has proven beyond a shadow of a doubt that she is loyal and dedicated to our magazine. I wish her the best as the future editor-in-chief of one of the fastest growing magazines in the country. *Enigma* is honored to have her."

Aliyah was lost for words. After receiving warm congratulations from Joe Simmons and the magazine publisher, Dotty was the first of her colleagues to wish her well.

"You deserve it," Dotty said. "You work harder than anyone I know, Aliyah. I wish you all the best."

Aliyah drove directly to her parent's home when she left work that evening. She wanted to share her good news with her mother. Betty had been so busy helping Sheniqua with her up coming wedding in December that she hardly had time for her daughter. Aliyah had been jealous at first. She was not used to sharing her mother with anyone other than Jamal. Finally, though, she had adjusted to the idea that her family was changing, and decided that she had better get used to it.

Aliyah found her mother working in her rose garden at the back of the house. Betty Neal's rose garden was spectacular. There were roses climbing up the trellises that covered the gazebo, and there were ornamental marble benches with rose bushes growing behind them. That whole section of the yard was beautiful with late-blooming roses in many colors and varieties. Her mother was cutting some of her prize-winning roses to bring into the house. Aliyah watched her for a few minutes before Betty looked up and spotted her on the deck.

"Hi, sweetheart," she said. "What brings you by on this beautiful day?"

"I have wonderful news, Mom," Aliyah said, walking toward her mother. "I'm going to be *Enigma*'s next editor-in-chief."

"Sweetheart, that's wonderful news. I knew you would be successful at whatever you chose to do," Betty said, tears welling up in her eyes. "Seeing all of your hard work pay off like this is an answer to my prayers. I want only the best for you." Betty embraced her daughter.

"I know you do," Aliyah said. "You are the best mom in the world. I can always count on your support."

"How do you want to celebrate?" Betty smiled at Aliyah.

"I don't want to celebrate, Mom. I just wanted to tell you. Besides I'm still tired from the long ride back from Virginia with Richard last night. It was after midnight when I got home.

"Oh," Betty said raising her eyebrows a little. "How did that work out?"

"I don't know Mom. It's all happening so fast. I've only known him for a short time, and I feel that he is pushing for a commitment. I'm not sure that he is the right man for me. I don't want to be rushed into something that I may regret for the rest of my life."

"Then don't let that happen," Betty advised her daughter. "You're a strong woman, Aliyah. You have good judgement. Trust your instincts and don't allow Richard to convince you that he knows what is best for you. I know that you are worried that your time to find a mate is running out, but believe me you have plenty of time to find the right man. Don't settle for less than what you want. Did you enjoy your trip to Virginia with Richard? Did you remember what your grandmother taught you."

"Before you get married, keep both eyes open. After you are married, close one." They both said in unison, and then laughed together.

"I kept my eyes open Mom, believe me. Truthfully I don't feel that I can fit into that family, and frankly I don't think I want to."

"Trust your instincts, Aliyah. In the meantime, enjoy your new job and make the best of the situation with Richard."

Back at the office, Aliyah found herself busier than ever. Joe Simmons behaved as though he had to teach her a lifetime of experiences in a few short months. Her first assignment as assistant editor was to find a replacement for herself. She was busy setting up interviews, finalizing copy, and planning for future editions. She barely had time to eat lunch each day, generally settling for a quick sandwich at her desk while working.

Dotty was proving to be a big help to her during the transition. One day while she and Dotty were working together on a story Dotty was finishing for the next deadline, she asked, "Aliyah, do you remember that article that you wrote a few months ago 'Red, Yellow, Black, and White: Why Can't We Be Sister Friends?'"

"Yes," Aliyah said, and looked up from the story she was reading. "If I remember correctly, it was you that suggested that I focus on equality."

"Right." Dotty smiled. "I'm wondering if I really believed that at the time. I really thought that I was going to get the promotion to editor in chief, but when I ask myself why, it comes down to racial superiority. I always knew that you work harder than I do, Aliyah. I guess I felt that I should have gotten the job just because I am white. How do you feel about that, Aliyah?"

"The fact that you could share this with me tells me that things are really changing. Did your therapist help you to see that, Dotty?" Aliyah shifted in her seat.

"No," Dotty said. "I decided that I didn't need to go into therapy. What I really needed to do was to be honest with myself. After I decided to do that, I found it easier to forgive my father and myself. I think that I am now ready to develop some true friendships. Do you think that we can be friends, Aliyah?"

"Sure, why not?" Aliyah gave Dotty a big smile.

Friendship was something that developed over time. Aliyah knew that from experience. She would try to be friends with Dotty, but she knew it would never be the kind of friendship she had with Claudia. The kind of friendship she had with Claudia was one of a kind. It was a friendship that encompassed a myriad of experiences that they had shared since they were eleven years old.

Aliyah had only seen Claudia once since they returned from the Bahamas. The last time they talked on the telephone, they agreed to get together soon to celebrate Aliyah's promotion to assistant editor. Aliyah's relationship with Richard and now her new job were taking up most of her time. She wanted to talk to Claudia about Richard. She knew that Claudia would be a good listener and that she could be open with her about her feelings. She also knew that Claudia's response would be honest, non-judgmental, and from the heart. Aliyah did not have an opportunity to spend time with Claudia again until a week after her promotion. It was a day she would never forget.

The morning of September 11 started like any ordinary day, but by the end of the day, the life of Aliyah Neal and countless other people all over the world would be changed forever. Aliyah arose at her usual early hour. She quickly put on her jogging suit, grabbed her trash to put at the curb, and was out of the house running through the streets of Newark before the sun rose. She took her usual route, southeast to Broad Street, east to the river, south along the riverbank for two miles and then back to her point of origin. Aliyah slowed down as she got closer to the corner of her street.

Parked right in front of her house was Jeremiah Jones' truck. As she walked up the street, she saw him leaning against the truck looking at her house. A slow smile started to spread on his face when he saw her approaching. His smile was contagious, and before she realized it, she was smiling back at him. His was a wonderful smile, baring beautiful white teeth. It brightened up his handsome face, making his eyes sparkle like stars.

"Were you looking through my trash bags again, Mr. Jones?" Aliyah said in a most charming manner. She walked up to him, her eyes fixed on his face.

"Actually I was waiting for you to get back. I saw you running while I was driving on the highway," he said, smiling. "I thought I would meet you back here and take a look at your recycling situation, if that's all right with you?"

For a few seconds they looked at each other without saying a word. Aliyah thought to herself *how handsome he is*. He had a milk chocolate complexion with beautiful dark eyes and eyebrows that a woman would kill for, perfectly arched, black and silky like his mustache. His forever-present shadow of a beard, that she found so sexy, reminded her of Eric Benet. His hair was midnight black and neatly trimmed on his perfectly shaped head. She was the first to look away.

"I only have a few minutes before I have to get ready for work." She began walking towards the house. "Why don't you come in, and we'll go out into the yard?"

He followed her into the large entrance hall and waited while she
locked the door behind them. Aliyah led the way to the back of the house.
Jeremiah's eyes scanned the living room, admiring her artwork.

"I see you like the art of the Benin," he said stopping to look at a
collection of African masks that Aliyah had decorating the wall leading up
the stairs.

"Yes, I do." Aliyah was surprised that he recognized the work. "Are you
interested in African art?"

"Yes, I am." Jeremiah looked at some of the other pieces in the collection
adorning the room. "I paint a little myself, but I am really fascinated with
African art, especially that of the Benin artists."

"You seem to know a lot about African culture." Aliyah remembered that
he read books on African religion.

"I guess you can call me a born-again African." He smiled, baring those
gorgeous teeth of his again.

Once in the yard, Jeremiah looked at the now five and a half, large
trashcans filled with cans and bottles. "How long have you been collecting
these?" he asked.

"I guess since I moved here about two years ago."

"I'll drive my truck around to the alley in back of your house. Do you have
the key to the gate?" He looked around the yard.

"How long will this take? I have to get ready for work," Aliyah said.

"Well, you can just give me the key to the gate, and I'll take care of
everything while you get ready for work."

They went back into the house, stopping in the kitchen while Aliyah
looked for the key.

"You have a very nice place here," he said. "I love the way you have
decorated it. It says a lot about you. I can tell that you are proud of your
African heritage. I like that a lot." He smiled at her.

"Thanks." Aliyah handed him the key. "I find it interesting that you
know so much about African culture, too," she said, looking right into the
sparkling eyes that had haunted her for weeks.

Jeremiah took the key from her, and their fingers touched, sending chills running down Aliyah's spine. She led him to the front door and stood in the doorway, watching as he climbed into his truck.

When Aliyah got out of the shower, she walked over to her bedroom window. She could see Jeremiah dumping a trashcan into the back of his truck. He was tall, not quite as tall as Richard, but at least six feet. He had long legs that appeared thick and well defined from the tight fit of his jeans. His logo T-shirt revealed a well-developed chest, and his arms were strong and muscular. He looked to be about her age or a little older. She wondered if he was married, she had noticed that he was not wearing a wedding band. Jeremiah looked up at her house, as he picked up the second trash can. Aliyah stepped away from the window. She didn't want him to see her watching him.

She hurriedly finished dressing, hoping to catch the 7:45 A.M. train to Manhattan. Jeremiah was pulling up in front of her house just as she stepped out of the door.

Handing her the key, he said, "Here's my business card in case you need my services again. I suggest that you start putting your cans and bottles out at the curb on a weekly basis. It will save you a lot of aggravation, and it won't be so unsightly in your yard."

"Thanks," Aliyah said putting the card and the key in her purse. "I really appreciate this." She rushed off.

"I can take you to the train station," he yelled from behind her.

"No thanks, you've done enough already." Aliyah was now running up the street. She didn't look at the card until she was seated on the train. Jeremiah Jones, it read, Environmental Engineer, and listed two telephone numbers, an e-mail address, and a fax number.

By 8:30 A.M. Aliyah was in the staff kitchen making a cup of tea. She was thinking about Jeremiah Jones and wondering if she had seen the last of him. She hoped that was not the case. She found him very attractive. Dotty came in just as Aliyah was preparing to return to her office.

"Hi, Aliyah," Dotty said. "I'm glad I caught you. I've wanted to talk to you, but you've been so busy I hardly ever see you anymore. How does it feel, being the boss?"

"I'm not the boss yet, Dotty. Joe's retirement is not effective until the end of the year. What did you want to talk about?" Aliyah took a sip of her tea.

"Well, I wanted to find out if you enjoyed your stay in the Bahamas, if everything was to your satisfaction."

"Oh, wow. How awful of me." She had sent Dotty a thank you card along with a dozen roses to express her gratitude for use of the beach house, but she hadn't mentioned a word of the vacation to her. "The trip was great, Dotty, and the beach house was wonderful. I must tell you all about it. How about lunch one day soon, my treat?"

"You're on. Oh, and another thing, Aliyah." Dotty smiled mischievously. "Can I move into your office when you move up to the executive suite?" She moved over to the stove to make herself a cup of tea.

"Sure. But why do you want to move? I've always thought your office was nicer, certainly bigger. I thought you got the better office because you were here before me."

"Your office has the better view though. I would prefer that to the extra space."

Suddenly the door to the kitchen swung open and one of the staff writers told them that a plane had just crashed into the World Trade Center. The rest of the afternoon of September 11 was one of mass confusion and shock. They turned on the television and watched the second tower being attacked. Soon the room was filled with crying staff members, many of whom had family or friends who worked at the Trade Center. Aliyah went back to her office, tears in her eyes, wondering *My God, what is happening?*

Her father called, "Honey, are you all right?" he asked, alarm coming through in his voice.

"Yes, Daddy. I'm fine." Aliyah tried to appear calm.

"I don't like having you in New York City now, especially in a tall building. Come home now," Bill practically demanded.

Aliyah assured her father that she would be fine. "I'll call you later, Daddy." She gently hung up the telephone.

The telephone rang again. This time it was her mother. "Mom, I'm all right. Please, don't worry."

Then Richard called. "Aliyah, do you want me to drive into Manhattan to pick you up?" he asked.

"No, Richard. I have work to do." Aliyah was able to maintain her composure. "I'll be just fine." She tried to convince him.

By noon, Aliyah knew that she wasn't going to get much work done. She couldn't concentrate on anything other than what was happening in New York City. News reports were alarming, especially after the Towers collapsed. Claudia called her, reporting that traffic in and out of New York was at a standstill. Trains were all off schedule.

"Come home with me, Aliyah, and spend the night. Don't try to get back to Newark tonight using mass transit."

Arriving at Claudia's house, Aliyah went directly into the den and lay down on the sofa. She was glad that she had agreed to go home with her. She had been confused, tired, and scared. Claudia fed and comforted Ebony, who was aware that something was going on but not sure of just what. Aliyah called her mother to let her know that she was spending the night in Manhattan. Kwame came in bringing bags of Chinese food for dinner. After checking on his family and finding Claudia reading a story to Ebony in her room, he joined Aliyah in the den, and they sat watching the news reports of the "Attack on America."

"This is scary, Aliyah. Everyone keeps asking how this could happen, who could hate us so much that they would do such a terrible thing?" he said. "We all know that America has done some very wicked things. The genocide of Native Americans and the enslavement of people of African descent for over two hundred years were sinful. In general, America has treated people of color horrible. People will be wondering if this is some sort of divine justice." Kwame kept his eyes glued to the television set.

"Maybe this is the first indication of a rude awakening that has to take place before Americans can come together in unity and love," Aliyah said.

"I finally got Ebony to sleep," Claudia said, coming into the room. "Are you still watching this? This is just too frightening. I don't think I can stand to watch that plane crash into the Tower one more time. Please turn the television off Kwame."

"This is history in the making, Claudia. I'm a history teacher. I can't turn the television off. I've got to watch this. The world is changing, and I have got to be a witness to it." Kwame never even looked up from the television.

"Come upstairs with me, Aliyah. We're not history teachers. We don't have to watch. I can't deal with this anymore tonight. I am overwhelmed with sadness. Ebony thinks it's the end of the world. I need to talk about something else for awhile." Claudia turned to leave the room.

Relieved for an opportunity to get away from the tragic events of the day, Aliyah followed her upstairs. Lying on Claudia and Kwame's king-size bed the two friends talked about how their lives were changing.

"Kwame and his associates have found a site in Ghana where they intend to build a school," Claudia told Aliyah.

"Does that mean that you will be moving to Ghana in the near future?" Aliyah asked.

"It will take them a little more time to raise the rest of the capital and to actually build the school. Kwame is estimating three years to complete the project. I guess we'll be leaving then." Claudia looked sad and excited at the same time.

"What about your job, Claudia? You have so much time invested there. Are you just going to quit?"

"That's the good part, Aliyah. I started working for NBC when I was only seventeen, remember? In two years, I'll have twenty years of service in the company. That will entitle me to full pension benefits. I will be able to retire in good financial shape. I've been taking courses at City College, you know. Before I leave for Ghana, I hope to get my bachelor's degree and a teaching certificate. I'm going to start a whole new career in Africa, Aliyah."

"I'm so proud of you Claudia." Aliyah reached out to give her friend a hug.

"I'm really very excited about it." Claudia returned the hug. "I can work in the new school with my husband, and my daughter can attend school there, too."

Aliyah listened to Claudia talk about the changes that were about to happen in her life, happy for her friend, but envious too.

"I'm so happy for you and Kwame, Claudia. Your life has worked out so well," Aliyah said.

"So will yours, Aliyah. Good things are going to happen to you, you'll see. Tell me what's happening with you and Richard?"

Aliyah told Claudia all about her dates with Richard. She told her about the trip to Richmond, Virginia. "Richard is a very hard working and ambitious man. He has definite ideas about what he wants for himself, but he has no clue as to what I want. He doesn't listen to me, and I don't think he respects my opinion. We're very different," Aliyah said, then rolled over on her back and stared at the ceiling.

"Do you have anything in common with him?" Claudia asked, filing her nails.

"We don't enjoy the same music, or share any other interests for that matter. Richard's family embraces the culture of his slave master great, great, great grandfather. They don't even acknowledge their African ancestors. If I were to marry him, I just know that his parents would hide pictures of me and my offspring in a desk drawer with the other dark members of the family. I don't want a husband who is not proud of his African ancestry. What would he pass down to our children?"

"Are you going to stop seeing him?"

"I don't know," Aliyah said honestly. "It's not like I have men breaking down my door and begging me to marry them."

"What about that guy you told me about in the Bahamas? You know the one that was going through your trash. Have you seen him lately?" Claudia was now putting a coat of clear polish on her nails.

The mere mention of Jeremiah brought a smile to Aliyah's face.

"Oh, oh, that smile says a lot." Claudia smiled, too.

Aliyah shared with Claudia the affect that Jeremiah Jones had on her. How he made her tremble when he looked at her, and how his touch sent chills down her spine.

"The chemistry between Richard and me is nothing compared to what I feel when I am in Jeremiah's presence. I hate the way Richard kisses, all wet and sloppy. Morgan says you can teach a man to be good with his pants off though. Truthfully, I don't think Richard will let me instruct him in anything. He is so macho, it makes me sick." Aliyah looked at Claudia as if she were ready to puke.

"Maybe you can get Norman Harris to teach Richard how to kiss." Claudia laughed. They were still laughing when Kwame came into the room.

"Have you two had enough of each other yet?" he asked.

"I'm out of here," Aliyah said, heading towards the guestroom, noting that it was well after midnight.

Returning to her office on September 12, Aliyah observed that the atmosphere was noticeably changed. People were walking around like zombies. Employee absenteeism was high. Dotty called in sick, as well as three other members of her department. The "Attack on America" was all that people were talking about in the rooftop café where Aliyah went to get a bun to have with her tea. When she returned to her desk, Richard called, demanding to know where she had spent the night.

"Why didn't you call me, Aliyah. I was worried about you. I didn't know where you were." Hurt and anger came through in his voice.

"I'm sorry, Richard," Aliyah said for the fifth time. "By the way," she changed the subject, "Kanmi called and wanted to know if we would have dinner at his place tomorrow night. I said yes, I hope you don't mind."

"I wish that you had checked with me first. You know I hate for you to make plans for us without checking with me first," he said, noticeably agitated.

"You don't have to go, Richard."

"But I want to see you. Don't you want to be with me, Aliyah?" he asked more sweetly.

"Then I'll see you tomorrow night." She rushed him off the telephone.

Dinner with Kanmi and Oya was delightful as usual. Aliyah had gifts that she had brought back from her vacation in the Bahamas. She played on the floor with Mwangi and Yori, while Oya put the food on the table. Richard and Kanmi were talking about the events of September 11 within their hearing range. Aliyah kept her ears open.

Richard was all for military retaliation on the terrorists. Kanmi felt that a softer approach was in order.

"War is not the answer. America has an opportunity to show the world that she can resolve conflict peacefully without force. I think it was Socrates who said "Civilization is the victory of persuasion over force," Kanmi said. "The whole world is looking to see how America handles this crisis."

"That is why we have got to use this disaster as a way to teach other countries that you don't mess with America. When we finish with the terrorists, every country in the world will know that America is the toughest and will not tolerate such acts," Richard said.

Aliyah was glad when Oya announced that dinner was ready. She was worried that the talk about terrorism and war was frightening the children, especially Mwangi, who kept looking up at the two men as though he were hanging on to their every word.

Kanmi blessed the food in his native Yoruba language, which Aliyah could tell made Richard uncomfortable. Over dinner, Kanmi told them how his belief in Ifa and the spirits of his ancestors had saved him from near disaster.

"How, Kanmi?" Aliyah asked.

"Remember when I told you about the opportunity that I had to invest a lot of money in a store in lower Manhattan, Aliyah." Kanmi put his fork down.

Aliyah acknowledged that she remembered.

"If I had made that investment I would have been wiped out financially after the events of September 11. The store was totally destroyed by the collapse of the Twin Towers and some of the surrounding buildings. The investment called for a very sizable amount of cash up front. As I told you before, Aliyah, I never make big decisions unless I consult with a *babalawo* and have him read my *odu*. My *odu* reading said I should definitely not make that investment. I was ready to go against my *odu*, thinking that I could make it work in my interest. Lucky for me, my wife and treasured friends like you talked me into going with what I knew. I pulled out of the investment just in time," Kanmi said, picking up his fork to resume eating his meal.

"Kanmi don't you think the building would have been insured to cover any losses you might have sustained?" Richard asked, skepticism showing in his voice.

"Insurance companies are going to be broke following the disaster of September 11," Kanmi said. "Many insurance companies will be forced into bankruptcy or rehabilitation. If anyone recovers their losses, it will be the old businesses, not newcomers like I would have been. I don't even know if I would have had any insurance on my initial investment. If I did, I still may have had to wait years before collecting anything. I am just glad that I followed the reading of my *odu* and never made the investment."

"So am I," Oya said, starting to clear away the dishes. Aliyah got up to help Oya, while Kanmi and Richard continued the conversation.

In the kitchen, Aliyah questioned Oya about Kanmi's *odu* reading.

"It is simple to do," Oya told her. "My mother taught me how to do it many years ago. You just have to use a fresh coconut and know how to read the pieces after they have been cast. Do you want me to do a reading for you, Aliyah? I have a fresh coconut right here." She picked up a coconut from the fruit bowl on the counter.

"Yes," Aliyah said. "I want to know if I should continue in this relationship with Richard."

Oya opened the coconut and reserved the milk in a covered container. "It is good for rinsing your hair after you wash it." She put the container in the refrigerator. "It helps to soothe the head and helps you to relax. Sometimes I use the milk for cooking. It has many useful purposes."

After breaking the coconut into four large pieces, Oya shaped them with a paring knife. When the pieces were ready she held them in both hands and cast them onto the kitchen table. Studying the pattern of the fallen pieces of coconut Oya said, "Okanran." She threw the coconut pieces again. Again she said, "Okanran."

"Aliyah, your ancestors are telling you, no, do not pursue this relationship if you want to fulfill your destiny." Oya gave Aliyah a look of genuine concern.

Aliyah went back into the living room to join the men. Richard was ready to go. They thanked Kanmi and Oya for a lovely dinner and left.

Once they were in the car, Richard said, "I know that you don't believe all of that African mumbo jumbo. Do you, Aliyah?"

Aliyah said nothing. When they arrived at the brownstone, Aliyah did not invite Richard in. He was disappointed and reminded her that he wanted to talk to her and that he was not going to wait forever.

"I know, Richard. I understand exactly how you feel."

As Aliyah got ready for bed, she thought about the reading of her *odu*. She asked herself the same question that Richard had asked her. Did she believe in "all that African mumbo jumbo"? She didn't know how to answer that question. All she knew for sure was that she was undergoing a spiritual change, and that Richard was definitely not her soul mate.

Chapter 11

New Beginnings

Three days after the attack on the World Trade Center, Aliyah was attempting to come to grips with all that had happened over the past few days. People all around her at work were behaving differently. Several people appeared to be in shock. People that had never said more than a courteous good morning to her were now stopping her in the corridors to talk. People were making decisions that they had put off making before. Four people in the department announced their engagements. Three people in her department decided to quit their jobs with no previous warning. Two of them had suddenly decided to move out of state. Absenteeism remained high throughout the building.

When she arrived at the office at 8 A.M. Friday morning, Joe Simmons was already in his office. Aliyah was surprised to find a message from him on her voice mail requesting that she come into his office as soon as she arrived.

The door to Joe's office was open when she got there. His office was huge with a spectacular view of midtown Manhattan. There was an oversized oak desk near the window. A leather couch and two armchairs were arranged nearby, creating a cozy conversational seating arrangement. A picture of the first colored senator and representatives to the 41st and 42nd Congress of the United States hung behind the sofa. Joe was busy cleaning out his desk and putting the contents into cardboard boxes. She knocked to let him know that she was there. He looked up and beckoned for her to come in.

"What's going on?" Aliyah sat down in a chair facing Joe's desk.

"I'm just making room for you." Joe barely glanced up from his task.

"But I thought you were going to stay until the end of the year, Joe."

"Officially I am. But in light of all that's happened in the past few days, I have decided that I am not going to wait another day, or postpone another thing. Time is not guaranteed to us, Aliyah." Joe finally looked at her. "When I think that on September 10, I was having breakfast at Windows of the World on the 110th floor of the World Trade Center at 8:30 A.M. I know that God is telling me something. Aliyah, I am seventy years old. I don't have a lot of time left. God is telling me to make use of the time I have left to make my family happy. I've spent the last fifty years of my life pursuing my dream. Well, my dream is over. I've fulfilled it, now it is time to move on. God has given me the blessing of a new beginning. I am going to take full advantage of it starting right now," he said emphatically.

"What about me? I thought you were going to help me make the transition to editor-in-chief." Aliyah stood up to emphasize her point. "Three important members of our department have just quit. What am I supposed to do? We still have a magazine to get out," she said.

"And you will do it without me. Aliyah, you were chosen for this job because I have faith in your abilities. I know you can do it. I have prepared you well. You have got to think of this as a new beginning for you, too. You have an opportunity to show your talent, your creativity without censorship. I know you wanted this job! Well now it is yours, make the best of it." Joe turned back to his task.

"Why didn't you warn me that you were leaving? I had no clue until I read the lead article in last month's edition. I thought you would be around for at least five more years. I was caught completely off guard, Joe."

"Well, so was I." Joe walked over to his file cabinets and opened a drawer. "No one expected what happened last Tuesday, but it happened. Don't worry, Aliyah, you'll do just fine. Like I said before, you are the best person to fill my shoes. Now get out of here and let me pack. You have some hiring to do, don't you?" he asked, without looking up.

Feeling completely overwhelmed, Aliyah turned to make her exit.

"This is officially your office now, Aliyah." Joe closed the drawer and walked back to his desk. "You have made it to the executive suite. I will be out of your way in about fifteen more minutes. Get your new office painted if you want. You can also get new furniture and carpeting. Take a look around and see what you want to change. I am sure that whatever you want will not be a problem. I haven't redecorated this office in ten years." Joe let out a sigh. "The men will be down to start moving your stuff out in a few minutes; that's why I called you up here. Welcome to the executive suite, Aliyah. Good luck and God bless!"

Returning to her own office, Aliyah plopped into her desk chair. *A new beginning*, she thought. *What should I do first?* It wasn't even nine A.M. and she already had five voice messages; two of them were from Richard. He was the last person she wanted to speak to now. The third was from the publisher requesting a meeting with the new editor in chief; the fourth was from Claudia, and the fifth from Teyinniwa, reminding Aliyah to come by for their monthly visit.

Aliyah picked up the phone and placed a call to the Human Resources Department, telling them that she needed people to interview for the three vacancies that were imminent. She then called the publisher and scheduled a meeting for 3 P.M. She returned Claudia's call and was told that she was at a meeting. She left a message for her. And then, in desperation, she called Dotty to invite her to lunch. Dotty had not been in since the attack on the World Trade Center. Aliyah expressed a sigh of relief when Dotty answered her phone.

"You're on, girlfriend," Dotty said, responding to Aliyah's lunch invitation. "Will noon be all right?"

"That'll be fine," Aliyah said.

They met at the Rooftop Café in their office building at exactly noon. The lunch crowd had not yet come in, enabling them to get choice seats. Aliyah chose a table putting them directly in the warm autumn sunrays. The sun felt good on Aliyah's face and helped her to relax a bit.

"Things are falling apart Dotty. Three of our key people have quit, and Joe has decided that today will be his last working day." Aliyah looked at Dotty, needing some assurance.

"I thought he was going to stick around until the end of the year," she said sympathetically.

"I thought so too, but I think we have seen the last of him until his retirement party."

"How can I help?" Dotty asked.

"We have four junior editors and we need to advance two of them to senior editor status," Aliyah said.

"I thought we only needed one other senior editor. Are you planning to fire me?" Dotty looked slyly at Aliyah.

"No. But the publishers and Joe created an assistant editor position and I intend to keep it that way. You will be the new assistant editor after Joe officially retires. Is that okay with you, Dotty?"

"I'm sorry to have to dump this on you now Aliyah, but I have been thinking about leaving, too. Not right now though," Dotty quickly added when she saw the look of alarm on Aliyah's face. "But soon, real soon. I have decided that there is no reason for me to remain in New York any longer."

"What about your job? Isn't that why you came to New York in the first place?"

"It was only part of the reason." Dotty said, her face becoming somber. "I came to New York to get away from some family problems." She looked down at the table and practically whispered. "I have a son, Aliyah."

"A son?" Aliyah's reaction was one of surprise. "Dotty I didn't know. Why have you never spoken about him before?"

"Right before coming to New York, I placed him in an institution in Canada. That's where I'm from you know." She looked up from the table.

"Yes, I knew you were from Canada."

"My son is autistic." Dotty looked at Aliyah and held her gaze. "His father left me when he was three years old. He could not cope with having a son who was less than perfect. I tried to raise him on my own for the two years following that, but it was too much. I just couldn't handle it. My father and I had a severe disagreement about my decision to place him in an institution." Dotty's eyes began to tear.

Aliyah reached over and covered Dotty's trembling hand with her own. "Raising normal children must be difficult. I can't imagine what you must have gone through. I'm sorry, Dotty."

"I decided to institutionalize him, and my father never forgave me for that. He said some really mean things to me, and I never forgave him for that. My son is fifteen years old now. I visit him once or twice a year. He does not respond to me. He shows no sign of recognition," Dotty said sadly.

"So you think if you were closer to home and saw more of him things would be different?" Aliyah continued to hold Dotty's hand.

"No. My parents visited him frequently, my mother continues to visit him, and he does not respond to her. It's just the way he is. He's severely handicapped."

"Well, if it isn't because of your son that you want to go home what is it?" Aliyah was confused. "You still have a job here. Is it because you didn't get Joe's job? Is that why you want to leave?"

"That's only a tiny part of it." Dotty became a little uncomfortable. "Shortly after I moved to New York, I met a man that I fell in love with. We had a ten-year relationship and now it is over," she said with tears in her eyes.

"Don't tell me." Aliyah let go of Dotty's hand and sat back in her chair. "He's married, and he's not going to leave his wife? Did he dump you?"

"Yes, he was married. But he did not dump me. He worked on the 102nd floor of the World Trade Center. He is one of the missing." Dotty was crying softly now.

Aliyah leaned closer to her, and held her hand again. "I'm so sorry Dotty. This must be awful for you."

"You are the only one I could tell, Aliyah. No one thinks about the mistress. Who comforts her at a time like this? Where do I go for help or information?" Dotty was still sobbing softly. "I keep praying that he will be found, but intellectually I know that he is dead. I was never sure of his love for me, because he stayed with his wife. He kept telling me that after the children grew up he would leave. We had terrible fights about it, but we stayed together. Now I miss him so much."

Aliyah could think of nothing to say that would comfort Dotty. After a few seconds of complete silence, Dotty said, "I have no reason to stay in New York now, Aliyah. At least in Canada I have my mother and my son." Aliyah still did not know what to say so she stroked Dotty's hand. Her heart ached for this woman that she had worked with for over eight years, but never got to know.

"Don't make a hasty decision, Dotty," Aliyah finally said. "Give yourself some time. I really think you need to see a therapist. This is a lot to deal with all by yourself."

"I don't need a therapist, Aliyah. What I need is a friend. I know that I have not made it easy for you to be friends with me, but do you think you can give me another chance? Can we start all over again, you know, a new beginning?"

"Of course we can." Aliyah smiled. "But only if you promise to stay on for at least another year to help me make the transition. How about it?"

"I'll guarantee another six months." Dotty committed herself. "Who knows what will happen after that."

"Good enough." Aliyah was relieved.

"Let's toast to a new beginning." Dotty raised her water glass for a toast.

The three o'clock meeting with the publishers turned out to be a three-hour affair. Aliyah met with them in the conference room on the eighteenth floor. Only the three of them sat at the long conference table with enough seats for a dozen people. The publishers were very reassuring about their confidence in her.

"You were very highly recommended for the editor-in-chief position," Aliyah was told. "As editor in chief your writing and research demands will be lessened tremendously, depending upon how well you utilize your staff. You have an initial advantage because of the recent vacancies in your department. You will be able to fill three positions immediately, for a staff of your choosing." The publishers smiled at her. "And you get a chance to hire your own replacement."

The publishers told her that a lot would be expected from her. She would have complete editorial freedom, but in addition to her editorial responsibilities she would also have social obligations to meet. She would be expected to represent *Enigma* at many public and private affairs not only in New York, but also across the country and sometimes abroad.

"This will be a wonderful opportunity to travel and meet people of status." The publishers appeared elated with her. "*Enigma Magazine* has grown tremendously over the past ten years," Aliyah was told. "We intend to continue the progress. You are a very important part of our future. One other thing, Aliyah, although much will be expected from you, the rewards will be plentiful. This is a new beginning for you. You have a chance to rise to the top of your field. This is your opportunity to shine."

Exhausted when she turned the key in the lock to her front door, Aliyah looked forward to a hot bath and an early retirement. It was a little after 7 P.M. She noticed the light on her telephone answering machine blinking and she instantly thought of Richard. There were three messages from him.

"Why haven't you returned my calls?" his voice said over the machine.

"Aliyah, are you trying to avoid me? Are you upset with me?" he said in his third message.

"I'll call him later," Aliyah said out loud. Kicking off her shoes, she went into the kitchen to fix herself a light dinner. As she washed greens for a salad and prepared to open a can of tuna, her doorbell rang. "Who can that be?" she said to herself. "I hope it isn't Richard. I don't feel up to him tonight."

She was surprised when she looked out of her front window and saw Jeremiah Jones ringing her doorbell. The sight of him gave her a new burst of energy. Checking herself out in the wall mirror over the credenza before opening the door, she was surprised to see how refreshed she looked.

"Mr. Jones, how can I help you?" she asked, looking into his sparkling eyes as they stood in the doorway.

"I came by to bring your money." Jeremiah thrust some bills towards her.

"What's this for?" she asked, surprised.

"This is the money you earned for recycling all those cans and bottles you saved," he said, the slow smile easing on his face.

"Oh no." Aliyah put her hand up as if to stop him. "That's your money. I am just grateful that you took those cans and bottles out of my yard."

"I can't take this money from you," Jeremiah insisted. "I just wouldn't feel right doing that."

"I insist that you keep it." Aliyah caught herself before adding, *you need it more than I do.*

"No," Jeremiah said adamantly. They looked at each other in silence for a second or two before he asked, "How about a compromise?"

"How?" she asked curiously.

"I'll keep the money only if you let me use it to take you out to dinner."

"I don't know about that, Mr. Jones."

"Why not? Are you married?" he asked.

"No."

"Neither am I. So what's the problem?"

"There isn't a problem. It's just that I barely know you."

"And I barely know you," he replied, smiling at her. "I hope that is about to change. How about tomorrow night? I'll pick you up at seven."

Thinking of nothing else to say Aliyah said, "Okay."

After Jeremiah drove off, Aliyah wondered, *what was I thinking about?* Just as she closed the door, the telephone rang.

"It's about time," Richard's voice came through the receiver. "Why haven't you returned any of my phone calls, Aliyah?" He sounded extremely frustrated.

"Richard everything has been so hectic at work. I just haven't had anytime to talk to you today."

"We've got to talk, Aliyah. I'll be getting off in a half-hour. I'll come right over when I leave here."

"Not tonight, Richard. I'm really tired. What about tomorrow morning for breakfast?"

"Saturday's are really busy for me, Aliyah. I have a client coming in at nine tomorrow morning and all day after that until about six. Can we have dinner tomorrow night?"

"No," Aliyah said. "I've made plans for tomorrow night. How about Sunday?"

"I'm not waiting until Sunday, Aliyah. I'm coming over tonight right after

I leave here," he shouted into the phone and then hung up.

It was eight thirty when Richard rang her doorbell. Aliyah had just cleaned up the dinner dishes and made a pot of tea.

She escorted him into the living room. "Would you like a cup of tea?" she asked, politely.

"No, Aliyah. I would like some answers. What is going on? Why are you avoiding me?"

"What do you mean, Richard?" Aliyah asked, giving him a puzzled look.

"You know what I mean." Richard's tone was harsh. "You have been acting strange since we left your friend Kanmi's house. What were you and Oya talking about in the kitchen?"

"Nothing that concerns you, Richard."

"Everything about you concerns me, Aliyah. You are a big part of my life. It's been months since your father introduced us, and I've begun to think of you in terms of the future. I want you to be a permanent part of my life, Aliyah. I have plans for us."

"What about my plans, Richard?" Aliyah began to get annoyed. "Or don't you think I have any? Well I do, and I don't see you in them. We're too different. I've been thinking that I want to end this relationship. It's just not what I want, Richard."

"How do you know?" Richard's face was becoming flushed. "You're not giving us a chance. We can make this relationship work, Aliyah. I know we can."

"I don't want to be in a relationship where it is hard work from the beginning," she said, leaning against the living room wall for support. "If it is this hard now, don't you think that's an indication of things to come? Richard, we have spent the last couple of months getting to know each other only to find out that we have nothing in common. Neither of us will be hurt if we walk away right now. If we continue like this, someone will get hurt."

"I will be hurt if we walk away from each other now." Richard was almost pleading. "I have a lot invested in this relationship, Aliyah. I plan to marry you and make a life with you. Don't deny me that, please."

Aliyah was becoming exasperated. "Richard, you are not making any sense. Marriage is something that two people enter into together. You can't decide to marry me without my consent. I have plans for my own future. I just got a big promotion on my job, and I plan to concentrate on that right now." Aliyah moved from the wall and walked into the kitchen to pour a cup of tea.

"You can quit that job if you marry me, Aliyah." Richard followed her into the kitchen. "I will be making enough money so that you won't have to worry about ever working again. I'll be able to provide for you the way your father provides for your mother."

"I love my job, Richard. It's what I spent a good part of my life preparing for. You don't know me, or what it is I want out of life. We have never even been intimate, Richard." Aliyah poured the tea into a mug, her hand shaking with anger.

"I'm not giving up on you, Aliyah." Richard began pulling her to him. He attempted to kiss her as she struggled to free herself from his grasp.

"I think you should leave, Richard. This is getting us no where." Aliyah moved toward the front door.

"Oh, so now you just want to kick me to the curb. Well, this is not over. I could have any woman I want, Aliyah, but I choose to have you. No one treats me the way that you have. I'm not giving up on you, do you understand?" He followed her to the door.

Aliyah opened the front door. "Goodbye, Richard. Please don't call me again," she said, on the verge of tears.

After Richard left, Aliyah felt troubled. She wanted to talk to someone. Not her parents, not yet. She didn't want to alarm them, and she didn't want her situation with Richard to affect his relationship with her father or his job for that matter. She called Claudia. Kwame answered the telephone and said that she was not home from school yet. Aliyah called Teyinniwa, but she was getting ready for bed. Aliyah made a date to come over the next morning for tea.

As she prepared for bed, she thought about Jeremiah Jones. What was going to happen with him? She knew that she was attracted to him, and it frightened her a little bit. It had been three years since she had been attracted to any man. *Is this a new beginning, too?* she wondered.

Teyinniwa served fresh corn muffins with the tea she and Aliyah were sipping. It was a gorgeous Saturday morning, enabling them to sit outdoors on the sun deck. It was only a little after ten when Aliyah arrived, but Morgan was already out shopping, so it was just the two of them. Aliyah told Teyinniwa about her ambivalence concerning Richard.

"Do you think I led him on?" she asked her friend. "I knew soon after I met him that he could never be my soul mate. I don't know why I continued to see him."

"Honey, you continued to see him because you were lonely, and you wanted to give him every opportunity to persuade you that he was the one," Teyinniwa said. "There is nothing wrong with what you did. He should have gotten the message that something was wrong when you refused to be intimate with him," she reassured Aliyah.

"Well, I hope this doesn't create any problems between him and my father. I don't want his job to be affected by my decision." Aliyah munched her muffin.

"That will be up to him." Teyinniwa poured them both another cup of tea. "If he continues to do his job and earn his pay, your father will keep him on. If he acts like a jerk, he will let him go, and that will be the end of it."

"You have a wonderful way of simplifying things." Aliyah smiled, feeling better.

"Life is simple honey. It's people who complicate things," Teyinniwa repeated the old cliché.

After leaving Teyinniwa's house, Aliyah ran a few errands. She got a manicure and a pedicure, got her hair washed and braided, and picked up groceries for the next week. It was half past five when she got home. She checked her answering machine and was relieved that there was no message from Richard. Claudia had returned her call, and her mother called inviting her to go to church with her the next day. After putting her groceries away, she called Claudia.

"What's up girlfriend," Claudia said.

175

"A lot is going on Claudia. I broke up with Richard, and I've got a date to go out for dinner with Jeremiah Jones tonight."

"What? When did all of this happen?"

"Yesterday," Aliyah said.

"Tell me everything. Aliyah, don't leave out one detail."

"I don't have time now, Claudia. Jeremiah will be picking me up in an hour. I have to get ready."

"Lunch Monday in the park if it doesn't rain?" Claudia asked quickly.

"Sounds good to me." Aliyah said, and hung up the telephone.

True to his word, Jeremiah rang her doorbell promptly at seven o'clock. Not knowing what to wear on a date where she would be riding in the cabin of a truck, Aliyah had decided to wear a short denim skirt with a white shirt and low-heeled shoes. It was a warm evening for September, and she decided to go bare legged and without a jacket. She was surprised when she opened her door to find Jeremiah dressed in a sports jacket, open collared shirt, and expensive looking dress slacks.

"I didn't know what to wear." Aliyah was embarrassed that she was dressed so casual. "I can change very quickly," she said.

"You look fine." Jeremiah flashed that gorgeous smile of his. He took Aliyah's arm to escort her to his vehicle, only the truck was not parked at the curb. Instead, there was a late model Buick.

Aliyah looked surprised. "Where's your truck?"

"I only use the truck for work." Jeremiah opened the door of the Buick for her to enter. "What do you feel like eating tonight, Aliyah."

"I'm not fussy, anything will do." She tugged at the short skirt, making sure her thighs were not overly exposed.

"Do you like fried catfish?" Jeremiah glanced at her as he drove.

"I love it," Aliyah said, looking straight ahead.

"Good. I know a place where they serve the best fried catfish in the city." John's Place was a nice little restaurant located in a section of Newark known as the valley. They served some of the best soul food in town and attracted a large crowd of mostly African Americans on weekends. The ride through downtown Newark to John's place had been rather quiet. Not more than a sentence or two was spoken between them. Jeremiah's car radio was tuned to WBGO, a jazz station in Newark, and one of Aliyah's favorite radio stations. John Coltrane's "My Favorite Things" was playing.

"Do you like jazz?" Jeremiah turned the volume up a little.

"Very much." The smell of Egyptian Musk and the mellowness of the music had put Aliyah in a relaxed and romantic mood.

Seated across from Jeremiah in the cozy restaurant, Aliyah avoided making eye contact with him. She looked around the restaurant at the décor. It wasn't as plush as some of the restaurants she had eaten at with Richard, but it was clean and sort of homey. They sat at a booth with vinyl upholstery. The waitress put down two paper place mats and stainless steel eating utensils wrapped in paper napkins. The water glasses were plastic. Finally her eyes rested on his handsome face. They looked at each other for a few seconds before she looked away again.

"What's the matter?" Jeremiah reached across the table for her hand. "Are you uncomfortable with me?"

"No," she lied, avoiding eye contact. Aliyah felt her pulse beginning to race at his touch.

"Then what is it?" Jeremiah forced her to look into his eyes.

"I don't know." Aliyah looked away again quickly.

"Okay, let's talk." Jeremiah released her hand. "That will help you to relax. Tell me about yourself, Aliyah."

"What do you want to know?" She sat back in her seat and tried to relax.

"What do you do?" he asked. "I see you rushing off to the train station in the early morning hours. Where are you going and what do you do?"

"I'm a writer." Aliyah reached into her purse and gave him one of her business cards. "Actually I was just promoted to editor-in-chief of *Enigma Magazine*."

"Congratulations! I know *Enigma*. I read it every now and then."

Aliyah was surprised. "You read a woman's magazine?" she asked, feeling more relaxed.

"How else am I going to know what women are thinking?" Jeremiah smiled his sexy smile. "What was the last article you wrote about?"

Aliyah told Jeremiah all about her last two articles on women in religion. He remembered reading the last one on women in spiritism. He was familiar with the religion of Ifa, and listened while she told him about her trip to Brazil and witnessing a Candomblé ceremony.

"That must have been very exciting for you," he said. "I became an Ifa follower myself about five years ago. I read a book about *Olodumare* written by a Nigerian *babalowo* and became intrigued with the religion."

"That's very interesting. Tell me in what ways do you consider yourself a follower?" Aliyah sat up in her seat, all ears now. She took a sip from her water glass.

"Well, I follow a monthly ritual of making an offering to my ancestors. I also make periodic offerings to my guardian *orisa*, Sango."

"Do you still pray to God?" Aliyah glanced at Jeremiah over her water glass.

"Of course, all the time." Jeremiah met her gaze. "My decision to make offerings to my ancestors and the *orisa* has not changed my faith in the creator. My belief in Ifa has enhanced my faith in God, and it has changed my life tremendously."

"How has it changed your life?" Aliyah asked, having no trouble making eye contact now.

"Well, for one thing I met you." Jeremiah looked up at the waitress who had come to take their orders.

After a delicious dinner of the best fried catfish Aliyah had ever tasted, and what turned out to be an exciting conversation, they left the restaurant. Aliyah felt more relaxed and did not object when Jeremiah held her hand as they walked to the car.

"It's not even nine o'clock, Aliyah, would you mind if we went somewhere else for a while? I'm not ready for the evening to end just yet." Jeremiah persuaded her.

"What do you have in mind?"

"I know a place where they play good music and you can dance. Do you like to dance?" He smiled at her.

Aliyah smiled back. "Yes."

"I know you are of the hip hop generation. The place I have in mind plays music from the sixties and seventies, the Motown sound. Is that all right with you?"

"I love the music of the sixties and seventies. My parents played it while I was growing up. My dad is a jazz fan, but my mother was big on Motown." They drove up Lyons Avenue to Irvington. They went into a restaurant and nightclub called Marlo's. When they walked in, people greeted Jeremiah as though they knew him.

"Hi, Jay." "JJ, where have you been?" "Hi, Captain."

Aliyah looked around the club. "Is this where you hang out?"

"Not really. I come up here sometimes when I have nothing else to do. Just to talk to some old friends. They found an empty table and Jeremiah ordered a club soda for Aliyah and a ginger ale for himself. A young man of about twenty-five came up to their table.

"Hi, Jay," he said. "I was hoping to see you around here again. I need a job, and I hear that you have your own business now. Can you help me?"

"Call me on Monday, Charlie. I'll see what I can do for you. Right now I want to dance with my date." Jeremiah grabbed Aliyah's hand and led her to the dance floor.

Smokey Robinson was singing "You Really Got a Hold on Me," and the dance floor was crowded with couples. Jeremiah pulled Aliyah into his arms, holding her close to him. She lay her head on his shoulder, and together they moved slowly to the music.

"I've wanted to hold you in my arms again for a long time," he whispered in her ear. "That's why I wanted to go dancing tonight."

"Again?" Aliyah asked, puzzled.

"Yes." Jeremiah pulled her closer. "Since I picked you up and carried you to your door. Remember when you hurt your ankle near the river?"

"Oh," Aliyah said, remembering. Then they were quiet. Holding each other. Listening to the music and swaying in perfect rhythm.

On the drive home, Jeremiah changed the radio station to one that played the music of the sixties and seventies. "I don't want to break the mood," he said, adjusting the volume to a soft tone. They sang "The Twelfth of Never" with Johnny Mathis. Then they sang "Wonderful World" along with Sam

Cook.

"Sam was a wonderful song writer," Jeremiah said. "I admire the way he wrote all of his own music and maintained the rights to it."

"He didn't write that song." Aliyah challenged him.

"Yes, he did," Jermiah said, authoritatively.

"A woman wrote that song," Aliyah insisted.

"Bet?" Jeremiah accepted the challenge.

"Bet what?" Aliyah was confident.

"If I am right, I will get another chance to take you out to dinner."

"What if I am right, what will I get?" she asked.

"What would you like?" Jeremiah flashed another sexy smile.

"How about you make me dinner if I am right?" Aliyah laughed.

"Bet's on." Jeremiah laughed, too. "Either way I win. I get to see you again." He looked at her and smiled.

At the front door to Aliyah's brownstone she invited Jeremiah in for a minute to take a look at her Sam Cook compact disc where the names of the writers were listed on the back. He let her lead the way to her collection of music, and faked dismay when they discovered that she was right. A woman had written the lyrics to "Wonderful World."

"I don't mind losing to you," Jeremiah said as they walked back to the front door. He stopped in the foyer, turned and reached for her, and she fell into his arms. His mouth covered hers, and his tongue found its way through her sensuous lips and into her mouth. Aliyah shivered. She was intoxicated with the smell of him, enraptured by his touch.

She felt like a starving child who had just been given her favorite candy, a Mr. Goodbar. She wanted to devour him, starting with small bites. She nibbled at his neck, and then she took tiny bites of his lips. He lifted her onto the credenza in the foyer, her short skirt rising above her slender hips as he did so. He stood between her legs, stroking her thighs, finally letting his fingers find her moistness. She purred like a feline as he touched her most sensitive parts, parts that had not been touched by a man in three years.

Jeremiah removed Aliyah's panties while she unbuckled his belt, allowing his pants to fall to the floor. He unbuttoned her shirt and sucked her nipples. She licked her Mr. Goodbar and took a few more tiny bites as they prepared to take a long ride together on a milky way to the stars. She fondled him until she couldn't wait another second.

"Now," she whispered in his ear. "I want you now."

He entered her most sacred cavity, and together they moved in perfect rhythm. Slowly at first and then faster staying in sync, she passionately kissed his neck, savoring each mouthful of her delicious Mr. Goodbar. Finally, in one gulp she swallowed him up, deep inside of her. "Aliyah, Aliyah, what are you doing to me?" Jeremiah moaned. When she had taken all that he had to give, she licked her lips like a satisfied cat and snuggled up to him while they both trembled feeling the aftershocks from the earthquake their lovemaking had created.

They remained tightly bound, enjoying the closeness of each other for what seemed like eternity. When she had sufficiently come down from the ecstasy of their lovemaking, she stirred in his arms. He gently lifted her down to the floor, his eyes fixed on her. They remained fixed on her as he arranged his clothing. She deliberately avoided his stare, smoothing her skirt over her hips. She picked up her panties that were sitting on the credenza. She felt his eyes on her as she walked towards the door, opening it for him to exit. At the door, he used his fingers and gently raised her chin up, kissing her lightly on the lips.

"Don't try to figure this out, Aliyah," he said. "It happened for a reason. This is not the end for us. This is a new beginning."

Aliyah watched as he walked out of the door and headed to his car.

Chapter 12

Passion

This has got to stop
Not the passion
Us not being able to
Resist each other
The endless craving in my groin
The hunger of my lips to taste you.

—Opal Palmer Adisa

"We never know when our time will come," Reverend Doggett said to the congregation of Metropolis Baptist church the first Sunday following the attack on the World Trade Center. The newly built, ultra-modern sanctuary was filled to capacity, and he used the occasion of a packed church, following a world disaster, to remind his congregation that they had better be ready if they intended to make that trip to the Promised Land.

"None of the victims of the World Trade Center, except those that committed the heinous act, had any previous warning that September 11, 2001 was going to be their last day on earth. How many of you are prepared to leave here without any warning? No time to get ready. Think about the last sinful act you committed. Have you asked God for forgiveness?"

Aliyah sat in the pew next to her Mother feeling disappointed in herself for having given in to the passion she felt for Jeremiah Jones the night before. She had a feeling of overwhelming grief for the victims of the events of September 11, and she felt sorry for herself for being a victim of her own passion. How could she have committed such an act of passion with a man she barely knew? Unprotected sex on her first date with a man that was almost a complete stranger. She had been so careful about that, especially after the abortion she had had when she was in college. How could she forgive herself, let alone ask God to forgive her?

"Are you all right honey?" Betty sensed that something was troubling her daughter.

"Yes, Mother," Aliyah answered. "It's just a sad time for everyone I guess."

"Yes, it is a sad time. It's a frightening time too. No one knows what tomorrow may hold in light of the attacks of September 11. But we have got to go on as though tomorrow is promised to us. To do otherwise would be to accept defeat. Are you coming home to have dinner with us? Jamal and Sheniqua will be by later. They need your input on their wedding plans."

When Aliyah arrived at her parent's home for Sunday dinner, her father was in the den watching the news on television.

"Hi, Daddy." Aliyah gave him a big hug.

"Hi, sweetheart." Bill glanced up from the television. "Come and sit with me for a while, let's talk."

"I really should help Mom in the kitchen." Aliyah looked at her Mother.

"It's all right, honey," Betty said. I did most of the cooking yesterday. Sit and talk with your father, while I set the table and finish up with dinner." She headed for the kitchen.

Aliyah walked over to the bar and took out a bottle of sherry. The spacious room had formerly been a den. Bill had it transformed into a media center that also served as a family room. Aliyah hoped that he did not want to talk about Richard. He was the least of her worries now. Of course, Richard Bishop was just what Bill wanted to talk about.

Aliyah poured herself a glass of sherry and made herself comfortable next to her father on the soft leather sofa. Bill got right to the point.

"What's going on with you and Richard, Aliyah?" he asked.

"Why are you asking me that question, Daddy?" She gave her father a look that she hoped would let him know she didn't want to talk about Richard.

"Richard has not been himself the last few days." Bill ignored the look. "He hasn't mentioned your name to me one time, which is highly unusual. I figured something must have happened between you two. Did you two have a fight?" he asked, turning the volume down on the television. "You don't have to tell me if you don't want to, I'll understand."

"Daddy, I told Richard that I don't want to see him anymore. He really isn't my type. We have nothing in common, and frankly the chemistry just wasn't there." Aliyah sipped her sherry.

"Honey, you're a grown woman, entitled to make your own decisions just like me. Are you sure though? Richard has a lot to offer as a husband."

"I'm sure, Daddy. Richard has nothing to offer me that I want or need."

"He didn't do anything that was inappropriate did he?" Bill scanned her face.

"No, Daddy, nothing like that. Like I said the chemistry just wasn't right. I really don't want to talk about Richard, do you mind?" Aliyah stood up, ready to go into the kitchen to help with dinner.

"Okay, honey." Bill turned the volume on the television up again.

Sunday dinner was delicious as usual. Betty served stuffed Cornish hens, corn pudding, fresh turnip greens, okra, and corn bread. For dessert there was homemade peach cobbler and ice cream.

"Did I tell you that Reverend Doggett has agreed to officiate at our wedding?" Jamal said, reaching for a second helping of corn pudding.

"Only five times," Aliyah said, moving the pudding within his reach.

"We're having the reception at the Mansion," Sheniqua chimed in. "Have you ever been there, Aliyah?"

"Isn't that the newly renovated nineteenth-century landmark in West Orange? If it's the same one I am thinking about, I know it was purchased about a year ago by a group of young black lawyers from Essex County."

"That's the one," Jamal said, digging into the corn pudding. "They use the second level for offices, and they rent out the first floor for banquets and weddings."

"It's a beautiful building, high on a hill with a gorgeous view of the Manhattan skyline," Betty said, cutting the peach cobbler into squares.

"Of course the skyline will be less interesting now that the twin towers are no longer there," Sheniqua said, shaking her head to refuse Betty's offer of dessert.

Before she left her parent's home, Aliyah had agreed to host the bridal shower at her house with input from the other bridesmaids. She also had agreed to make arrangements for one of *Enigma's* photographers to take all the pictures at the wedding and the reception. She had looked at several designs for dresses that Sheniqua wanted the bridesmaids to wear. She had selected one that she thought would be the most flattering to her figure. Sheniqua had said she would take it under consideration.

It was after 9:00 P.M. when she returned to her brownstone. All she wanted to do was go to bed. She pressed the button on her answering machine to listen to her telephone messages before going upstairs to her bedroom.

"Hi Aliyah," Jeremiah's voice came over the machine. "I just wanted to make sure that you were all right and to hear your sweet voice. Call me when you get a chance."

The sound of Jeremiah's sexy voice caused Aliyah to tremble. She stared at the credenza where just twenty-four hours ago she and Jeremiah had made mad passionate love. She could almost feel his arms holding her and his breath on her hair, his lips on her mouth. She felt herself getting aroused at the thought of him.

Aliyah rushed up the stairs, removed her clothing and stepped into her shower. How was she going to deal with this man? The sound of his voice was all it took to arouse her passion.

Sitting on their favorite Central Park bench the next day eating lunch, Aliyah bared her soul to Claudia.

"What am I going to do, Claudia?" Aliyah looked helplessly at her friend.

"Call him back," Claudia said.

"But Claudia I'm afraid to be near him. I don't think I can resist him. I barely know him." Aliyah put her face in her hands.

"Now, Aliyah, you've been out with him once, you must have gotten to know something about him." Claudia took a bite of her sandwich.

"We spent the whole evening talking about me. He wanted to know all about me. He didn't tell me anything about himself. Do you think he's hiding something?"

"Oh, Aliyah, you complained because Richard didn't want to know anything about you. You said that he only talked about himself. Now Jeremiah is doing just the opposite, and you are still not satisfied." Claudia shook her head in disbelief. "Give the man a chance. Call him back and ask him whatever you need to know."

"I can't see him again, Claudia. I know what will happen. The only thing that I know about him is that he is great with his pants off. I don't want to end up in another 'good fucking relationship.' What should I do?"

"Don't worry girlfriend, everything will work out fine. Just give it time," Claudia said putting her arm around Aliyah.

Returning to her office, Aliyah began to prepare for her first staff meeting as editor in chief of *Enigma Magazine.* She had called the meeting for 3 P.M. This meeting, she thought, would be the opportune time to show that she could pull together all the different facets of the magazine to produce her first edition as editor in chief. She wanted everything to be perfect. She had helped Dotty complete the feature article, and now she needed to bring in the other staff writers to make sure that everything was moving along to meet the deadline. What she wanted most was for her staff to have confidence in her ability and to feel comfortable knowing that she was in charge.

She tried to focus in on what she needed to do, but thoughts of Jeremiah holding her, touching her, caressing her, kept coming to her mind. Fleetingly these thoughts would come to the forefront of her brain, causing her to pause for a few seconds and lose her concentration. She had to force herself not to let the passion she felt for Jeremiah take complete control of her. Work had been a great distraction for her during her period of loneliness, now it would have to distract her from the passion she felt for a man she barely knew.

The staff meeting went better than Aliyah had expected. When she returned to her office, the telephone rang and she picked it up herself, forgetting that she had a private secretary who would do that for her now.

"Aliyah, don't hang up, please." Richard's voice came through the receiver. "I just wanted to apologize to you for anything that I may have said that upset you. I thought about what you said, and although I am very sorry that it couldn't work out with us, I want you to know that I respect you and your right to make your own choices. I would like for us to be friends. At least be on speaking terms in case I see you when you come to visit your father. What do you say?"

"Of course we can be friends, Richard. I'm sorry that it didn't work out, too, but I know that this is for the best." Aliyah stared out of her window.

"Aliyah, I tried to reach you Saturday night. Where were you?"

"I went out with a friend Richard," she said expressionlessly.

"Was it with another man, Aliyah? I need to know if you are dumping me for someone else."

"Who I went out with is none of your business, Richard."

"I know. I'm sorry. I won't be bothering you again Aliyah."

"Goodbye, Richard."

"Goodbye, Aliyah."

On the train ride back to Newark, Aliyah thought about her brief relationship with Richard. She had never felt the kind of passion for Richard that she was feeling for Jeremiah. The chemistry was never there with him. She could barely tolerate his kisses, and she had discouraged any other intimate contact with him. She was glad that it was finally over between them, she would rather be lonely than be with a man that she could not tolerate.

Jeremiah, now, he was something different. The chemistry was certainly there, but what else was it about him that made him so attractive to her. He was certainly good looking. His voice was so smooth and mellow. He had interesting things to say. He enjoyed reading and studying African culture, something Aliyah enjoyed too. They both enjoyed the same music, jazz and rhythm and blues. They had things in common; perhaps a relationship was worth considering.

By the time the train arrived in Newark, Aliyah had decided that she would not discourage Jeremiah from pursuing her. She would keep it at a distance for a while. She was adamant that she did not want to develop a sexual relationship with a man that for all she knew could be a serial killer. She had to find out more about him, but from a distance. Getting off the train at Newark's Penn Station, she picked up the local newspaper and walked the few blocks to her house. After eating a dinner of the reheated food she had brought home in a doggy bag from her parent's house, Aliyah retired to the living room with the newspaper and a cup of her favorite chamomile tea. She had been reading the paper for about twenty minutes when the telephone rang.

Before she even picked up the receiver, she felt herself becoming aroused; somehow she knew it was Jeremiah Jones.

"Hello," she said, a little too sweetly, into the phone.

"Is this really you or is this the answering machine?" Jeremiah's voice came through the receiver.

"Yes, it's me."

"Good. I hate talking to machines. How long have you been home?"

"Oh, about an hour or so." Aliyah stretched out on the sofa.

"Why haven't you returned my telephone call?" Jeremiah asked, sounding more hurt than angry.

"I got in a little late last night, and I was so busy today that I didn't get around to making any personal calls," Aliyah said, reaching for a pillow to hug.

"What are you doing now?" Jeremiah asked.

"Just reading the paper and drinking some tea."

"Anything interesting in the news?" he asked.

"Most of the news is about what happened on September 11," Aliyah said, picking up the paper again. "There are at least six thousand sad stories that came out of that one event."

"Did you know anyone that was personally affected by the tragedy?" Jeremiah asked.

"Yes, I knew a couple of people that worked in Tower One that have been reported missing. My assistant editor has a loved one that is missing, and I had some business contacts at the Trade Center, but I don't know how they have been affected yet." Aliyah said, laying the paper down and hugging the pillow again.

Jeremiah's down to earth conversation and his non-threatening questions helped to put her at ease. She felt perfectly comfortable asking him a few questions herself now.

"What are you doing?" she asked.

"I was painting before I decided to try and call you again."

"What are you painting?"

"I'm working on a picture of a tree. I have a photograph of a tree that I took in Ghana some years ago. I've always wanted to paint it, and now I am."

"What's so interesting about the tree?" Aliyah tried to visualize him painting.

"Well, the Ghanaians call it 'God's Tree' because it is noticeably larger than any other tree in the area. It looks as though it reaches heaven. Its branches extend into the clouds."

"How long were you in Ghana?" she asked.

"Three weeks in 1990."

"My best friend will be moving to Ghana in about three years. I'm sure that I will visit her once she relocates. Did you like Ghana?"

"What's not to like about Ghana? It was one of the most beautiful places I've ever visited. Maybe when you go to visit your friend in Ghana, you can take me along." Jeremiah teased.

Aliyah did not respond, but her pulse began to throb a little faster at the thought of traveling to Ghana with him. "It's getting late and I have to get ready for work tomorrow," she said, releasing the pillow.

"I'll call you again tomorrow, okay."

"Okay," Aliyah said, before hanging up the telephone.

She felt a little better about Jeremiah after talking to him on the telephone. A feeling of ease came over her after learning more about him. Now she knew that he painted, and that he had traveled to Ghana in West Africa. "He seems to be a very interesting man," she said to herself." *I like the fact that he is not pressuring me to let him come over or go out with him again. He must be a very sensitive man,* she thought.

That night Aliyah dreamed that she and Jeremiah were in Ghana. She had never been to Ghana before, but the tree that he told her about was in the dream. They were dancing under the tree. There were flowers and exotic plants all around them. She was wearing a white organza dress that was very sheer. She didn't appear to have on anything under it. Jeremiah was wearing white slacks and a white shirt that was unbuttoned down to his waist. His bare chest was exposed. They were dancing barefoot and laughing. They were so happy.

The next day and for days thereafter, thoughts of Jeremiah would find their way to the forefront of Aliyah's brain. The thoughts would only last a few seconds, but she would get a tingling in her groin, and she could feel her body temperature rising. She would turn the air conditioner up only to turn it back down again when the thoughts passed, allowing her to concentrate on her work again.

She loved her spacious new office with its magnificent view of the city. The carpet was plush, and the furniture was expensive and heavy. She set up her calendar for the next week, marking the dates to interview new writers, submit reports to the publishers, and review final copy for the next issue. She took her new secretary out to lunch to get to know her better while at the same time establishing a sense of loyalty. Aliyah felt good when she left the office at 6:00 P.M. She had accomplished a lot in spite of the temporary interruptions caused by her passion for Jeremiah. She could enjoy the train ride home and think about him without feeling guilty. Knowing that he was going to call her that evening made her break out in a cold sweat.

It was 7:00 P.M. when Aliyah walked through her front door. She immediately went up to her bedroom, changed into her lounging pajamas, and began to prepare something for dinner. She wanted to be relaxed and comfortable when the call from Jeremiah came. After eating a salad with a piece of broiled fish and a baked potato that she prepared in the microwave, she poured herself a glass of sherry, picked up a competitive magazine and perched herself on the living room sofa to wait for his call. When the telephone finally rang at about 8:45, she jumped up and took a few deep breaths before saying "hello" in her sexiest voice.

"You must have been expecting someone else," her Mother's voice came through the receiver.

"Hi Mom," she said, ignoring the comment. "What's up?"

"Have you made an appointment to go for your dress fitting?"

"Not yet." Aliyah said, only half-listening. *I should have gotten call waiting. What if Jeremiah calls while I'm talking to Mom?* Aliyah hated call waiting on home telephones. She disliked being put on hold when she called her friends and she refused to subject her friends to the discourteous service when they called her. She now had second thoughts.

"Mom, I'm expecting an important telephone call, can we talk about this another time?" Aliyah said, glancing at the clock on the mantle.

"I thought so from the way you answered the telephone. Are you waiting for a man to call you?" Betty asked her daughter.

"Just a friend, Mother."

"I know you well enough to know that when you call me 'Mother' like that you don't want to talk about it, right?"

"Yes, Mother dear," she said sweetly, and rushed her Mother off the telephone.

She read the entire magazine from cover to cover without the telephone ringing again. She dozed on the couch for a few minutes before she woke up, looked at the clock again, and decided that he was not going to call. At 11 P.M., Aliyah went upstairs and climbed into her bed. She was disappointed that Jeremiah had not called her, but she was determined not to let it get her down. As soon as her head hit the pillow, she dozed off and the dream reappeared. She and Jeremiah were sitting under "God's Tree," she dressed in the white organza dress and he in the white slacks and shirt. He was smiling at her, and just as he reached out to touch her face, Aliyah woke up abruptly. The telephone was ringing. She picked up the receiver, still half asleep.

"Did I wake you," Jeremiah said. "I'm sorry to call you so late, but I was babysitting, and I didn't have your telephone number with me. I didn't want to go to bed without hearing your voice, Aliyah."

"Babysitting? Do you have children, Jeremiah?" she asked, sounding a little alarmed.

"No, I was babysitting my niece and nephew, my sister's children. She and her husband had an emergency, and she called me to come and baby-sit."

"Oh. Is your sister older or younger than you?" Aliyah asked.

"She's seven years younger than me," Jeremiah responded.

"I have a younger brother, and he is getting married before me, too." Aliyah smiled, thinking, we have something else in common.

"I was the first to get married, Aliyah."

"I thought you told me that you were not married," Aliyah said apprehensively. She sat up in her bed and turned the light on. She could not help feeling disappointed.

"I'm divorced," he said.

"How long have you been divorced?" she asked, feeling a little relieved.

"About ten years now," he said.

"How long were you married?"

"Ten years."

"Where is your wife now?" Aliyah asked as she fluffed up her pillows and leaned back on the bed.

"My ex-wife," Jeremiah said. "She moved out west after the divorce, I think she lives in Seattle, Washington."

"You have no contact with her?"

"No, she remarried about three years ago."

"Are you over her?"

"Completely!" Jeremiah said emphatically.

They were quiet for a few seconds before Jeremiah said, "Why don't you go back to sleep now. We both have to get up early, and it is well past midnight. I will call you tomorrow, okay?"

"Okay." Aliyah turned off the light and closed her eyes hoping she could recapture the dream. She was sure Jeremiah was about to kiss her, and she wanted to taste his sweet lips on hers.

As the days went by, Aliyah began to live for the nightly phone calls from Jeremiah. With each call, she learned more about the man for whom she had such burning passion. The passion she felt for him was overwhelming, and she could tell by the questions that he was beginning to ask her that he was feeling the same thing.

On Sunday night, a week after she had received the first call from Jeremiah, she lay on her bed talking to him on the telephone, hugging her pillow. She was telling him about her brother's wedding plans, describing the dress that she would be wearing, and how she was beginning to get excited about the whole event, when suddenly he asked, "What are you wearing now, Aliyah?"

"Now?" She sat up in the bed.

"Yes, right now."

"I have on my nightgown."

"What color is it?"

"Pink."

"What color pink, dark, light, or medium?"

"It's like an ice pink." Aliyah got out of bed and looked at herself in the mirror.

"Is it long or short?"

"Short."

"How short? Above the knee, or thigh high?" he asked.

"Thigh high," she said.

"Is it lacy or plain?"

"It looks like a slip," she said.

"Oh. I've got the picture."

Two nights later, after they had been on the telephone for over two hours discussing world affairs, the World Trade Center disaster, and local politics, Jeremiah whispered into the telephone, "Aliyah I want to see you. I need to see you. When are you going to let me see you again?"

"I don't know," she said.

"What are you afraid of?" Jeremiah's voice softened.

"I don't want to jump into a relationship with someone I barely know."

"Neither do I. But I know all I need to know about you for now. I know that you are beautiful, intelligent, and very passionate."

"Maybe too passionate." Aliyah hugged her pillow.

"Why do you say that, Aliyah? There is nothing wrong with passion."

"I like to control my passion." Aliyah put her pillow between her legs and squeezed it tightly.

"Are you concerned because you feel you let your guard down a little when we were together last time?"

"A little? I would say that I let my guard down more than just a little. Unprotected sex with someone I hardly know is completely out of character for me."

"You don't have to worry about the unprotected part," Jeremiah reassured her. "I'm clean, drug free and disease free."

"Still, I don't want that to happen again."

"I promise you, Aliyah, nothing will happen until you are ready for it to happen. We'll both be on guard. I just want to see you."

"Maybe."

"How about Friday? Can we go out for a bite to eat and go see a movie maybe?"

"Maybe," Aliyah said again.

"I'll call you tomorrow." Jeremiah said before hanging up the telephone. Aliyah was happier than she had been in a long time. The time she spent talking to Jeremiah on the telephone was relieving all of her anxiety about him. She felt blessed. I love my new job, she thought, and I am falling for a guy that might be my soul mate.

The day after Jeremiah told her that he needed to see her, Aliyah was making her daily run through downtown Newark. She stopped at the riverbank. Looking deeply into the water, she poured Osun an offering of honey, watching as the current quickly snatched it up. After swallowing the offering in one gulp, the water continued to move swiftly and smoothly downstream. "Yes," Aliyah said out loud to herself. "I have got to snatch Jeremiah up like Osun snatched up the honey. She is telling me that he is the one. I won't keep him waiting any longer. I will confirm our date for Friday night."

195

The following day Aliyah was getting a little anxious about seeing Jeremiah again. The date had been confirmed the night before. *What should I wear when I go out with Jeremiah tomorrow night?* She wondered as the train sped her to Manhattan. *I'm certainly not going to wear a short skirt or anything that will be too revealing.* She wanted their second date to be nice and proper, like the first date should have been. *Maybe I'll just keep on my business attire,* she thought.

A message from the publishers asking her to call as soon as she arrived was waiting for her when she got to her office. She wondered what could be so urgent that it required a telephone call before 8:00 A.M. Apparently Joe Simmons had agreed several weeks ago to travel to San Francisco to accept an international publishing award for *Enigma*. The publishers needed her to attend in Joe's absence. The award was being presented at a banquet at the Hyatt Regency Hotel in San Francisco on Friday. She would have to be ready this afternoon for a 3:15 flight out of Kennedy Airport.

"Why wasn't this on my calendar?" she asked her secretary.

"Mr. Simmons insisted on keeping his own calendar, Ms. Neal," was the only explanation she received.

By the time the limousine arrived to take her back home to pack a few things, and then to Kennedy airport for the flight, Aliyah was exhausted. She had put the finishing touches on her report to the publishers, canceled one of her morning appointments, and interviewed two people for the existing vacancies in her department. It was eleven o'clock before she headed down to the garage to get in the limousine.

She arrived at the brownstone at eleven thirty, packed a dress appropriate for the banquet, with matching accessories, an extra business suit, running shoes, lingerie, makeup and toiletries into two pieces of luggage and started out the door. She remembered to call her Mother to let her know where she would be in case of an emergency, and was on her way to the airport by twelve thirty.

She did not think of Jeremiah until she was comfortably seated in the limousine and speeding towards Kennedy Airport. The minute he entered her mind, she frantically pulled out her case of business cards looking for his. Jeremiah Jones, Environmental Engineer, she sighed a sign of relief.

She would be placing her first phone call to Jeremiah that night.

When she arrived at the hotel it was 6:15 San Francisco time. She hung up her clothes and discovered that she had not remembered to pack her jogging suit. On the flight out to the West Coast, Aliyah had thought about running through the streets of San Francisco on Friday morning. She was looking forward to it. *Maybe I can still find a store open where I can purchase one*, she thought to herself. She quickly changed into her running shoes and headed out into the city.

The cool air blowing off the bay made her shiver. She had forgotten how cool San Francisco could be, especially in the evening. Walking towards the Embarcadero, Aliyah looked up and saw that the sky was a beautiful orange. The color was emanating from the sun's descent. She walked down to the wharf where a few remaining fishermen and vendors were packing up their gear from the day's activities. Then she walked towards Market Street, hoping to get a glimpse of the hills and maybe see the Twin Peaks. Finally she found a small variety store on a side street that was still open. She hastily purchased an inexpensive jogging suit and headed back to the hotel.

On the way back, she discovered a bookstore that was open, went in and browsed for a few minutes before selecting a copy of *A Man of the People* by Chinua Achebe. Her father had recommended she read the book some time ago, but she had never found the time. Well, now she had the time. When Aliyah returned to her room, she ordered a light dinner from room service, showered, and put on her white silk pajamas with matching robe. She took Jeremiah's business card from her purse, picked up the telephone and dialed his number. Aliyah laughed at the surprise in Jeremiah's voice when he heard her on the other end of the receiver.

"Is everything all right?" he asked her. It was 7:30 P.M. in San Francisco, but 10:30 P.M. in Newark, later than the time he usually called her.

"I was just getting ready to call you again," he said.

"Everything is just fine. Unfortunately I will have to cancel our date for tomorrow night."

"Are you having second thoughts?" he asked, sounding disappointed.

"No," she said, and explained to him her hasty trip to San Francisco.

"That's all right darling," he said. "We'll have plenty of time to be together when you get back. I'm a very patient man. What are you going to do in San Francisco all by yourself?"

"Well, the banquet is not until tomorrow evening. I plan to run in the morning and maybe do a little shopping. I purchased a book to read tonight and on the flight back."

"What book did you purchase?" he asked.

"*A Man of the People* by Chinua Achebe," she said. "Are you familiar with him?"

"Chinua Achebe is one of my favorite African writers. I love his books. I've read *Things Fall Apart* and *The Writings of Chinua Achebe*, but I've never read *A Man of the People*. Let me know if you like it, then I will read it for sure."

When she hung up the telephone, Aliyah had a big smile on her face. Jeremiah had called her darling. She could feel her passion rising and the yearning in her groin.

Chapter 13

Jeremiah Jones

"Can I get something else for you?" the flight attendant asked for the second time in less than a half-hour. There were few passengers on the return flight to New York. Air travel had decreased tremendously following the events of 9-11. The flight attendants were more friendly than usual, trying to ease the tension.

"No, thank you," Aliyah said, and sipped her tea. She was trying to read Chinua Achebe's book, *A Man of the People*, but every few minutes thoughts of Jeremiah Jones would interrupt her concentration, and she would smile broadly. Knowing that he was going to pick her up at the airport filled her with anticipation, excitement, and happiness. She hadn't seen him in two weeks. Her telephone conversations with him certainly had increased her desire to be with him. They had talked so much over the last two weeks, and she had found out so much more about him that she felt as though she had known him for a very long time. He didn't feel like a stranger to her any more. She felt connected to this man in some mysterious way.

Aliyah walked out of the terminal, luggage in hand, and the first person she saw was Jeremiah, smiling at her. A broad grin spread across her face. He strode up to her, grabbed her around the waist, and gave her a big kiss right on the lips. They embraced for a few seconds. She snuggled her nose and mouth to his neck, breathing in his delicious smell and enjoying the hardness of his body. Jeremiah threw her garment bag over his shoulder, grabbed her remaining piece of luggage in one hand and used his other hand to hold her around the waist as they walked to his car parked at the curb.

Once in the car, Jeremiah asked Aliyah if she were tired. She had risen at 4:00 A.M. after talking to him on the telephone until midnight.

"A little," she replied, putting on her seat belt.

"Are you hungry?" he asked, starting the car's engine.

A light lunch had been served on the plane, but Aliyah had been too excited to eat much.

"A little," she said again.

"How about I take you somewhere to get a bite to eat, and then take you home to get some rest?" Jeremiah asked, putting the car into gear.

"Sounds like a plan to me."

They drove to Newark's Jazz Garden, a restaurant and bar on Halsey Street, not far from her brownstone. The first thing that Aliyah noticed when they entered was an upright piano in a corner in the front of the restaurant near the bar. There was a step leading up to a platform where about ten tables, each seating four people, were attractively arranged. The walls were exposed brick, and along one of the walls there was a fireplace with a wood-burning fire that took the chill out of the early fall evening.

It was barely five o'clock and only a few people were in the restaurant sitting at the bar. The bartender looked up when they entered, and smiled at Jeremiah. "Hi Jay," he said. Jeremiah returned the greeting as he led Aliyah to a table near the fireplace. The waitress immediately came to their table.

"What are you having this evening, Mr. Jones?" she asked, appearing to know Jeremiah as well.

"Do you like New Orleans style gumbo?" he asked Aliyah.

"I don't know if I've ever had any."

"It's the specialty of the house here. They make a big pot every Friday. Try it, you'll like it." He convinced her. "Brenda, bring us two large bowls of gumbo," he said to the waitress.

"I don't think we have any left," Brenda said.

"Ask Cook. I told him to put some away for me." Jeremiah watched as Brenda walked toward the kitchen.

"Everyone here seems to know you, do you come here often?" Aliyah looked around the restaurant.

"Yes. I eat most of my meals here."

"Do you live nearby?" She wondered why she had never asked him where he lived before.

"I live upstairs. There's a loft above the restaurant where I have an apartment and a studio." Jeremiah followed her gaze to the stairway leading up to his loft.

"Oh," Aliyah said, thinking, *He lives very close to me.*

"If you want, I'll take you upstairs to see my place after we eat." Jeremiah looked at her.

"Okay." *I am going to go with the flow,* Aliyah thought.

The gumbo came and turned out to be all that Jeremiah said it was. She ate all of hers and half of his.

"I love a woman with a healthy appetite who still manages to stay in shape." Jeremiah looked at her in amazement.

"I guess I was hungrier than I thought." Aliyah ate the last of the gumbo. When they finished eating, Jeremiah, with his hand gently placed on Aliyah's lower back, led her to the staircase that led up to his loft. Aliyah was immediately impressed with the comfort of the loft. Exposed brick walls, also with a fireplace, gave the loft a homey appearance. A comfortable brown leather sofa and chair made up a cozy and attractive seating arrangement near the fireplace. A huge baby grand piano faced the wall of windows that looked out on Halsey Street and down a side street to Broad Street. The shiny oak floors looked as though they had recently been polished.

At one end of the loft was a kitchenette that was separated from the main living space by a counter and two barstools. At the other end was a door that Aliyah assumed led to the master bedroom. Next to the bedroom was a flight of stairs leading up to the roof.

"Is there something on the roof?" she asked.

"There's a solarium that I use for a studio. Come, I will show you."

The solarium was a brick and glass structure with a sky roof providing plenty of sunlight. The only furniture in the studio was a comfortable looking divan against a bright blue wall, an artist's desk, and a long table with lots of paint and other supplies. Stacked against another wall were blank canvases. Finished paintings were lined against the opposite wall and others were on easels placed throughout the room.

"Someone must have invested a great deal of money to build this studio, Jeremiah. Did the landlord pay to have this solarium built?" Aliyah admired the studio.

"I am the landlord," he said. "I purchased this building five years ago. I rent the restaurant out to some friends, but I help to manage it." He led her to view some of his paintings.

Jeremiah's paintings completely awed Aliyah. He was so talented. She admired his landscapes, still lifes, portraits of old men and women and some of children.

She was completely taken aback when she found herself looking at a painting of a perfect likeness of herself. She stared at a face so familiar to her that she thought for a minute that she was looking in a mirror. The beautiful portrait was still on the easel. It was her face and body dressed in a pink nightgown, almost identical to the one she had described for Jeremiah. She was lying on the grass under what could only be "God's Tree."

"When did you paint this?" She stared at Jeremiah in amazement.

"I started it shortly after I met you. Remember when you caught me going through your trash? For days, your face haunted me in my dreams, until I captured your beauty on canvas. I finished it last week after you described the pink nightgown you were wearing. Do you like it?"

"This is so unbelievable," Aliyah kept saying. She told Jeremiah about the haunting eyes dream, and the dream she had had of the two of them dancing under God's tree.

"It was destiny that we meet, Aliyah." Jeremiah smiled at her. "I knew that as soon as I saw you making the honey offering to Osun. Sango, my guardian *orisa*, was married to Osun you know? Sango and Osun are both highly sexual *orisas*. Children of Sango and Osun are very compatible and often have very satisfying relationships."

"It's been a long time since I have had a satisfying relationship," Aliyah said.

"I have not had a satisfying relationship with a woman since my wife left. I think I can have that again with you, Aliyah. We were destined to come

together, and I believe that it was Osun and Sango that brought us together."
Jeremiah smiled again.

"Why did your wife leave you, Jeremiah?"

"She believed that I loved my job more than I loved her. I was a Newark policeman for twenty years until I retired on permanent disability two years ago. Unfortunately, I was injured twice very seriously. I promised her that I would quit after the first injury, but I couldn't do it. When she realized that I wasn't going to quit, she left. Eight years later, I was injured again. It was then that I made up my mind to leave."

"Why didn't you and your wife have children?" Aliyah was curious.

"She felt that if she stayed with me she would end up a widow. She didn't want to raise children alone. I couldn't blame her for that, so I never pushed the issue of having children." Jeremiah started towards the door that would take them back to his apartment.

When they returned to Jeremiah's apartment, Aliyah felt that she knew all she needed to know about the man that destiny had brought into her life. While he poured them a glass of wine and put on a Sarah Vaughn compact disc, she looked at the photographs he had on display.

"Is the attractive woman in this picture on the coffee table your wife?"

"No, that's my mother when she was a young woman. She died in a car accident when I was fifteen years old." Jeremiah looked over Aliyah's shoulder at the photo.

"Who raised you and your sister after your mother died?" Aliyah replaced the photo.

"My father took us to live with his mother in the South Ward of the city. My father is a musician, and at that time he traveled a lot looking for 'gigs' as he called them. My grandmother took very good care of my sister and me." Jeremiah removed a picture of his grandmother from atop the piano and showed it to Aliyah. "She died three years ago," he said sadly.

"Do you have a picture of your father?" Aliyah studied the picture of Jeremiah's grandmother for a resemblance.

"Here's a picture of my father and me, taken when I graduated from Weequahic High School." He handed her the photograph. "I went to Essex County College for two years after that to study criminal justice. Then I joined the police academy."

"There is a strong resemblance between you and your father, Jeremiah." She gave the picture back to him and took a seat on the sofa. "When did you find time to get married?"

"I married Kathy, who was my girlfriend all through junior high and high school, a week after I graduated from the police academy."

"Do you have a picture of her?" Aliyah hoped she wasn't too beautiful. "No."

Jeremiah sank down into the leather sofa next to Aliyah. "Do you want to stretch out on the sofa and take a little nap? Or you can lie down in the bedroom for a while if you prefer."

"Will you lie down with me?" Aliyah asked brazenly.

"If you want me to." Jeremiah got up taking her hand. Together they walked into the bedroom.

Jeremiah's bedroom was huge. There were large glass panel windows overlooking the street. The huge king-sized bed was facing the windows. On the wall behind the bed was a mural of a beautiful landscape. It looked like the Garden of Eden, and there smack in the middle was "God's Tree."

"When did you finish this?" Aliyah could hardly contain her emotions.

"Two days ago. I was hoping I could get you to lie down with me under God's tree when you got back. I wanted it to be ready." He closed the blinds against the last of the sun's descending rays.

Aliyah removed her clothes carefully, taking each piece off slowly, with her eyes on Jeremiah the whole time. He did likewise, making sure to put on a condom when he finished undressing. When they lay down together on the bed, they heard piano music and the sultry sound of a female jazz singer singing "Heaven, I'm in heaven" coming from the restaurant below. As Jeremiah took Aliyah into his arms under "God's Tree," she hummed, "I'm in heaven," before she got lost among the stars and drifted to the moon.

It was almost midnight when they awoke from their nap. The piano downstairs was still playing and the sultry singer was singing again. Aliyah snuggled up to Jeremiah for one last bit of his loving before they showered and dressed.

Aliyah and Jeremiah went downstairs. The restaurant and bar were packed. A young man was playing the piano and a heavyset, attractive woman was now singing "Misty." When they entered, Jeremiah was greeted over and over again by the patrons of the restaurant. When the singer finished her song, someone asked him to play some Duke Ellington. The piano player relinquished his seat at the piano, and Jeremiah took over. He wanted Aliyah to sit next to him on the piano bench while he played. He played and played, and Aliyah thought, *He's so talented.* It was 2:00 A.M. when they left the nightclub.

"I'll drive you home now," Jeremiah said once they were seated in the car. "Are you sleepy?"

"Not really. That nap did me a world of good, in more ways than one." Aliyah stretched.

"Me too." Jeremiah grinned at Aliyah.

"I didn't know you were such a talented pianist."

"My father is the pianist in the family. What little I know I learned from him. That's his piano in my loft. I'm just keeping it for him until he sends for it."

"Where is your father?"

"Right now he is in Senegal, West Africa. He married an African French woman five years ago. He met her in Paris, but they travel back and forth between France and West Africa. He's sixty-six years old, but you would never know it. The man is phenomenal. He has so much energy. He loves playing jazz music, and he is talented on the trumpet as well as the piano." Jeremiah started the engine.

"Do you get to see your father often?"

"Not as often as I would like. I took my sister and grandmother to his wedding five years ago in Senegal, and I visited him in France last year. He has been to visit us twice since he got married. I hope that he will be coming to the States for Thanksgiving. I don't know if they will be coming to Newark or going to New Orleans though. I speak to him on the telephone two or three times a month. I'm sure he'll give me his itinerary when he calls again. I would love for you to meet him, Aliyah. He really is an extraordinary man."

"He sounds like an extraordinary man." *His son appears to be pretty extraordinary too,* she thought to herself.

"My father was a wonderful husband to my mother and a loving father to me and my sister." Jeremiah headed towards Broad Street. "Even though he spent a lot of time traveling, we always knew that he loved us. That made it a lot easier to accept his intense love for music. We didn't mind sharing him with his work."

"Was he away for long periods at a time?"

"Once he toured Europe for a year. He called home often, as I recall. My mother never seemed unhappy, though, as long as he called home and provided for us."

"Do you think he was faithful all of that time?"

"I believe he was. I remember once, a few months after my ex-wife left, my father had one of his father-son talks with me. I was going through a difficult time. He saw me with a different woman every other week, and he was concerned. He talked to me about sexual abstinence, and I came away believing that he knew what he was talking about from his own experiences. I have come to appreciate abstinence. Before you, I was abstinent for quite a while." Jeremiah looked at Aliyah.

"How long did you abstain?" Aliyah asked, wondering if his period of abstinence had been three years like hers.

"Long enough. Long periods of abstinence drain the energy from Sango's children. You have definitely replenished my energy," he said, smiling at her.

They drove in silence for a few minutes, just listening to the sounds of the radio playing mellow jazz from WBGO.

Breaking the silence, Jeremiah said, "I had always hoped that my ex wife would understand how important my work was to me, like my mother understood how important music was to my father, but it didn't happen."

"Your situation was different, Jeremiah," Aliyah said. "Your work was so dangerous. I can empathize with your wife. I think I would have felt the same way if I were in her shoes."

"But would you have left me, Aliyah?"

"I don't know. I don't know the kind of pain she must have felt when you got hurt. I can only imagine. What I do know is that I am glad that you are no longer a police officer. The thought of your getting hurt is painful to me. Tell me about the times you were injured."

"Better yet, I'll show you." Jeremiah turned the car around.

They drove through the Central Ward of Newark. "This is the West Ward Precinct." He pointed out the building where he had worked for twenty years. Then they drove over to Spruce Street, and Jeremiah pointed out the eleven-story building in the Stella Wright Housing Projects where he almost lost his life.

"My partner and I were responding to a call from a tenant reporting drug activity in a vacant apartment in this building." He looked up at the building remembering. "When we got here, we discovered that it was a crack house. I spotted a young man that appeared to be actively engaged selling crack. When I approached him, he bolted out the door. I chased him up to the roof. When I got to the roof, I saw him standing near the edge. My gun was drawn, and I asked him to put his hands up. He complied. But as I approached the suspect, someone else emerged from the shadows and shot me from behind. The bullet entered my right side and exited my chest barely missing my heart. Three young men picked me up and were going to throw me off the roof. My partner got there just in time and shot two of them; the third one fled."

"How long were you hospitalized?" Aliyah broke the silence that followed.

"I lost consciousness in the ambulance and remained unconscious for five days. When I regained consciousness, my wife, my sister, and my father were all standing over me. I later learned that my wife refused to leave the hospital until I regained consciousness. They let her stay at the hospital the whole five days. She made me promise, while I was only semiconscious, that I would never put her through that again. She reminded me every day of the forty-five days that I was hospitalized that I had promised I would quit the force. Six weeks after I was released, I was ready to go back to work."

They sat in the car, parked across the street from the building where he had almost lost his life. Aliyah looked up at the boarded up building, now completely abandoned and scheduled for demolition. She thanked God that she had met Jeremiah when that part of his life was over.

"What about the second time you were injured?"

"That happened eight years later." Jeremiah started the car engine and headed towards downtown. "I was a detective by then, and I was involved in a homicide investigation when someone I was questioning drew a knife on me and stabbed me in the stomach. He ran and left me alone to bleed to death. Luckily, I was able to walk and crawl to a nearby home and get help. I remember my father coming to the hospital to see me. He looked at me and asked, 'Boy, haven't you had enough of this police stuff yet?' That's when I seriously began to entertain the idea of leaving the police force."

"Do you miss being in law enforcement?" Aliyah looked at Jeremiah, as they turned onto her street.

"Not really. I like what I am doing now. I have always been interested in the environment. After I did some research, I decided to start my own recycling business. That keeps me pretty busy for a good part of the day, and I spend the rest of the day painting and managing the restaurant. I receive excellent retirement benefits, and what I make recycling and selling my paintings enable me to live a very comfortable lifestyle.

"Have you sold many of your paintings?"

"Yes. As a matter of fact, there is an exhibit of some of my work at a gallery on Academy Street tomorrow. Would you like to go?"

"Yes." Aliyah did not hesitate in her response.

"Good. The owners are friends of mine. They do a wonderful job of providing emerging artists like me an opportunity to exhibit their work. They focus on artists of color; you know, Black, Latino, and Asian. You'll enjoy visiting the gallery." Jeremiah parked his car in front of Aliyah's house.

Jeremiah carried Aliyah's luggage into the brownstone, it was after 3:00 A.M. and neither of them was the least bit tired. "I know you must be sick of me by now." Jeremiah followed her into the living room still carrying the luggage.

"Not in the least," Aliyah said, recalling the words of Morgan. "There will never be a time when you won't want to be with him, and there will be little about him that you will want to change" was what she had said about meeting Mr. Right. "I hope you don't have to rush off; I'm not ready for you to leave yet."

"I have nothing better to do." Jeremiah smiled. "It's already Sunday morning, and I usually sleep late and have a nice leisurely breakfast, what about you? What do you do on Sunday mornings, Aliyah?"

"Sometimes I go to church with my mother, but I think I will skip it this Sunday. Maybe I'll sleep in, too, and make you breakfast a little later. How about that?" She led the way to her bedroom.

"Sounds like a plan," Jeremiah said, ascending the stairs to her bedroom.

At 9:00 A.M. Aliyah awoke to the sound of the telephone ringing. She rolled over and smiled when she saw Jeremiah's nude body sleeping next to her. She quickly answered the telephone, not wanting to wake him.

"Aliyah, where have you been?" Her mother's voice came through the receiver. "I have been so worried about you. I thought your plane was due to arrive around three-thirty yesterday afternoon. I have been frantic with worry. I left at least two or three messages for you, why didn't you return my call?"

"I'm sorry, Mom," Aliyah whispered into the phone. "A friend picked me up at the airport and we went out. I didn't get home until late, and I haven't checked my messages yet."

"Why are you whispering? Is someone with you?" Betty was curious.

"Yes, Mother, if you must know."

"Is it a man?" Betty didn't bite her tongue.

"I'll talk to you later, Mother." Aliyah was about to replace the receiver on its hook.

"Are you coming for Sunday dinner?" Betty asked quickly, anticipating her daughter's reaction.

"No," Aliyah said politely and hung up the telephone.

Jeremiah continued to sleep on his side, while Aliyah scrutinized his naked body. He was so beautiful. Long and lean with a nice trim waist and beautiful round buttocks. There was a little hair on his chest and legs, but not much. Jeremiah stretched and changed positions, now lying on his back. Aliyah could see the scar where the bullet had exited his chest. She looked further down and saw the knife wound on his stomach. She touched the scars lightly causing Jeremiah to stir. He opened his eyes and smiled when he saw her looking at him.

"Pretty scarred up body, huh?" He smiled at her.

"Beautiful body." She licked his wounds.

Jeremiah moaned and pulled Aliyah onto his gigantic erection. Aliyah reached over to her nightstand and pulled out a box of condoms that she had purchased just for such an occasion.

After a breakfast of pancakes and turkey sausage, Aliyah put the dishes in the dishwasher while Jeremiah checked out her library. "You have quite a collection of books here," he yelled into the kitchen.

"Yes, I do." She joined him in the library. "I have always been an avid reader. I noticed that you have quite a collection yourself."

"I see we have many of the same books." Jeremiah continued to browse the shelves. "I enjoy reading biographies, and I see you have Zora Neal Hurston, Malcolm X, W.E.B. DuBois, and Marcus Garvey. I have read all of them."

"Do you like fiction?" Aliyah picked up a copy of *Two Thousand Seasons*.

"Some of it. I think I told you that I like Chinua Achebe, but I also like James Baldwin and Walter Mosley."

"I finished Achebe's book, *A Man of the People*, on the plane. I really enjoyed it."

"Good," Jeremiah said. "I'll switch with you. I'll give you my copy of *Things Fall Apart* if you give me the book that you just finished."

"Okay."

While Aliyah dressed, Jeremiah went home to get ready for their visit to the art gallery. *How blessed I am*, he thought as he drove the short distance to his loft. *Aliyah is the perfect woman for me.* It had been a long time since a woman had made him feel the way Aliyah did. *She is so beautiful*, he thought. *She's intelligent, sensitive, and passionate, all the things I admire in a woman. Plus she is sensible, caring, and charming.* He smiled to himself. He, too, was glad that he was no longer a police officer. He did not want anything to threaten his budding relationship with Aliyah. They had so much in common. He loved being with her. Talking on the telephone with her for the past two weeks had given him an opportunity to really get to know her.

When Jeremiah came back to the brownstone for Aliyah, he suggested that she bring her jogging outfit with her.

"What on earth for?" Aliyah gave him a puzzled look.

"You just may have to do your Monday morning jog from my loft." He looked at her with a serious expression on his face. "I am not ready to let you go yet."

"Okay." Aliyah ran upstairs to get her jogging suit and the pink nightgown.

She was impressed with the art gallery. It reminded her a lot of Jeremiah's loft, exposed brick walls and hardwood floors. The paintings were exquisitely framed and arranged by subject on the walls. There were portraits by several different artists on one wall. One of Jeremiah's portraits caught her eye. It was of a very attractive woman of about sixty years old.

"I love this painting," she said to Jeremiah, as he approached her, bringing two glasses of champagne.

"It's a portrait of my mother." He handed her one of the glasses.

"I thought your mother died when she was young."

"She did. I progressed the years on her. That's how I think she would have looked if she were still alive today."

"What a wonderful tribute to your mother. Wherever she is, I am sure that she must be very proud of you." Aliyah smiled and squeezed Jeremiah's arm.

"Thank you." Jeremiah took her arm and led her to the next exhibit.

"This gallery resembles your loft." Aliyah could not help but notice.

"Yes, it does. One day I would like to turn my loft into a gallery like this, but I'll have to find another place to live. Is there anything available in your neighborhood?" Jeremiah joked, giving Aliyah an amused look.

"I don't know, but I'll keep my eyes open." Aliyah blushed.

They left the gallery with Aliyah feeling that she was embarking on a venture that would fulfill her desires and, perhaps, be more than she had ever dreamed. Jeremiah was the best thing that had happened to her in a very long time, and she wanted to scream it to the whole world.

They had dinner at the Jazz Garden and then retreated to Jeremiah's loft for the remainder of the evening. He played his father's piano while Aliyah read the Sunday papers. Later she made brownies, and they snuggled up in his king size bed and watched a movie on television, munching the brownies and sipping glasses of milk. For the second night in a row, Aliyah slept peacefully in Jeremiah's arms, content and satisfied. *Things cannot get any better than this*, she thought, as she was consumed by dreams of her and Jeremiah laughing and dancing under God's tree.

Chapter 14

Acts of Love

"Why didn't you wake me?" Aliyah asked Jeremiah when she joined him in the kitchen of his loft at 5:00 A.M. the Monday morning following her return from San Francisco.

"I knew that you would get up when the time was right for you," he said, handing her a glass of freshly squeezed orange juice. "You have a built in alarm like I do." Noticing that she was already dressed in the jogging suit she had brought from her brownstone he said, "I see you're ready for your morning run."

"Yes. It's already five and I want to get home before six in order to catch the 7:20 train into Manhattan." She sat on one of the barstools at the counter, and quickly drank the glass of juice.

"What's your schedule like today?" Jeremiah asked.

"I have a lot to do at the office. I probably won't get back to Newark until about seven." Aliyah did some stretching exercises on the floor.

"Is there something special you would like to do tonight?" Jeremiah said, sipping his juice.

"No. What do you have in mind?

"How would you like to meet me for dinner tonight downstairs at The Jazz Garden at seven thirty?" he asked.

"That's fine," said Aliyah, putting on her jacket in preparation for her run.

"Do you have a new route mapped out for your run?"

213

"Just about," she said. "Do you have any honey in the house? I want to make a special offering to Osun. She has been so good to me lately." She smiled at him.

"I know what you mean. Those six red apples in the dish on top of the piano are my offering to Sango." Jeremiah reached into the cupboard to get the honey. "Red apples are a favorite of his, you know."

Leaving Jeremiah's house, Aliyah ran south on Halsey Street, then east, and then north to the river, thinking about him the entire distance. Just thinking about him brought a smile to her face. When she got to the river, she poured the honey he had given her into the Passaic River, thanking Osun for responding to her pleas. The short time she had spent with Jeremiah Jones had been the happiest time she had experienced in a very long time. She felt exhilarated and content. She prayed that the feeling would be lasting and that nothing would go wrong in the relationship she was beginning to develop with Jeremiah.

At 7:15 A.M. Aliyah was heading to the train station. She was settled in her office by eight. A half-hour after she arrived at the office, Dotty called and asked if she could see her for a few minutes.

"Sure, Dotty, why don't you come up now." Aliyah wondered what was up.

Dotty knocked on her door at the same time her private telephone line rang.

"Come in," Aliyah called out to Dotty, picking up the telephone.

"I just wanted to make sure you arrived at your office safe and sound." Jeremiah's voice came through the phone.

"Yes, I did." Aliyah's face broke out into a broad grin at the sound of his voice. "Where are you?" She motioned for Dotty to take a seat.

"I'm in the truck talking to you on my cell phone."

"Don't talk on the telephone while you're driving," she said to him. "That's a very dangerous thing to do, and I don't want anything to happen to you."

"Don't worry. Nothing is going to happen to me now that I have found

214

you. I am blessed."

Aliyah was still grinning when she replaced the receiver in its cradle and turned her attention to Dotty.

"Now, don't tell me that was your father?" Dotty said, matching her grin. "I can see love written all over your face, Aliyah. When did this happen?"

"I don't know exactly." Aliyah said, still smiling. "I think it was love at first sight, but I do know that I want this feeling to last forever."

"I am so happy for you. You deserve it."

"Thanks, Dotty." Aliyah sat back in her chair. "Now, what can I do for you?"

"Do you remember me telling you about my missing friend that worked in the World Trade Center?" Dotty became serious.

"Of course." Aliyah looked at her, remembering.

"Well, his family is finally having a memorial service for him next Thursday morning. I want to attend, but I don't want to arouse the suspicions of his family. I don't want to go alone. You are the only one who knows about the two of us. I wonder if you would go with me to the service. It would look better if I was with someone, and not just a lone, weeping female grieving for another woman's husband."

"Of course, I'll go with you Dotty," Aliyah said sympathetically. "I wouldn't want you to be alone during such a sad occasion anyway. You know I care about you, don't you?"

"If I didn't know before, I do now," Dotty said, sincerely. "Accompanying me to the memorial service will mean so much to me, Aliyah. It really is an act of love, and I hope you will be blessed with many such acts for your generosity and kindness," she said. She smiled at Aliyah and then got up to leave the office.

"Acts of Love." *Such a nice phrase,* Aliyah thought after Dotty left the office. Those words came to her mind frequently over the next few weeks. She and Jeremiah developed a routine where they spent every night together. As to where they would sleep, they alternated between her brownstone and his loft. On Sunday morning, when they woke up together in the brownstone, Aliyah fixed breakfast, while Jeremiah read the Sunday papers.

"I hope you like pecan waffles." She put the tray down on the bed.

"Aliyah, whatever you fix is fine with me." Jeremiah said, wasting no time digging into the waffles. "It's been so long since anyone has served me breakfast in bed, I would have been happy with just bread and water."

"I will never serve you just bread and water, my darling," Aliyah said. "I am going to spoil you. You'd better get used to such 'acts of love.'" She joined him on the bed.

"I can't wait," he said, wolfing down a forkful of waffles.

The next Sunday morning, they woke up at the loft and Jeremiah served breakfast in bed while Aliyah read the papers.

"I hope you are ready for the Jones breakfast special." He placed a tray with a plate of grits and salmon smothered in onions in front of her.

"I love a man that can cook." Aliyah relished the smell of the food.

One day when Aliyah did not drive into Manhattan, Jeremiah met her at the train station in Newark and together they walked to the Jazz Garden for dinner.

"You two are the talk of the Garden," Brenda said as she took their orders.

"What do you mean?" Aliyah asked.

"Well, everyone has noticed the halo over the two of you whenever you walk in that door together. It must be love," she said, before leaving to place their orders.

"What do you think she meant by that?" Aliyah looked at Jeremiah who said nothing, but the smile on his face spoke volumes.

One Wednesday evening, Jeremiah prepared dinner for her in the loft apartment. After dinner they sat in the living room playing a game of scrabble.

"U-T is not a word," Aliyah said. "It's the abbreviation for the state of Utah."

"Are you challenging me?" he asked, giving her a look that said, "I dare you."

"If you don't change the word, it will be a challenge. I'm an editor,

Jeremiah. I think I know a little more about words than you do."

"Then challenge it."

"Okay, I will." Aliyah reached for the scrabble dictionary.

"Don't assume you know every word just because you're an editor." Jeremiah laughed at the look of astonishment on Aliyah's face when she found out she was wrong.

One of Aliyah's favorite things to do was to listen to Jeremiah play the piano. Occasionally he would play while she sang, badly.

"It's a good thing you didn't want to be a singer," Jeremiah kidded her after she finished singing her own rendition of Sarah Vaughn's "Broken Hearted Melody."

"Was I that bad?"

"Sarah must be crying in her grave." Jeremiah took her into his arms and smothered her with kisses when he saw the hurt look on her face. "You can't be great at everything darling," he said.

They went to see the movie *Love Jones* at the old drive-in, as Jeremiah referred to the multiplex cinema located in the ironbound section of the city.

"I love romance movies, don't you, Jeremiah?" Aliyah asked, walking back to the car.

"Sometimes," he said. "This one was especially nice because the good guy got the girl at the end of the story." Jeremiah opened the car door for her to get in.

"Are you a good guy?"

"You know I am, otherwise I would not have gotten you."

"How do you know you got me?" Aliyah smiled.

"You're with me aren't you?"

On the days that she drove into Manhattan, Aliyah would return to her brownstone and prepare dinner for Jeremiah. Once, just as she was finishing up, he arrived bringing a bouquet of fresh cut flowers and a bottle of her favorite Merlot wine.

"Just a little 'act of love,'" he said when she protested that he was spoiling her.

In return for the "acts of love" that Jeremiah showered on her, Aliyah reciprocated with her own "acts of love." Once, he sat down to dinner and exclaimed, "You made yellow turnips for dinner? I thought you didn't like them."

"I'm trying to acquire a taste for them because you love them so much." Aliyah had called her mother to get the recipe. Her mother also gave her recipes for fresh baked bread, cakes, and pies. Aliyah was thrilled when she saw the look of love in Jeremiah's beautiful eyes when he tasted her "acts of love."

On Saturdays, Aliyah and Jeremiah would spend the whole day together. One rainy Saturday, he accompanied her to Bloomingdales at Short Hills Mall and helped her shop for clothes to wear to work. He sat patiently outside the dressing room reading a book while she tried on different outfits, coming out to model them for his approval.

"The navy blue one looks better on you." Jeremiah decided after seeing her model two different suits. "The shorter skirt shows off your long gorgeous legs."

Before leaving the store, he wanted to visit the lingerie department.

"I want to see you in this." He held up a cute little sky blue teddy. "This color looks good against your bronze skin."

On alternate Saturdays when Aliyah would get her hair washed and re-braided, Jeremiah would unplait her hair to cut down on the time she would have to spend away from him in the beauty salon, the one place he refused to accompany her. Aliyah loved feeling Jeremiah's fingers in her hair.

"This reminds me of when I was a child sitting on the floor between my mother's legs letting her condition my scalp," she said.

"Well, having you between my legs does not make me feel very maternal." He squeezed his knees around her body, enabling her to feel his hardness.

Aliyah got her nails done at the same salon, but now she skipped the airbrush designs, preferring to let Jeremiah paint original designs on selected nails. Once he painted a barely noticeable erotic design on her right pinky.

"What's that design on your pinky?" Dotty asked one day at a staff meeting.

"Nothing," Aliyah said, blushing, and then giggling uncharacteristically, causing everyone to wonder what was going on with her.

Jeremiah purchased Aliyah's favorite body wash, deodorant, and other toiletries to keep at his loft in order to make her as comfortable as possible when she was visiting him. He kept a supply of her favorite herbal teas and soft drinks in the pantry, and he made sure to have a supply of honey on hand for when she wanted to make an offering to Osun.

He took out a subscription to *Enigma*, as well as *Essence* and *Oprah* magazines, in order to stay abreast of current issues relating to women. He became an excellent source of information for Aliyah. She loved being able to discuss her work with him. In return, she became the subject of many of his paintings. She even posed for a semi-nude portrait that he wanted for his private collection.

Aliyah learned the game of football so that she could not only be with Jeremiah while he watched the games, but enjoy them too. Whenever they watched television together, she gave him complete control of the remote. She really didn't mind this "act of love" for in return he gave her back rubs and massages that were as arousing as they were relaxing.

Jeremiah taught Aliyah how to play poker. They would play for loose change. After a few games, Jeremiah would have won all of Aliyah's change that she generally used for train fare. He would feel so bad that he would deliberately lose so that she could win her money back. Of course he would deny that he lost on purpose, and she would know that it was another "act of love."

"Being in love is so wonderful when it is reciprocal," Aliyah said to Claudia as they sat in Central Park having lunch one late October afternoon. It was a beautiful day, sunny and mild.

"I know exactly what you are talking about." Claudia smiled at her friend. "Kwame and I are blessed the same way. Aliyah, I am so happy for you. When will I get to meet him?"

"Soon, Claudia. I just want to be sure that this is the real thing before I introduce Jeremiah to my family and friends. Besides he hasn't introduced me to his family yet, and although I know he loves me he hasn't said it yet. I don't want to take anything for granted. I'm too vulnerable right now."

"What do you mean he hasn't said it yet? I thought he told you that some of the things he does, like slipping your favorite candy bar in your jacket pocket before you leave for work, are 'acts of love.'"

"That's true Claudia, but he hasn't said 'I love you, Aliyah' to me. There are so many 'acts of love,' like meeting me at the train station with an umbrella on rainy days, rubbing my feet when I am tired, and fixing me breakfast in bed, but I still want to hear those four words before I am truly convinced that he loves me."

Aliyah said almost the same thing to her mother when Betty phoned and pressured her daughter to meet the new love interest in her life. "I want to be sure before I bring him around the family Mom. I hope you understand. I just don't think I can take another big disappointment at this point in my life, but if I have to, it will be easier if he has not bonded with my friends and family as well. Please, be patient and wait until I feel more secure in the relationship."

"Of course, I understand," Betty said to her daughter. "But does this mean that we won't get to see you until you feel secure in your relationship with this man? It's been weeks since you have been to church with me, or come over for Sunday dinner. Your brother's wedding is only a few weeks away and we have had little input from you."

Before ending the telephone conversation with her mother, Aliyah promised that she would break away from Jeremiah the very next Sunday to attend church with her mother and have dinner with her family. She had similar conversations with Kanmi, Oya, and with Teyinniwa. When Teyinniwa called to find out if their monthly social visits had ended, Aliyah assured her that they had not.

"I've been so worried about you," Teyinniwa said over the telephone. "I thought you might be still brooding about the disappointment with Richard Bishop. Morgan, however, seemed to know, somehow, that you were preoccupied with a new love interest. I'm so glad that she was right. I hated the idea of you sitting around brooding about that Richard man. From what you told me about him he didn't deserve you. Tell me, my dear, what is this

Jeremiah Jones like?"

"He's wonderful, Teyinniwa," Aliyah said. "He's so talented and very intelligent. He loves to travel and read. We have so much in common. He's gentle, kind, and financially independent. Please, tell Morgan that he is wonderful with his pants off and with them on." Aliyah laughed.

"How old is he?" Morgan was asking in the background. "Does he have any children from previous relationships, because that can be a problem sometimes, you know?"

"He's forty-two and he does not have any children," Aliyah said in response to Morgan's inquiries. "He has a sister, a niece, and a nephew that live in the area. His father lives between Paris and West Africa from what he tells me."

"Hmm!" Teyinniwa exclaimed loudly. "Dad sounds interesting. Is he married?"

"Yes, he's married to an African French woman and, from what Jeremiah tells me, they are very happy."

"Oh, well." Aliyah detected Teyinniwa's disappointment. "That's the story of my life. Please, bring Jeremiah over soon so Morgan and I can check him out to make sure he is good enough for you."

"Oh, I will. Soon, very soon." Aliyah hung up the telephone, smiling.

Kanmi was not as subtle in his approach to finding out why Aliyah had suddenly become unavailable to her friends. "What the heck is going on with you, Aliyah? Why have you been avoiding your friends? Even Mwangi wants to know if you have found another godchild to replace him." Aliyah detected disappointment.

"I hope you told him that it will never happen, Kanmi."

"Then when are you going to bring this guy for a visit?" Kanmi was persistent.

"Please, don't make a commitment until we have a reading of your *odu*." Aliyah heard Oya's voice in the background. "The blessings of the ancestors are essential if you wish lasting happiness."

"Soon, soon, you will meet him," Aliyah assured Kanmi and Oya. "Believe me, I will not make a commitment without casting the coconut to consult with the ancestors first." She reassured Oya.

Hanging up the telephone, Aliyah wondered if Jeremiah would be receptive to the idea of having Oya do a reading for both of them.

Aliyah explained to Jeremiah that her family wanted her input for her brother's up-coming wedding nuptials. He agreed that she should spend not only Sunday, but all the time that was necessary to accomplish what she needed to get done with her family.

"It'll give me a chance to do some things around the loft that I have been putting off," he said. "Call me when you get in Sunday evening, okay? If I am not in the loft, I'll be at the Jazz Garden. I'll miss you, but I understand I have to share you with your family."

"Do you think that we'll be able to get together later Sunday evening?" Aliyah asked, not wanting to be separated from Jeremiah overnight.

Sunday service at Metropolis was inspirational as usual. Reverend Doggett was out of town, and a visiting woman minister delivered the morning sermon.

"God wants us to be happy," she said. "If you are unhappy don't blame it on God. You probably need to search within yourself to determine what it is you are doing to cause your unhappiness. Perhaps you are relying too much on someone else to make you happy. Perhaps you are not taking responsibility for your own happiness. Happiness is too necessary for our overall well-being to entrust it to anyone else. Your happiness can only come to you through God. Your prayers to God for guidance will lead you to your greatest good, and from within that goodness, happiness will come."

"Amen," the congregation said in unison.

"Thank you for answering my prayers," Aliyah whispered to God.

"Did you say something?" Betty whispered to her daughter.

"No, Mom. I was just listening to the sermon." Aliyah turned her attention to the minister.

"Your prayers for guidance will lead you to make decisions that will directly impact on your happiness. So if you are unhappy, ask yourself are you following the guidance that God is providing or have you decided to let someone else guide you? There are those who follow the word of God, and those that follow their own way. When you have a choice to make, do you ask yourself, is this the choice that God would want me to make? If the answer is no, and you decide to make that choice anyway, then you have to take responsibility for your unhappiness."

The service ended and the congregation stood holding hands singing, "God Be With You Until We Meet Again." Aliyah looked around at all the smiling faces, thinking, *How fortunate I am to belong to a race of people that can so openly show their love for each other.* The black church was the only place she knew of where one could go and get such a large dose of love that it could carry a person from Sunday to Sunday. She looked at her mother, beautiful and beaming with love, and wondered, *What does God have in store for me? Is the happiness I am experiencing now real?*

Aliyah explored her feelings further as she helped to prepare Sunday dinner in her mother's kitchen.

"Mom, I don't want to depend on Jeremiah to make me happy, but I have to admit that I am so happy when I'm with him." She sliced the duck her mother had prepared for dinner.

"Sweetheart, were you unhappy before he came into your life?" Betty asked, putting chocolate frosting on a cake.

"No," Aliyah admitted. "But I was so lonely, and I don't want to go back to that."

"Honey, if this relationship with Jeremiah works out, you will find that even though you are together, there will be times when you will experience loneliness. Believe me, I love your father, and we have been married for almost forty years, but there are times when I am so lonely. Don't believe that being in love will solve everything. Many people are very happy and not in love. They find their happiness in doing other things, like being useful in the community or the church, or helping needy children. You are a very independent and creative person, Aliyah. Don't feel that you can't be happy unless a man validates you. You've got so much to offer." Betty finished icing the cake just as the rest of her family joined the two of them in the kitchen, demanding food.

It was almost 9:00 P.M. when Aliyah returned to her brownstone from her parent's home. She had helped Sheniqua and Jamal pick out floral arrangements, select silver patterns, table linens, and music for the wedding that was now less than eight weeks away. The invitations were ready to be mailed, and the dates were set for the bridal shower and the rehearsal dinner. They still hadn't decided on the menu, but the caterer had invited the whole family to a food tasting at the Mansion the week before Thanksgiving. The final selection of menu items would be made at that time.

Aliyah and Bill had one of their infrequent father-daughter talks, and Aliyah had listened as her father cautioned her not to be in a hurry to marry because her younger brother was taking the plunge.

"Daddy, no one has asked me to marry them yet. Why are we having this conversation?" She had looked at her father.

"I just don't want you to think that we expect the same thing of you because Jamal is getting married. As long as you are happy, I don't care if you never get married." Bill had tried to reassure his daughter.

Aliyah was tired when she got home, but she wasn't in the house more than five minutes before she began to miss Jeremiah. He did not pick up the telephone at the loft when she called there. She hung up without leaving a message, and called the Jazz Garden. She could tell that the music in the background was Jeremiah playing the piano. He sent a message that he would call her back in ten minutes. When he returned her telephone call, Aliyah was relaxing on her bed dressed in the blue teddy Jeremiah had selected for her.

"Are you coming over?" She lay sprawled across the bed.

"We're a little short of help here. One of the bartenders called in sick. They really need me to help out tonight. Why don't you get some rest, and I'll call you later."

"Okay." Aliyah was disappointed, but hoped it didn't show in her voice. It was the first night since her return from San Francisco that they would not be together. "Don't forget to call me when you finish up," she quickly said, before he hung up the telephone.

The built-in alarm in Aliyah's head woke her up at 5:00 A.M. She was alone in her bed for the first time in weeks. She didn't like the feeling of waking up without Jeremiah. He hadn't called her either. "What could have happened?" she asked herself aloud as she dressed in her running clothes. The air was damp and there was a slight drizzle. With no hesitation, though, Aliyah started her run through the park and southeast on Broad Street. By the time she reached the Art Center, the drizzle had turned into a steady flow of rain. She hesitated for a second or two before proceeding towards the river. In a matter of seconds, the rain had increased to a steady downpour. She was getting drenched. Closer to Jeremiah's loft than she was to her brownstone, she headed back across Broad Street and up to Halsey Street.

By the time Aliyah climbed the stairs to Jeremiah's loft she was drenched to the bone. Her hair was soaked and dripping. It was about 5:20 A.M. so she assumed that Jeremiah would be up preparing to do his recycling. She knocked softly on the door. When there was no answer, she knocked harder. After a few minutes she heard the lock turn and the door opened. Standing there in one of Jeremiah's T-shirts with his environmental logo covering large well-developed breasts was a very attractive young woman. Her mouth was moving and she was saying something, but Aliyah did not hear her. Could not hear her. Her mouth dropped open in disbelief. Tears welled up in her eyes. Her knees had turned to Jell-O. She felt faint.

Aliyah looked beyond the woman, who was wearing only the T-shirt, and noticed that the bedroom door was open. Her eyes came back to the woman who was now looking at her very peculiarly. Her rumpled hair was naturally curly and cut very short. Her skin was caramel colored and her eyes were dark and deeply set in her face. She was barefoot and her bright red toenails revealed a recent pedicure.

"Who are you looking for?" The caramel colored woman yelled out as Aliyah turned and stumbled back down the stairs and out into the pouring rain.

"Not again, oh Lord, not again," she kept saying to herself as she ran up Halsey Street. She had run almost five blocks before she realized that she was running in the wrong direction. She was running away from her brownstone in the pouring rain. She was now on the south side of Market Street. She turned and ran east across Broad Street, further down pass Mulberry Street and on to the riverbank.

"Oh, why, Osun? Why have you betrayed me? What did I do to deserve this?" Aliyah cried. At the riverbank she stood in the rain looking at the water rushing past her for what seemed like hours, when actually it was only a few minutes. Just as her knees gave way, and she began to sink into the mud she felt strong arms grab her from behind. Even in the rain with all the wetness she could smell the Egyptian musk oil. She turned to face him. He held her at arms length by the shoulders. Her fists pummeled his chest.

"How could you, Jeremiah? How could you do this to me? I trusted you." Aliyah shouted over his words. His words would not sink in. He kept repeating the same words over and over again, until finally they began to sink in.

"She's my sister Aliyah. Aliyah, she's my sister." Jeremiah held her until she realized what he was saying.

"But, but, she had on your T-shirt," Aliyah said between sobs. "She came out of your bedroom."

"She came over last night, after I talked to you on the telephone," he said. "She had the children with her, and she was very upset. She and her husband had a fight. I was up most of the night calming her down. I finally settled her and the kids down to sleep in my bedroom. I slept upstairs on the divan in the studio. I didn't hear you when you knocked on the door. I was still sleeping." He loosened his grip on her shoulders.

His words now taking effect, Aliyah continued to sob, only more softly now. Jeremiah gathered her in his arms, holding her close. "Aliyah, I love you, darling. Don't you know that? I would never do anything to hurt you. You are the answer to my prayers. You are my gift from Sango. I will never hurt you darling. I love you, Aliyah."

Together they stood in the pouring rain, holding on to each other for what seemed like an eternity. Finally, feeling Aliyah shiver from the coolness of the early November morning and the chilling rain, Jeremiah said, "Let's get out of this downpour before we both catch pneumonia."

Taking her hand, they ran across the highway, across Broad Street, through the park, and to the brownstone. Once inside, they stripped off their soaking clothes and wrapped themselves in matching oversized terrycloth bathrobes that Aliyah had purchased for chilly mornings such as this. While Jeremiah brewed hot cups of tea for them, Aliyah laundered their soggy clothing.

They took a long hot shower together. In the shower, he rubbed a lavender scented gel all over her body until it was slick and foamy. She did the same to him. They moved closer together under the hot water, now pouring down over them, washing the soap off their smooth brown bodies. Jeremiah kissed her neck, her lips, and her nipples. He dried her with a large fluffy bath sheet, and she dried him. They lay on her bed looking at each other, touching, but not saying a word. Finally, Aliyah broke the silence.

"Why did you come out in the rain after me, Jeremiah?"

"I awoke to the sound of voices coming from downstairs. Then I heard my sister asking, 'Who are you looking for?' When I came downstairs, she told me that a rather distraught looking woman with long braided hair ran out into the rain. I knew it was you, and I didn't want you to be distraught for one minute more than necessary. The mere thought of your believing that I had another woman in my bed was enough to send me running out into the rain to look for you. I knew you would go to the river, so I headed there, too." He rubbed her shoulders.

"Your coming after me was an 'act of love,' Jeremiah. I hope our life will be one continuous circle of such 'acts of love.' I once read that when you love someone you do things that will make your partner happy. In turn, he or she is so happy that they do things to reciprocate, creating a circle of reciprocity. Love is a continuous circle of 'acts of love.'"

Chapter 15

*"A soul mate is someone who can read
you without your telling
them what you are feeling,
Someone who empathizes with you,
Who wants for you what you want for yourself"*
— *Oya*

"This appears to be a pretty fancy wedding that you two are planning. Have you been engaged long?" Jeremiah asked Jamal.

"Only about six months," Jamal said.

The Neal family had finally come together at the Mansion for the food tasting for Sheniqua and Jamal's wedding. Aliyah thought it would be the perfect opportunity to introduce Jeremiah to her family. She had been a little worried that her father and Jamal would ask Jeremiah a lot of questions concerning his intentions and make it uncomfortable for him. She knew, though, that it would only last a couple of hours at the most, enabling them to make a quick get away if necessary.

She need not have worried though. Jeremiah was perfectly charming and her parents were obviously receptive of him. Even her father was on his best behavior, asking only the most pertinent questions. Aliyah could tell, though, that her father was dying to ask Jeremiah his intentions regarding his daughter, but he refrained.

"We don't believe in long engagements," Sheniqua said.

"Neither do I," Jeremiah said surprisingly. "I feel that most people know right away when the right person comes along. There is no reason to prolong the inevitable, especially when you are old enough and established enough to make a commitment. What do you think?" Jeremiah asked, looking directly at Bill Neal.

You could see the look of delight on Bill's face when Jeremiah himself brought up the subject so early in the evening. It was during the tasting of the hors d'oeuvres to be exact.

"Well, Jeremiah, I guess I have to say that I agree with you," Bill said, smiling. "I fell in love with this lady the first day I laid eyes on her. It was definitely love at first sight." He looked lovingly at his wife. "But, we were still in high school and certainly not ready to make a lifetime commitment. I knew, though, that as soon as I was through school and established in my chosen field, that I was going to make this woman my wife, and I did just that." He reached over and held Betty's hand.

Jeremiah had showed no apprehension when it came to meeting Aliyah's family. As a matter of fact, he had told Aliyah that he looked forward to the day when he could meet her parents and her brother. He wanted to show them how much he loved her and to obtain their blessings as well. He was anxious to prove to them and to the world that he was the right man for Aliyah.

By the time the desserts were put on the table for tasting, Jeremiah had become like one of the family. Aliyah could not keep her eyes off him. He teased and cajoled her mother telling her that the recipes Aliyah was getting from her were every bit as tasty as the gourmet food they had been sampling.

"I keep telling Aliyah how much her cooking reminds me of my mother's cooking." He smiled at Aliyah. "I know she uses your recipes. Your recipe for peach cobbler could put all of these desserts to shame."

"He's right, Mom." Jamal agreed with Jeremiah. "I hope that you will share your recipes with Sheniqua, too," he said.

When they left the Mansion, everyone went to their respective cars and went their separate ways, but it was with the understanding that they would all meet at the Neal home for Thanksgiving dinner the next week. Jeremiah was instructed to invite his sister and her family, as well as his father and stepmother if they arrived in town.

Once settled in the car, alone with Jeremiah, Aliyah reached over and pulled his head toward her and gave him a long passionate kiss that left her trembling when they broke their embrace.

"What was that for?" Jeremiah asked.

"Just for being you," she said. "I hope your family will like me as much as my family does you."

"Why wouldn't they?" Jeremiah put the car in gear.

"I'm a little apprehensive about meeting your sister again, especially after the way I behaved when I saw her at your apartment."

"You don't have to worry about that." Jeremiah attempted to reassure her. "I am sure she received a favorable report about you from the children, and that she will like you as much as they do. Women are like that you know. If you treat their children nice, they will automatically like you." Jeremiah glanced at her for a moment before turning his attention to the road.

Aliyah smiled, thinking back to her meeting with Jeremiah's niece and nephew two days after she had acted so hastily and run out into the rain from the loft. Naomi, Jeremiah's sister, had stayed with him for almost a week while she worked out problems with her husband. Jeremiah had baby-sat at the loft one evening, providing Naomi and her husband an opportunity to go out and talk.

"Come and keep me company while I baby-sit." Jeremiah had persuaded her over the telephone. With what she thought was good reason, Aliyah was a little apprehensive about meeting his family.

"I acted like such a fool." She had confessed to Jeremiah. "Your sister probably thinks that I am some love-struck adolescent who is infatuated with her brother."

"Nonsense," Jeremiah had said. "She knows that you are not an adolescent," he had kidded her.

"Come over," he had insisted. "You have got to get over your apprehension."

Despite her anxiety, she had gone by the loft after leaving her office. The children were delightful. As soon as she had arrived, they warmed right up to her.

"Can we call you, Aunt Aliyah?" Rachel, the youngest, had asked.

"Mommy says that you and Uncle Jay are in love. I guess that means that you will probably be getting married, right?" Noah, the oldest, had asked.

"Mind your own business, Noah," his sister had quipped.

"Yes, Noah," Jeremiah had agreed with Rachel. "Don't ask personal questions of people you just met; it isn't polite." Jeremiah gently scolded his nephew.

"But can we call you Aunt Aliyah?" Rachel had insisted on knowing.

"It's up to your uncle," Aliyah had said, looking at Jeremiah.

"Okay, Aunt Aliyah it is." Jeremiah gave in.

Jeremiah was wonderful with the children. He had played chess with Noah while Aliyah and Rachel played jacks on the hardwood floor. Then Jeremiah had played the piano while they all sang. Finally, Aliyah had helped Jeremiah put the children to bed. Afterwards, they had lay on the leather sofa in front of a warming fire and talked about their own dreams of having children.

"I think you would make a wonderful father." Aliyah laid her head in Jeremiah's lap.

"And I know you will be a wonderful mother." Jeremiah had stroked her hair. "I love you Aliyah. When I get married again I want it to be for keeps. I want my wife to have children for me. Do you think you might want to have children with me one day, Aliyah?" he had asked.

"Most definitely," Aliyah had said. "I'll be thirty-six my next birthday, you know. My biological clock is ticking away, and I want to be young enough to enjoy children, like we do with Rachel and Noah," she had said.

"We have a lot to think about," Jeremiah had said as Aliyah started to doze off in his arms.

"Let's talk about this again real soon okay, Aliyah?"

"Real soon," Aliyah had said.

Aliyah did not hear Naomi when she had come in. When Jeremiah awakened her Naomi had retired to the bedroom. Aliyah and Jeremiah had gone to the brownstone to spend the night.

The Monday before Thanksgiving, Jeremiah's father and stepmother arrived from Senegal, West Africa. Jeremiah picked them up at JFK Airport and insisted that they stay at his loft rather than at his sister's larger home. Jeremiah thought that his sister and brother-in-law, newly reconciled, needed their privacy. Besides, he expected to be spending most of his nights at the brownstone with Aliyah during his father's visit.

Jeremiah Senior and his wife, Simone, were planning to fly to New Orleans after the Thanksgiving holiday. Aliyah got her first chance to meet them at the Jazz Garden where Jeremiah planned for them to have dinner the night of their arrival. Jeremiah picked her up at the train station and drove directly to the restaurant. He telephoned the loft from the bar to ask his father and Simone to join them for dinner. Naomi and her husband had arranged to join them for dessert.

Aliyah knew right away that the distinguished looking couple entering the Jazz Garden was Jeremiah's father and stepmother. Mr. Jones was a handsome, older version of his son. He had a full head of silvery hair and a silver mustache. Simone Jones was beautiful. She was tall, slender, and very dark. She wore her hair in an intricate Senegalese hairstyle. It was braided and beautifully wrapped around her head. She appeared to be in her mid-fifties. She was wearing a lovely African print dress that flattered her trim figure, and gorgeous gold jewelry.

When Jeremiah introduced Aliyah to his father and stepmother, Simone smiled, revealing beautiful, pearly white even teeth and dimples. Aliyah liked her right away. Mr. Jones did not smile, but his eyes were warm and kind as he looked over the woman his son had undoubtedly told him all about.

"It's a pleasure to meet you, my dear," he said, not taking his eyes off her.

"It's wonderful to finally meet both of you," Aliyah said. "Jeremiah has told me so much about you."

During dinner, Aliyah learned that Jeremiah's father, although semi-retired, had accepted an engagement in New Orleans. He was going to be the opening jazz pianist for a new restaurant that a good friend had recently purchased on Bourbon Street. He expected to be in New Orleans through the New Year's celebration. Mr. Jones was a fascinating man. He told story after story about his life in Senegal. Although Simone was born and raised in Paris, her parents were originally from Senegal, West Africa. She had met her husband in Paris fifteen years earlier, where she had been employed as a music teacher in a conservatory. Since their marriage, they had been living between two continents. They had spent the last four months in West Africa, where Simone still had family.

"I have taken up fishing," Mr. Jones told them. "We live in Dakar, the capital of Senegal," he said to Aliyah. "Although it is a big city, we live about twenty-five miles from a fishing village right on the ocean. Simone's father grew up there. Her uncle is a retired fisherman; he is eighty years old now. He still lives in the village, and he is teaching me to fish."

"He goes fishing everyday," Simone said. "We have fresh fish to eat all the time."

Mr. Jones appeared to enjoy the specially prepared meal that Jeremiah had requested of Cook. He told them that he had forgotten what it was like to have so much variety in a meal. He had become accustomed to a steady diet of Jollof rice.

"Jollof rice is the traditional Senegalese meal prepared everyday," Simone said. "We make it fresh for dinner every night, and whatever is left over will be eaten for lunch the next day. The main ingredients are rice, tomato, onion, and other vegetables like cabbage or green beans, and generally carrots or yam. You can add fish or meat if you choose." She looked at Aliyah while she talked. "The only variety is in the choice of vegetables that are added or the meat or fish. Sometimes I use shrimp."

"In Senegal and most other places in West Africa, dinner is a meal that is always eaten together," Mr. Jones said. "Families eat off of one large platter. You remember that from your visit don't you, Son?"

"Yes, I do," Jeremiah said. "I would love to take Aliyah to West Africa."

"That would be wonderful," Mr. Jones said. "Will you be able to get away from your business for any length of time? When can you come?" He became excited.

"Getting away will not be a problem for me, especially since I hired Charlie to help me out. You remember Charlie don't you, Aliyah?" Jeremiah asked. "You met him at Marlo's on our first date," he reminded her.

Aliyah said nothing. There was only one thing that lingered in her mind about that first date.

"Well, Charlie has proven himself to be a very dependable and loyal employee since I hired him," Jeremiah said, not waiting for a response from her. "I can go away and leave him in charge without a worry. So, how soon before we can go would depend on Aliyah's schedule. Aliyah is the editor in chief of a well-known New York magazine." Jeremiah looked at her with pride. "She has responsibilities that do not allow her to take off from work for many vacations."

"That's why I never allowed my wives to work," Mr. Jones said, looking at his son. "Your mother never worked and neither does Simone. I like my women to be available to travel with me whenever I get an urge to go. It was only after you and your sister started school that your mother insisted on staying home to care for you. Otherwise she would have traveled with me wherever I went." He nodded his head as if to confirm what he had just said.

"Aliyah loves her job," Jeremiah said. "She has worked very hard and accomplished a lot in a short period of time. Whatever makes her happy makes me happy," he said to his father.

This man is truly my soul mate, Aliyah thought looking at Jeremiah. *He wants for me what I want for myself.* "Perhaps I can arrange to do a feature article for the magazine that will require me to travel to West Africa," she said.

"That would be wonderful," Simone said. "What would you write about?"

"I don't know yet," Aliyah said. "*Enigma* is a woman's magazine. Perhaps you can enlighten me about some of the issues pertaining to the women of West Africa." She looked at Simone.

"I would love to discuss it with you," Simone said, just as Naomi and her husband joined them for dessert.

After the initial embarrassment of meeting Jeremiah's sister again, Aliyah could tell from Naomi's smile that they would be friends.

Thanksgiving dinner at Betty and Bill Neal's home was a very happy occasion. Naomi and her husband came with their children. Mr. Jones and Simone arrived with Aliyah and Jeremiah. Jamal and Sheniqua were radiant only one month before their wedding, and Betty and Bill were in their glory. Their children were happy and their family was expanding. What more could they ask for? They were truly blessed.

Betty had prepared a wonderful dinner, which included the traditional roasted turkey, all golden brown, with cornbread stuffing, roasted potatoes, macaroni and cheese, fresh cranberries, candied yams, three different kinds of vegetables, and grilled fish. There was sweet potato pie, homemade pound cake, and her fabulous peach cobbler for dessert.

"When did you find the time to do all of this?" Simone asked.

"I have been preparing for this all week long," Betty said. "Nothing is too good for my family when I can get them all together." After everyone was seated at the dining room table, Betty looked around the table with a look of contentment on her face. "Let's give thanks to God." She looked at her husband and signaled him to say grace.

While the food was being passed around the table, the blended family shared stories and got to know each other.

"Jeremiah was always a good kid," his father said. "He never gave me any serious concerns. He accepted responsibility at an early age, caring for his mother and younger sister whenever I was away from the home. I have always been able to depend on my boy to do the right thing." He looked proudly at Jeremiah. "The only time I ever worried about him was when he was a Newark police officer. I never prayed as hard as I did the two times he was injured in the line of duty. I am so glad that he is no longer a policeman. I love what he is doing now to protect the environment, and his paintings never cease to amaze me." Mr. Jones smiled at his son.

"Pop, please," Jeremiah, said. "You're embarrassing me."

"It is all so true though," Naomi took up where her father left off. "Jeremiah has always been a wonderful big brother to me, especially when we were children. He always took very good care of me. I want you to know, Aliyah, what a wonderful man you have gotten; they don't come any better than my brother."

Not to be outdone by the Jones family, Betty and Bill told stories of their own children's achievements. "Aliyah was so smart as a child that she was reading before she started kindergarten," Betty said. "She amazed our friends and family members who would drop by and find her lying on the floor reading the Sunday comics when she was only four years old." Betty smiled at her daughter.

"Jamal could take things apart and put them back together from the time he was a little boy," Bill said of his son. "He fixed all the neighborhood children's bicycles, and later he fixed their cars when he was just a teenager himself. He is the best mechanic in this state, if I say so myself," he bragged about his son.

Aliyah and Jamal just beamed.

After dinner, they retreated to the large living room for an after-dinner cordial. The living room was hardly used by the family since Bill had renovated the den into an entertainment center. The living room had become much too formal. It was decorated with antiques for which Betty had carefully shopped. She had tried to recreate the living room her grandmother once had.

The room had her grandparents' wedding portrait hanging over the large fireplace. The mantle held beautifully framed photographs of her and Bill's ancestors. Photos of Bill and Betty's deceased parents, grandparents, siblings, aunts, uncles, and cousins adorned the heavy oak mantle. Everyone pictured on the mantle was dead. Betty said that her grandmother once told her that you should keep pictures of the dead and the living separated. If you put a picture of a living person among those of the dead, it meant that the living person would soon join the ancestors. She never mixed them.

Pictures of the living were in the den, and in numerous albums Betty had filled up over a forty-year period. She brought out the family photo albums. Aliyah stood over Jeremiah's shoulder while he looked at pictures of her and Jamal as children growing up in their parent's home. When he got to one of her lying on a blanket, naked at three months old, he whispered in her ear, "You had a sexy body even then."

The first week in December was a busy time for Aliyah. She spent

Thursday and Friday helping the publishers at *Enigma* prepare for a reception in honor of some very important sponsors of the magazine. The clients had flown into New York City from Hong Kong on Thursday. The reception was to be held in the presidential suite at the Plaza Hotel at noon on Friday. Aliyah had the responsibility of hosting the affair. She had ordered a divine lunch, which included oysters, lobster, caviar, and other delicacies from the hotel's menu.

Weather reports for the day had not been favorable. The clients from Hong Kong had expected to depart from JFK Airport on Saturday afternoon. The prediction of an early snowstorm for the New York area was causing them to reconsider their plans. The snowstorm was moving in from Canada, and weather reports indicated that Buffalo was already buried under twenty-seven inches of snow. The Hong Kong clients finally decided to take an earlier flight, leaving New York right after the luncheon reception on Friday.

It was already beginning to snow lightly when the reception started. By the time the reception ended there were about two inches of snow on the ground. It was just after 3:00 P.M. when the honored guests departed for the airport. Shortly afterwards, the reception began to break up and all the guests began to leave. Aliyah thought it was a good time to make her own departure. She had driven into Manhattan that morning and was anxious to get on the road, knowing that traffic would be horrendous. When the publishers suggested that she spend the night at the Plaza in the presidential suite that was already paid for until the next afternoon, she reconsidered. *Why not?* she thought, it would probably take her hours to get home, and she hated to drive in the snow.

After everyone had left, Aliyah looked around at the decor of the presidential suite, made herself comfortable on the luxurious sofa, and then called Jeremiah. He was disappointed that she would not be coming home that night, but he agreed that she should not drive back to Newark with the weather being what it was. He promised to call her later.

When he hung up, Aliyah could not help but wish that he had thought to join her at the Plaza, despite the snow. There was still plenty of food and champagne left from the reception. She looked in the master bedroom and marveled at it's opulence. The presidential suite was the most expensive suite at the Plaza, one of the most expensive hotels in New York City. Here she was all alone; how could she enjoy it? To help pass the time, she turned on the television, and before she knew it she had fallen asleep.

It was 7:30 P.M. before Jeremiah called her back.

"Did I wake you?" He detected the drowsiness in her voice.

"Yes." Aliyah looked at her watch. "I guess I fell asleep."

"Are you tired?" he asked.

"Not really. I guess I was a little bored." Aliyah yawned.

"What will you do there all by yourself?"

"Probably watch television, or maybe read one of the magazines that's here." She picked up one from the coffee table.

"What would you do if I were there with you?" he asked.

"Well, there's a great looking Jacuzzi in the master bathroom, big enough for two," she said. "And there is plenty of champagne and good things to eat," she added.

"Hmm. It sounds wonderful. Why don't you turn the Jacuzzi on, and put some champagne on ice, but first open your door." Jeremiah laughed. Aliyah flew to the door, and when she opened it, Jeremiah swept her up into his arms and carried her back into the presidential suite.

The next morning, Aliyah looked out the window of the master bedroom of the presidential suite that overlooked Central Park. It looked like a winter wonderland, so beautiful. She looked at Jeremiah still sleeping in the king-size bed. The look of satisfaction on his beautiful face conjured up images of the blissful night they had just shared. How wonderful it had been. *Thank you, Osun, goddess of pleasure, for all that you have done for me. I am so blessed,* she thought.

She gently nudged Jeremiah to wake up, and coaxed him to join her at the window to see the magnificent view. An hour later they were in the park, playing in the snow. Only a little over five inches had fallen in the city. Jeremiah showed her how to make snow angels, and they threw snowballs at each other, laughing and running like children.

When they had their full of the snow, they walked to the Museum of Natural History, where Jeremiah pointed out a statue of a lion that graced the entrance to the museum.

"This is one of my favorite displays," he said.

"He certainly looks fierce," Aliyah said.

"And proud," Jeremiah said. "Few people know that this statute is one in a series of three placed throughout the museum. Come, I'll show you the other two." He took Aliyah's hand and pulled her into the museum.

The other two statues were of the same lion, only different. The second statue in the sequence depicted the lion being trapped. The third statue in the sequence showed the lion captured. "This exhibit reminds me of the African slave trade," he said sadly. As Jeremiah told her the story of the lion's capture, he became more and more animated. She could not help but smile as she watched the excitement building in him as he told the story. *I adore him*, she thought.

When they left the museum, Aliyah called Claudia and invited Jeremiah and herself to lunch at the Harlem brownstone.

As they drove up to Harlem, Jeremiah pointed out some of the places with which he was familiar. "This is the Audubon Theater where Malcolm X was shot in 1965, Aliyah. Do you remember that?"

"Jeremiah, I wasn't even born when that happened. You couldn't have been more than five or six yourself; how could you remember?" Aliyah looked at the building from her window.

"I remember," he said. "My father was so upset. He used to talk about Malcolm all the time. Malcolm was his hero. Have you ever seen one of the shows at the Apollo Theater?" He pointed it out as they drove up 125th Street.

"No, but my parents did, they often talk about the shows they saw at the Apollo."

When Claudia opened her front door and saw Aliyah and Jeremiah standing there, tears came to her eyes. "You two look so beautiful together," she said. "Jeremiah, I am so happy to finally meet you." She didn't wait for an introduction. "I have prayed so hard for my girlfriend to find her soul mate, and now, all praises due to God, it has happened." Tears were streaming down her face now.

Kwame took their coats and ushered them into the den where a roaring fire greeted them. While they munched on delicatessen sandwiches and

drank hot apple cider with cinnamon stick swirls, the two couples talked
and talked about everything, including politics, locally and abroad. They
talked about music and books, relationships and dreams. While Claudia and
Kwame got to know Jeremiah, the two couples bonded in the process. When
the visit finally ended, they had discovered that Jeremiah and Kwame shared
many of the same viewpoints and interests.

"I am so glad that you and Aliyah got together," Kwame said to Jeremiah.
"These two women are closer than any sisters that I have ever known, and I
am just happy to have a male to make us a foursome now."

"Thank you for your wonderful hospitality," Jeremiah said. "I hope you
will let us reciprocate soon."

The week after the visit with Claudia and Kwame, Aliyah brought Jeremiah
with her for her monthly visit with her good friends Teyinniwa and Morgan.

"So you finally found some time to visit us," Teyinniwa said, scolding
Aliyah.

"I can see why she hasn't been around." Morgan stole a glance at Jeremiah
over her sister's shoulder. "What a hunk," she said unabashedly. "Our girl
has landed a winner from what I can see."

"I'm the winner in this situation," Jeremiah laughed.

"Oh, I like him," Teyinniwa said. "I'm glad to see that you recognize
quality goods. Aliyah is the best!" She took their coats.

During the course of the evening, Teyinniwa and Jeremiah talked about
their travels abroad, and Aliyah told her friends about the trip she and
Jeremiah were planning to West Africa. They talked about Jeremiah's
desire to open a gallery that would give African- American artists more
opportunity to exhibit their work in Newark.

"There are so many talented young men and women in this city that just
need a break," Jeremiah said.

"The Daughter's of Africa have been very successful in our effort to help
abused and displaced African-American women and their children,"
Teyinniwa said proudly. "I am glad that you, too, are interested in doing
something positive that will help in the development of our people."

They talked about relationships and how some people never find their
soul mate. Morgan kept them laughing with stories of the close calls she had

made only to find out that wishful thinking could sometimes make one feel as though one had found the right person, only to discover that it was not the one. Before the evening ended, Aliyah found an opportunity to let her friends know how grateful she was that she had listened to the people she loved. Taking the advice of her family and friends, because she knew they loved her, was the best thing she could have done.

The very same weekend Aliyah and Jeremiah visited Kanmi and Oya. Not surprising to Aliyah, Kanmi and Jeremiah hit it off very well together. They appeared to have a lot in common. Jeremiah was astounded to hear about Kanmi's art collection, gathered from all over the African continent.

"People come from around the tri-state area to see my collection," Kanmi told Jeremiah. "I have a whole floor in the store that is devoted to African art. The pieces that we keep at home are constantly changing. Whenever I sell a piece from the store, I replace it with something from home. I keep only a few pieces for my private collection; everything else is for sale."

"I would love to see your collection," Jeremiah said.

While Kanmi took Jeremiah on a tour of the house to show off his collection, Aliyah and Oya retreated to the kitchen.

"What do you think, Oya?" Aliyah smiled at her friend. "Do you think that Jeremiah is the one for me? Is he my soul mate?"

"What do you think, Aliyah?" Oya answered the question with one of her own. "What do you feel in your heart?"

"I feel only love for this man, Oya. There was something special about him from the first time that I met him. You remember me telling you about the haunting eyes that followed me until I saw him again?"

"I remember," Oya said.

"It took a little while for us to get together, but since our first date, not one day has gone by when I have not enjoyed being with him. He has shown me nothing but love."

"That is certainly a good sign." Oya smiled. "Has he openly professed his love for you?"

"Oh yes," Aliyah said. "Over and over again. I have no doubt that he loves me. Remember when you defined the term soul mate for me? You said that a soul mate is someone who can read you without your telling them what you are feeling, someone who empathizes with you, and who wants for you what you want for yourself."

"I remember." Oya encouraged Aliyah to continue.

"Well, Jeremiah does all of those things."

"Shall I prepare the coconut to see what the ancestors have to say about him?" Oya picked up a fresh coconut from the counter.

"Yes," Aliyah said.

As Oya prepared the coconut for the reading of the *odu*, Aliyah's anxiety grew. *What if the reading is not favorable?* she asked herself. *Will I go against the reading, and continue to see Jeremiah?* "I don't think I can bear to give him up." she said, looking at Oya for reassurance.

"If it is meant to be, the ancestors will let you know." Oya tried to reassure her friend.

"My only concern is that I have not known him that long. We have only been dating three months. Can you really get to know a person in such a short time?" She watched Oya and waited for an answer.

"Some people date for years, and never get to know each other." Oya used the paring knife to round the coconut sections.

Just as Oya was about to cast the coconut pieces, Kanmi and Jeremiah entered the kitchen. "Why are you casting the coconut?" They both asked in unison.

"It's for me," Aliyah said. "I want to ask the ancestors if you are my soul mate." She looked at Jeremiah.

"Don't you think that this is something we should do together?" Jeremiah asked Aliyah. "Why don't we ask the ancestors if this relationship has their blessing?"

"Okay," Aliyah said. "That would be much better."

Aliyah and Jeremiah held hands as Oya cast the coconut pieces on the mat. Aliyah held her breath. *"Ejifa,"* Kanmi and Oya said in unison after they studied the pattern of the fallen coconut pieces. From the broad smiles on their faces Aliyah knew that the reading was favorable.

"Don't you have to throw the coconut pieces again to be sure?" Aliyah asked.

"The ancestors have given you an absolute yes," Oya said.

"*Ejifa* is a definite yes; it means you don't have to ask again. Your relationship is blessed. I am very happy for you," Kanmi said.

One week before Christmas, Aliyah lay on the bed in her bedroom reading the Sunday newspaper while Jeremiah prepared breakfast downstairs. It was the week before her brother's wedding day, and Aliyah was thinking about a gift to give the couple. She had already decided to give them money, but was now having second thoughts. She wondered if she should give them something special that they could cherish forever. She wished Jeremiah would come upstairs so she could consult with him. As if in answer to her wish she heard Jeremiah ascending the stairs. The smell of scrambled eggs, grits, buttered toast, and coffee wafted upstairs. The feeling of nausea that swept over her sent her running to the bathroom. When she came out, Jeremiah was munching on a piece of toast and reading the magazine section of the newspaper.

"Are you okay?" he asked, without looking up from the paper.

Picking up the editorials, Aliyah responded, "I think I'm pregnant."

Looking right into her eyes, Jeremiah said, "Let's get married?"

And they did.